REDEEMABLES

REDEEMABLES

THE BOHICA CHRONICLES™ BOOK THREE

C.J. FAWCETT   JONATHAN BRAZEE

MICHAEL ANDERLE

DISRUPTIVE IMAGINATION®

REDEEMABLES TEAM

Thanks to the JIT Readers

John Ashmore
Dave Hicks
Diane L. Smith
Jeff Eaton
Peter Manis
Kelly O'Donnell
Dorothy Lloyd
Deb Mader0
James Caplan
Micky Cocker
Jeff Goode
Paul Westman

If we've missed anyone, please let us know!

Editor
Skyhunter Editing Team

CHAPTER ONE

The Zoo

"Take that, motherfuckers!" Walker "Roo" Demopoulis yelled and hurled a grenade at the approaching monsters.

Only four remained in the oncoming wave. They clawed their way over the bodies of their three fallen companions, snarling and hissing. They were as big as Clydesdale horses, light green, and scaly. They could spit acid, and the only warning was the expanding blue sacs under their chins and between their shoulder blades.

The grenade exploded and knocked back the first beast that surged forward. Its right front leg was blown off and the sac on its back ripped open. The acid ate through its tough hide and burned the other lizards as they came forward.

"Way to show the wanker, mate," Mick Bennelong said and paused in shooting his F88C to give his fellow Australian a fist-bump.

"For fuck's sake, now isn't the time for a bleddy tea party. Take the rest down." Eustace Percival Coddington,

1

Booker to the others, all but growled. One of his rounds found its mark in a lizard's expanding acid sacs. It writhed and fell and he ejected the empty magazine from his M5, shoved in another, and continued to fire.

The last two lizards leapt over the other corpses and uttered a hiss. They kept themselves within spitting range but moved no closer. The boiling water sound of their sibilant defiance couldn't distract from the glowing blue acid sacs. Charles Tillman and Serenity "Reen" Nguyen stepped forward to meet them. He chambered a slug in his Remington MCS and she sighted down her M492. With near-perfect synchronicity, they fired. Both former Marines struck their targets.

The animals screamed and lunged forward. They still attempted to claw the humans while being rapidly dissolved by their own acid.

The duo high-fived.

Roo rolled his eyes. "Americans. Always fucking showing off. We get it. You think you're fucking badasses."

"How many times do I have to tell you, babe? I don't think I'm a badass. I *am* a motherfucking badass," Reen said and winked at him. He flipped her off.

"We need to keep moving," Booker said. "That wave hit faster than the others. What the bleddy hell is going on in here today? This is worse than it normally is."

"It's the Zoo," Charles said with a shrug. "Does it ever make sense or behave the way we think it will?"

"All unpredictable alien-ness aside, you have to admit that it's not its usual MO," the Brit pointed out.

"This sucks balls," Roo said. "Why are we retreating again?"

"Because I'd rather not die today and getting paid for a few Zoo plants isn't high on my list of things I'd die for," Booker said. "Besides, we're running low on ammo. We need to get out on the double or become Zoo fertilizer."

"I thought Marines were all about that 'Retreat, hell' bullshit?" Mick asked Reen as he jogged through the jungle beside her.

"That might be our slogan," she said, "but we aren't fucking morons. We know which hills to die on and which hills to leave the fuck alone."

"Fudge, I'm going to be sore tomorrow," Charles said and easily overtook his two teammates with his longer stride.

He fell into step beside Booker at the front of the small procession.

"You getting soft, cowboy? Maybe you should focus on leg day," the Aussie snarked. "I know you're trying to beef up to match my fucking awesome physique, but we can't all be gods."

His teammate made an obscene gesture over his shoulder.

"How far are we from the wall?" Reen asked.

"Three klicks," the Brit answered.

Booker let Charles set the pace. He lengthened his stride and kept them running at a speed that was fast for the terrain but still easy to maintain for a longer distance.

Roars sounded from the jungle nearby.

"Fuck," Roo said, "not again! Can't these assholes give us a fucking break?"

A creature that resembled a porcupine—if porcupines were the size of hippos and had fangs, glowing yellow eyes, and massive claws—sprang out of the jungle ahead of them. It screamed and flexed its back to whip its thick tail up and over its head. Foot-long obsidian quills rocketed through the air.

Taken by surprise, Charles and Booker barely had time to dive out of the way. Mick shoved Reen aside but the movement slowed his own escape and exposed his right arm. One quill sliced through the fleshy portion of his upper arm. Another pierced his forearm to shatter bone and lodged there. The Aboriginal screamed in pain.

Roo swung his AK-47 forward from its place at his side, held the trigger, and let the rounds rip the new animal to shreds.

"Mick! Mick, are you all right?" Reen asked. She leaned over him and inspected his right arm.

"What the fuck kind of question is that?" He gritted his teeth against the pain. "Fuck me dead. You try to do one fucking good thing and this is what happens. That stupid bitch karma can get stuffed."

Reen used her Bowie knife to cut strips of cloth from the extra shirt she had in her pack.

"What are you doing?" Mick asked. He gritted his teeth again but still managed to glare at her. He was pale and sweating from more than the humidity and physical exertion.

"I'm going to bind these wounds. Hopefully, there wasn't any poison."

"Hopefully? Fuck."

She cut his sleeve away and winced when she saw the tattered flesh of his upper arm. Blood flowed freely down the elbow where it dripped to the dirt.

"How bad is it?" he asked.

Roo came over, saw the arm, and grimaced.

"Jesus, it's that bad, huh?"

"We have to pull this quill from your arm," Reen said.

Mick's eyes grew wide and he tried to push away from her. "No fucking way. Nope. GFY. Don't you fucking touch me!"

She glanced at the Aussie, who nodded.

He pinned his teammate to the ground.

"Hey!"

Charles and Booker moved to stand over the three and keep watch while they tended to the injured man.

With Roo holding Mick secure, Reen took a firm hold of the back of the quill and with a quick shove, pushed it forward until the tip appeared on the other side of his arm. Too quick for him to react, she shifted her grip to the tip and yanked the quill through and out.

The Aboriginal screamed. "Motherfucking cock-sucking son of a slag! *You bitch.* Jesus Christ, was that necessary?"

"Oh, come on, Mick. If you can still talk, it's not as bad as you think it is." She retrieved a bandage roll from her medkit and bound the cloth tightly around the wound. "You're lucky you're injured. Any other time and I'd punch you so hard your grandma'd see stars."

"Yeah, I'm real fucking lucky."

"Should we splint it?" Roo asked.

Reen looked at the foliage around them. The Zoo plants crept forward and vines already pulled at their clothing.

"I don't know if I trust any of this stuff to use as a splint," she said. "Who knows what it might do to him?"

"Here, use this," Booker said. He passed her a push dagger in a sheath.

She raised her eyebrow.

"It'll keep his arm from moving," the Brit said. "Worst case scenario, he can use it. But hurry it up. We can't stay here much longer."

Seeing the sense of it, she ripped the bandage in two, positioned the knife as a splint, and used the remainder of the bandage to keep it in place. The strapping stayed white for a few moments before blood began to seep through.

A few howls sounded in the near distance.

"Okay, people. Time to wrap it up!" Charles said and glared into the jungle.

Reen sat back on her heels and inspected her handiwork. "It'll have to do."

"Can you walk?" Roo asked. He helped his teammate to his feet.

"My bloody arm was caught, you bogan, not my fucking leg. Of course I can still fucking walk. Jesus."

"Just checking," he said. "You were acting like such a wombat I needed to make sure."

His friend found a good use for the middle finger of his good hand.

They started at a run again and held formation in a tightly-knit group with Mick in the center.

"I'm not bloody useless," he said but didn't try to force his way to the perimeter.

Vines dropped from the canopy and tried to snatch the running humans into the trees. Some had round mouths with three rows of teeth and tried to take chunks out of them. Charles fired buckshot to scatter them and leave them in tatters.

"I won't be able to keep them off for much longer," he said.

"We're just over a klick out," Booker said. "There shouldn't be vines when we get closer."

Five massive demiwolves burst through the trees, snarling and howling. They kept pace next to the humans easily and their eyes glowed red against their matted black fur. Their long dark horns spiraled down their backs to end in wicked, sharp-looking tips.

"Fuck these mangy mutts," Reen grumbled and fired at the mutants.

Charles leveled his shotgun but hesitated, trying to see if Thor was among the animals that bounded alongside them. He didn't think his erstwhile pet would attack them and he wasn't sure what he'd do if he did. To his relief, he didn't see him. It was weapons-free, then, as far as he was concerned.

They howled and snapped, lunged at the humans, and looked for an opportunity to bite.

One of Reen's rounds caught a creature in the temple and its skull imploded. Its body rolled away to trip another of its pack mates.

Booker fired his M5 and stitched the side of another demiwolf with progressive strikes and it fell back. The remaining three howled in anger and pounced recklessly at the humans.

A demiwolf tried to leap across their path. Charles rammed the butt of his Remington into the animal's side. He followed the movement through and pounded his shoulder into it too. The monster was thrown off course and landed on its back with a yelp.

Mick tried firing at the attackers but his aim was off as his injuries forced him to use his non-dominant hand. He let the rifle hang at his side and snagged a grenade with his good hand. He forced the fingers of his right hand around it and pulled the pin with his left. His movements were awkward but he didn't let his injuries stop him from helping. He lobbed the grenade at two of the oncoming mutants. It exploded and they were showered with blue— almost black—blood, fur, and chunks of body parts. The last creature ran into the jungle, howling.

"Shit, I think some of that got into my mouth," Roo said and spat with disgust.

The Aboriginal stumbled and Booker caught him by his good arm. The wounded man was pale and sweated heavily. Blood flowed down his arm, having soaked completely through the bandages.

"He's lost a lot of blood," the Brit said. "We need to get him help."

As if to prove his point, the man stumbled again.

"Charles, you might have to carry him."

The American nodded and moved toward them, then stooped to pick the other man up.

Mick sidestepped away from him. "Fuck that," he slurred. "I'm not being carried like some goddamn baby."

"Come on, Mick. Letting Charles carry you the rest of the way out isn't going to knock you down any in our eyes," Booker said.

"It's unmanly," he protested.

"I thought you were above all that macho bullshit," Reen said.

"Turns out, I'm not."

"It'll be fine," Roo said.

"Course you'd say that! You're not the one who has to be carried! Besides, it's just my arm."

He took a few steps forward to demonstrate that he was fine. His knees buckled and Reen grabbed the back of his shirt to haul him up before he face-planted in the dirt. They all exchanged concerned looks.

"He looks paler than he should for just blood loss," Charles said, his brow furrowed.

"Poison?" Roo asked.

"It's probable," she said.

"What?" Mick asked and glared at his teammates.

Roars sounded closer to their location.

"Enough waffling," the Brit said. "We need to move. Sorry, Mick, but Charles is going to carry you."

Charles picked him up in a fireman's carry. He grunted and widened his stance to accommodate the other man's weight.

His unwilling passenger groaned. "This is fucking embarrassing, mate. Not to mention, you're bony as shit. What the hell's up with that? You have so much muscle I shouldn't be able to feel all your bones digging in."

"It doesn't help that you're pretty heavy, man," Charles said.

"Rude. You fat-shaming me?"

"We've got to make tracks. I think he's going into shock," Booker said. He looked at Mick on Charles' broad shoulders and frowned. "You've already lost too much blood. That quill probably nicked an artery or something. It's a bleddy miracle you haven't bled out already. Just hang on. We're nearly there."

They started off again at a jog. The rest of Charles and Mick's extra ammo was given to Booker, Reen, and Roo since neither man could properly fire a weapon.

The foliage around them began to thin. The spaces between the trees grew larger. They caught glimpses of the ten-meter-high concrete wall that separated the jungle of the Zoo from the human base on the opposite side.

"Almost there!" Charles said.

Mick made a noise between a gasp and a groan and went limp.

"Shit," the American said, "I think he passed out."

Reen smacked the injured man on the back of the head and he opened his eyes.

"Whassat for?" he mumbled.

"Stay awake," she commanded.

He made a half-hearted effort to flip her off.

"Come on, mate. We're right here. Just hold on five more minutes," Roo said. He frowned at Mick and his brow furrowed with worry for his friend.

Something big screamed behind them, followed by a bellowing roar.

"We definitely don't have enough ammo to take care of whatever the fuck that is," Reen said.

"We'll be out of here dreckly," Booker said as the tree line broke and they stumbled across the sand toward the gate.

They crossed the twenty or so meters of partially burned sand that rimmed the jungle of the Zoo in a gold and black-charred ring. The guards manning the anti-tank gun at the top of the wall signaled them to run faster. One of the Ma Deuces opened fire and the machine gun's stuttered cry jarred Mick awake again, but not for long. Another Ma Deuce fired, but they didn't look back to see what the guards had targeted.

They reached the wall as the gate slid open.

The flamethrowers coughed to life and a wall of heat enveloped their backs as the team of five slipped into the dark passageway. There were several roars, and the ground trembled as the gate snapped shut behind them.

The blue running lights were a stark contrast to the blinding Saharan sun they'd been in moments before. The cool of the concrete passageway was a welcome feeling.

"We made it," Charles said, but he still didn't put Mick down.

Booker pressed his fingers to Mick's neck. "We still need to hurry. His pulse is slowing."

"You can't fucking die on us now, mate," Roo said.

"I'm not dying," the man moaned. "Can't a fella rest his goddamn eyes?"

"Just keep talking," Reen said.

"Fuck you."

The gate ahead of them slid open and they were again in the blinding sun. The guard nodded to them but went back to looking at the men on top of the wall.

They walked along the designated path, careful not to step off or become victims to whatever lay in wait beneath the sand. Warning signs glared at them from the walls, each bright color promising death.

"Can you radio for a vehicle?" Booker asked the guard

at the second wall. "We need to get our man to the infirmary as quickly as possible."

"You got it, boss," the guard said and punched in the code to let them through the second wall.

They wound their way through the concrete obstacles that filled the sandy space between the second and third walls. Then they were through and into the Harvesters Camp.

An old ambulance, the side riddled with bullet holes, screeched to a stop in front of them as they exited the final wall. Two burly men in black scrubs leapt out and rushed to get Mick off Charles' back while he told them hastily what had wounded his teammate. They loaded him onto their stretcher and raced back to the ambulance.

The vehicle accelerated and the team followed on foot.

Charles pulled his shirt off.

"Uh, what are you doing?" Booker asked.

"I don't want his blood on me anymore," Charles said. He threw the shirt into a firepit as they walked past and shook his arms an in attempt to get his blood flowing again. "I'm really getting tired of carrying people around."

"Too bad you're a hulking black dude who's built like a linebacker," Reen said. "I think you can handle it."

"I *was* a linebacker."

"See what I mean?"

"Do you think he'll make it?" Roo asked. "I don't know what I'd tell his ma and pa if he didn't. I'm the reason he's here."

Booker clapped him on the shoulder. "I'm sure he'll be fine. We got him in just in time. The French Quarter might not be the most high-tech place, but their docs know their shit."

"It's just too bad we won't be getting anything for that shit show," Reen said.

"Doesn't matter," Charles said. "A man's life is more important than material gain."

"Yeah, about that," the Aussie said.

The three looked at him with raised eyebrows and he smiled. He opened his pack and revealed three sample containers full of silver plants with small purple flowers.

"Where the fuck did you get those?" Booker asked.

"I ripped them up during the first attack. You guys were doing such a bang-up job distracting the wankers and I took advantage of that," he said. "So it won't have been for nothing."

They arrived at the infirmary and Booker asked the nurse at the main table about Mick.

"The Aboriginal guy?" the nurse asked.

They nodded.

"Yeah, you brought him in just in time. Doc got him stitched up and we're addressing his broken arm. He also had to have a blood transfusion. You guys were lucky with your timing. Any longer and he would've lost too much blood to save. Lucky for him, the poison on whatever attacked him was pretty mild, and we were able to administer a general antidote to neutralize it. He should be out of surgery in an hour."

"So, he'll be fine?" Roo asked.

The nurse held his hands up. "Don't see why not. We're giving him an extra help up with some new medicine that's apparently been synthesized to speed up healing or something—some new cutting-edge trial they're running or whatever."

"That's not going to turn him into a mutant or something, right?" Reen asked.

The nurse laughed, then seemed to realize she wasn't kidding. "Oh. Uh. No. It'll just speed up the healing process. Help knit everything back together faster. I don't know the whole science of it, but someone apparently thinks they've discovered something that can make a difference and I guess they want to test it in the field before the Army accepts it."

"If it does anything to fuck him up, I'll come find you," Roo said. "I don't forget a face easily."

"Right. Well, I'll leave you to wait, then." The nurse hurried away but looked over his shoulder once as if wondering how serious he was.

"I'll go take the containers to Franco's, then," Booker said. "I'll be back in time for Mick to be ready to go home."

"Want to grab me a shirt while you're at it?" Charles asked.

He nodded and walked out of the infirmary.

"You really going to cover up so soon, Charles?" Reen asked.

Roo rolled his eyes and the American laughed.

"You like what you see?"

"Oh, for fuck's sake," the other man said.

"Jealous, Roo?" she asked.

He merely raised an eyebrow challengingly.

"Besides," she said, "I'm definitely in a ginger phase at the moment."

The man stood a little straighter and ran his fingers through his short, red hair.

She smirked at him and winked at a nurse who walked past, her strawberry-blonde hair in a bun on top of her head. The woman giggled and waved at her.

Charles laughed. "You should see the look on your face, Roo."

"Fuck you," his teammate retorted and his two companions laughed at him.

After half an hour, Booker returned to wait with them and confirmed that they had been paid. They saved the details for later, though, as nurse came up to them soon after he arrived.

"You three here with Mick?" he asked.

"We are," the Brit said. "I'm Booker. We're with BOHICA Warriors."

"Right. Sure. Well, he made it through just fine and the drugs are wearing off," the nurse said. "He'll need some time to rest, but he should be okay. We put a few screws in his arm to hold the bone in place. His arm's in a cast at the moment, but he should have that off in a month or so. Just make sure he doesn't do anything too strenuous. He'll also have to take medication for the next two weeks to make sure the poison has been completely flushed from his system and no alien crud takes ahold."

Mick was wheeled out from the back of the infirmary. Booker was about to stand but the nurse pressed him back into his seat.

"We'll need you to pay for his treatment," the nurse said. "Ivan can take your payment."

A tall man with a scan pad approached him.

"Let me guess," he said, "you're Ivan?"

"At your service. Your friend's care will be eighty grand. How would you like to pay that? Cash or electronic transfer?" the man asked with a grin.

The Brit sighed. "Electronic transfer."

Roo helped Mick out of the wheelchair. "How you feelin'?"

His teammate shrugged, then winced. "Like I got hit by a truck and the wanker backed over me again just to be sure he ran me over properly."

"You want the good news or the bad news?" Reen asked.

"What? There's bad news?"

"Sure," she said. "The good news is, you'll get better and out of that cast in a month. The bad news is you'll be better and out of the cast in a month."

"Oh, joy."

"Let's take this party back to home base, shall we?" Booker suggested.

"Please," Mick said. "I feel like I can sleep through that month of this cast."

They walked out of the infirmary and to their building.

CHAPTER TWO

The Zoo - Thor

The need for blood pounded through Thor's veins and pulsed in the forefront of his mind. The whole Zoo thrummed with it—bloodlust, revenge, and self-preservation were a potent cocktail.

He raced through the jungle with his pack. The older demiwolves led the charge, snarling and howling. He wasn't as fast as the others but did his best to keep pace.

The others reached the humans first, but he stopped. He became confused. The Zoo pressed him to attack and rip the humans apart for trespassing. Thor only had one reason to hesitate—Charles.

The man was there with the other humans and some of their scents were still familiar. It was Charles who had made a lasting impression on his mind, though. He wouldn't attack that man.

So, he pulled back from the fighting. He paced alongside the others, deeper into the vegetation, and watched as the other Zoo animals answered the call to which he was unwilling to respond.

Thor rammed his horns into a nearby tree because he needed to channel his aggression somewhere. He scraped against the tree. His horns were knotty, unlike the curling horns of his pack. Their obsidian color swirled with red at the tips. They started between his ears and curved back in an arc, following the shape of his spine like an ibex's horns. He tossed his head and scored the tree's trunk until sap oozed out.

Caught in the overwhelming urge, he snorted and growled and attacked the tree again. Finally, with a groan of complaint, it shuddered and fell to land solidly with a thud. The noise snapped him from the near trance-like state he'd been in.

He looked around and no longer heard the sound of fighting. The desire to destroy the humans had diminished so he went to investigate.

A path of destruction followed the humans. The bodies of the Zoo animals were already being re-absorbed by the Zoo. The path was riddled with half-dissolved carcasses.

Thor stood over what remained of three of his kind, their bodies twisted and broken. The ground lapped up the blood and fur and churned the bones into dust. They weren't from his pack—their scent was unfamiliar—but it still bothered him. He raised his head and uttered a mournful howl. Several calls answered his call.

He needed to rejoin his pack but for some reason, continued to follow the trail the humans had taken. The smell of the injured Zoo was heady, the air thick with the scent of crushed plants and the herby-metallic odor of dead animals.

A different type of scent, clashing with the others, reached him and Thor's heart rate accelerated. It was human blood. He rushed forward to investigate. It was slowly being absorbed into the ground, but there was enough of it there that he could still make sense of it. He sniffed at the dark stain and a feeling that could have been categorized as relief filled him. It was human blood, but it wasn't Charles'. The scent that clung faintly was completely unfamiliar.

Driven by an inward need he didn't understand, he followed the trail until it led him to the wall. He stopped in the tree line, immediately before the sand, and remained in the shadows. His gaze focused on the wall and he was filled with longing to cross the barren space. He wondered if it was because he missed Charles. On some level, he missed playing fetch with the old tire and he missed Charles always having food for him. But there was something else, too. It wasn't completely about wanting to be reunited with him and the other humans. In the jungle around him, other animals moved forward. His pack soon joined him and fanned out in a line.

A giant, scaly monster crept forward, surprisingly silent for its size. Thor watched as the black, iridescent scales on the creature's body began to change. They shimmered and deepened in color, then lightened dramatically. The gorgorex stretched a leg forward and dragged one long talon through the sand. The scales covering its foot turned the same buttery beige color as the desert. It clicked its sharp teeth together and stared at the wall. Strings of milky blue saliva dripped from its jaws.

Thor looked at the wall again. He sat and prepared to wait—but for what, he wasn't sure.

CHAPTER THREE

Fiddler's Green, Harvesters Camp

Roo closed the door to Mick's room. He'd had it to himself since Lester was killed, the BOHICA Warrior's first fatality. The Aussie went to the dining area where Charles, Reen, and Booker were waiting.

"He's sleeping," he said. He scrubbed his hand over his face. "What exactly happened out there, huh? What made those bloody wankers go apeshit like that?"

"I feel like the monsters in the Zoo have been more aggressive lately," Booker said. "That's the fifth or sixth time something's tried to breach the wall. The guards keep repelling them, but do you think they can keep it up?"

"I don't see why not. They've lasted this long. I wouldn't want to be on the receiving end of a Ma Deuce," Reen said.

"It seems like all the attacks are in small numbers," Charles said. "If the animals worked together as a big wave, the guards'd be hard-pressed to push them back, I think."

She sighed. "Don't be such a Debbie Downer, Charles."

He ignored her.

"I don't think we'll be able to figure it out just by gabbing about it. I need a fucking drink." Roo stood from the table and stretched. He cracked his neck. "Do you think Mick'll be fine if we leave him alone?"

"He's a grown-ass man. He'll be all right for a few hours. Besides, he just broke his arm. It's not like he's completely incapacitated," she said.

"To the Wateringhole we go," Booker said.

The Aussie opened the door a crack to check on the wounded man on their way out. He snored softly so he shut the door again.

The usual crowd of off-mission mercenaries filled the bar. The four made their way to the back and settled at a corner table. A waitress swung past and took their order.

"I definitely think something's changed," Booker said.

"What are you talking about?" Roo asked.

"With the Zoo," he answered. "I mean, think about it. The last couple of missions we've run have ended in near-disaster."

"I think Lester being ripped to shreds would be considered a disaster," Charles pointed out.

"Exactly. Something's bleddy off. We consistently get attacked in the Zoo but lately, it's been extra ferocious. It's like the whole jungle wants to destroy anything foreign."

"Ironic, isn't it?" Reen said. "They're the aliens but we're foreign material."

The waitress brought a pitcher of beer and four glasses to them. Roo winked at her, but she ignored him and walked away. He glanced at the others, hoping they hadn't seen the interaction.

Reen grinned. "Losing your touch there, Casanova?"

He gave her a two-finger salute and she laughed.

The table beside theirs was full of drunk men. Their conversation grew louder and Roo, who was seated closest, glanced at them when he realized that the BOHICA Warriors were the subject of their conversation.

"Look at them," a man said, "they think they're hot shit. But they sure as hell aren't. They're just pretending like they're still the best."

"Let's be fair now, Craig," another said, "they *used* to be the fucking kings. Pride comes before the fall."

"BOHICA, my left foot," Craig scoffed. "Seems they're the ones on the receiving end."

The others at the table laughed.

"BOHICA Warriors? More like BOHICA Wimps! What fuckwads."

Roo, who grew redder the longer the conversation went on, stood. He turned to the table of drunks. They looked at him expectantly and laughed.

"Listen up, you fucking wankers," he stated belligerently. "I don't see you assholes doing anything on our level. In fact, you're so goddamn below us we're on a different planet."

"Oh, yeah?"

"Roo, sit back down," Booker said.

Charles pulled him back into his chair.

"Yeah, sit back down, little man," Craig said. "We don't want you hurting yourself."

"Fuck me dead," he muttered and ground his teeth together. His hands were in tight fists.

Reen raised an eyebrow. "Three...two...one," she said to Charles.

The Aussie launched himself out of his seat, bull-rushed Craig, and knocked him on his ass. The other man didn't have time to react before he cold-cocked him. His opponent's three companions jumped forward to pull Roo off.

Charles stood and intercepted one man before he reached his teammate. The large man threw a quick right hook and his target reeled back.

Craig managed to get out from under Roo. They struggled to their feet and squared off.

"This is almost déjà vu," Booker said. He drained the rest of his drink. "Right. Here we go."

The loudmouth was focused on the Aussie and paid no attention to the others so he didn't see Booker's front kick coming. He stumbled sideways and barreled into another table to spill their beer and food. The table collapsed under him.

Reen stood beside Charles. "Your lip's bleeding, Roo."

He ignored her comment and stood on a chair. "Anybody else have something shitty to say about us?" he yelled at the rest of the bar.

"Sit the fuck down!" a man from across the room yelled.

"Hey, asshole!" A member of a crew they'd been with to capture a gorgorex slugged the heckler.

The bar filled with the sound of toppling chairs and knuckles smacking into flesh as an all-out brawl erupted. The mercenaries were always on edge and it didn't take much to set them off.

A man stormed toward Reen. He was twice her size and

Charles was about to step in front of her, but she pushed him out of the way. She grinned at the approaching assailant, shifted her weight, and snapped a leg up in a roundhouse kick. It landed across the large man's jaw and he collapsed. She waded into the fighting with deadly grace to throw elbows and kicks and clear a space around her.

Craig had resumed his attempt to get the better of Roo. They punched each other and traded blows in equal measure. The mouthy merc used his height advantage, pinned his opponent against the wall, and began to knee him in the stomach.

Charles tackled him. He snapped his elbow across the man's face and he immediately went limp.

"You good?" Charles asked Roo.

His teammate nodded and pinched the bridge of his nose to try to stop the bleeding.

Booker flipped a man over his shoulder. Another approached him from behind and landed a kidney punch before the Brit could deliver his back kick. Despite being hit, he had enough force in the kick to catapult his attacker into a table, which buckled. He stood beside Charles and Roo. "You'd think they'd invest in sturdier furniture around here."

The corner of the American's mouth twitched.

"Where's Reen?" Roo asked and tilted his head back. "Fuck, I think my nose is broken."

"Maybe it'll improve your features," Booker said.

"Fuck you."

She appeared in front of them, holding a man in a head-lock. "This scene is getting old," she said. The man tapped her arm. She sighed and removed her arm. He dropped to all fours and gasped for air before she kicked him out of her way.

A gunshot rang out above the noise of the fight. The bartender stood on top of the bar, a Smith and Wesson .500 in his hand. "Enough! Who the fuck started this shit?"

"I think that's our cue to exit, gentlemen," Booker muttered.

The fighting petered out. Chairs and tables were set to rights and the mercs shifted and glared at one another.

"As this is the closest bar, we can't afford to get banned," the Brit reminded them. They slipped out into the night before fingers could be pointed.

"I'm getting too old for this shit," Roo said.

"You fucking started it, you bleddy wanker."

He made a dismissive gesture with his hand. "That cocksucker had it coming."

Reen vibrated with unused energy. "I haven't been in a bar fight in ages."

"Stick around this one and I'm sure it won't be the last you'll have," Charles said and threw an arm around Roo's shoulders. His teammate shoved him away.

"I've definitely had enough excitement for a while. It's been a long fucking day," Booker said.

"You've gotta do a better job of controlling your temper, Roo. It's too much after a mission as intense as that one. What would your daughter think about you getting into so many fights?" Charles asked.

The Aussie gave him a black look. "Fuck off, cowboy. You don't get to say shit like that to me. Leave Cassie out of this."

The other man held his hands up in surrender.

"I think we all need some R-n-R," Reen said. "We'll all feel better about this in the morning."

"I feel fucking fine," Roo said.

No one bothered to contradict him.

CHAPTER FOUR

Fiddler's Green, Harvesters Camp

Booker shoved the scrambled eggs around his plate with his fork. "I miss a proper English brekky," he muttered.

"You don't like my scrambled eggs? Next time, make something for yourself," Reen said.

"No. It wasn't a reflection on your cooking. You're a better cook than Roo is."

"I never said I was a fucking chef," Roo said. "Whose idea was it to rotate who cooked for everyone?"

The Brit pursed his lips. "Who knows?"

"It was probably yours," she said.

"Let's be real, none of us are great at cooking," Charles interjected. "I think we could all use a break. I miss my ma's cooking. She makes the best spaghetti pie you've ever had in your life."

"What the fuck's a spaghetti pie?" the Aussie asked.

"Pretty self-explanatory. Ma uses fresh basil and her

own ricotta. It's the best. Add some fried okra on the side and you have the best freaking meal you could want."

"I could go for a few fried fillets of King George whiting with some chips. Or spit-roasted lamb and orzo." Roo sounded wistful.

Reen groaned. "Talking about this isn't going to help anything."

"She's right," Booker said. "So maybe we should talk about something else. I think we all need a break. It's been too long. A lot has happened and I think we're all feeling the effects of that."

No one argued with him.

"So, what's your solution?" Charles asked.

He opened his mouth to answer but was interrupted by a knock on the door and frowned.

"Hold that thought."

His frown still in place, he went down the stairs to the first floor of their building and opened the door. A tall, grim-looking man in green-and-brown fatigues stood on the stoop. He had a bright red bandana around his neck and an equally bright green beret on his head.

"Can I help you?" Booker asked, a hand still on the door.

The man saluted. "I'm looking for the BOHICA Warriors Company."

"You've found us. I'm Booker. What can I do for you?"

"I am Emam, I'm in the Benin Armed Forces and I've brought a letter from the President of Benin—Arhambault Okonkuo." Emam held out a cream-colored envelope addressed to the BOHICA Warriors Company. It was sealed with the Benin crest.

"Thanks," he said. "Did you want to come in and wait for our answer, or…"

"No, sir. Thank you. I've got to be heading back. I believe there is contact information in the letter." He saluted again, turned on his heel, and walked away.

The Brit closed the door and ripped the envelope open. He read it as he walked up the stairs to rejoin the others.

"What's wrong?" Reen asked.

"Who was that?" Roo asked at the same time.

He frowned and sat at the table. "We just got a letter. From the president of Benin."

"No shit. For real?" the Aussie demanded. "Where's Benin?"

"South-east from here. Little country, next to Nigeria," she answered.

He raised an eyebrow and she shrugged. "I'm half-African. I like geography. Why not learn the geography of Africa?"

"Huh," he said.

"And the president of this tiny country sent us a letter?" Charles asked.

Booker nodded.

"Well, what did it say?" she prompted impatiently.

In reply, he pushed the letter across the table toward her. She read it quickly and frowned.

"Will someone just bloody tell us what the fuck is going on?" Roo demanded.

"It seems about thirty Catholic boarding schoolgirls have been kidnapped by the insurgent group, Ansaru. The Benin Army's hands are tied, apparently. It would appear that forces from within Benin are assisting the Ansaru,"

Booker said. "President Okonkuo heard about us from a Russian diplomat. It seems no one else is willing to provide an assist—too mired in world politics. And with the Zoo relatively close, no one wants to step on anyone else's toes. So that's where we would come in. The president wants us to go rescue the girls."

Charles pressed his lips into a thin line and a vein pulsed in the side of his neck. "Thirty schoolgirls?"

The Brit nodded. "They think. At least thirty from the school, that is. From the information in the letter, it looks like most of them are under the age of fifteen."

"There could be more?" Reen asked.

"The letter doesn't do a good job of laying out the details."

"Fuck," the large man said. "I remember when my sister was that age."

"So, what? They just expect us to swoop in and rescue these girls? What's in it for us besides feeling okay about ourselves at the end of the day?" the Aussie challenged.

Charles scowled at him.

"They're offering us about three hundred million West African CFA francs for the completion of the job. Which translates into roughly half a mill in American dollars," Reen said.

"I think we should do it," the American said.

"I mean, as much as I agree that kidnapping young girls is a fucking shitty thing to do, I don't think we should do it," Roo said.

Everyone stared at him.

"Look. The BOHICA Warriors weren't created to play superhero. We were—we are—a company of badasses

32

whose sole purpose is to kick ass in the motherfucking Zoo. We aren't equipped for a civilian rescue against terrorists. Especially not when those civilians are young girls."

"You have a daughter! You should be the most up in arms about this out of all of us!" Charles yelled. "She's even the same age!"

He winced. "I know, I know. I'm just not sure how effective we'd be able to be. I don't want to do more damage."

The large man stood from his seat and leaned across the table toward his teammate, who held his ground.

Reen grabbed the back of Charles' shirt and pulled him back. "Relax, Charles. Roo's making some good points."

He folded his arms pointedly over his chest but sat again.

Booker massaged his temples. "The money's good. And it would be a brilliant thing to do. I just don't know."

"What's not to know?" the American retorted. "It's either we go rescue these poor, innocent girls. Or we leave them in the hands of a terrorist group."

"I think it's too political, on top of us not being properly outfitted," Roo said.

"I don't think we should make a decision on it right now," Reen interjected.

"I agree," the Brit said. "Let's table this and come back to it. Maybe when Mick's back on his feet. I'm sure he'd probably have an opinion about this too."

"Can you live with that, Charles?" she asked.

The American heaved a sigh. "Fine. But we shouldn't wait for very long."

"We won't," Booker said. "The president has asked for an answer by the end of the week. In the meantime, I think we should take some time off. Maybe until Mick is a little more recuperated. It's been a good ten days now and he's much better but could do with a little more recovery. We can afford to take the time, so let's do that. Sound good to everyone?"

"Works for me," she said, stood, and stretched. "Come on, Charles. Let's go work out some of that aggression, yeah?"

"You two aren't going to go rut, are you?" Roo asked.

"Fuck off, Aussie. We're going to spar."

"Want to join in?" Charles asked and stretched his muscular arms.

"I'll watch," he said.

The Brit looked toward the ceiling. "Christ, you're such a bleddy perv."

The other man simply grinned. "Who wouldn't want to watch Reen kick Charles' ass?"

"In that case," he replied, "maybe I'd like to see that."

"You guys don't think I can take her?"

The two men exchanged a look and watched Reen bend to wrap her hands around her ankles. She snapped to a standing position and adjusted her curly mohawk.

"I choose not to answer that question," Booker said.

"I think she's going to fucking kick your ass," Roo said.

Charles let his fingers do the talking.

CHAPTER FIVE

Fiddler's Green, Harvesters Camp

"It's been two fucking weeks. I'm fine. I finished that dumb-ass medicine. I'm ready to go back into the Zoo and kick ass," Mick announced from where he stood at the end of the table in the dining room.

Charles looked up from his whittling project and stared pointedly at the cast that was still on his right arm. His teammate glowered at him and shifted his body so the cast wasn't in direct line of sight.

"Glad you're feeling better, mate," Roo said. "And as much as I hate being such a bogan, I don't think we're quite ready to go back into the Zoo. Not until you're at least at eighty-five percent."

The Aboriginal groaned. "Fuck percentages! I'm fine."

"You can't shoot for shit with your left hand," Reen pointed out. "Plus, your arm isn't completely healed yet. Imagine what diseases lay in wait in the fucking Zoo. You wouldn't want to pick up something flesh-eating or some shit like that."

"Uh, GFY."

"Right back a'tcha, buddy," she said with a wink.

Booker walked into the room, scrolling through something on his tablet. "Let me guess. Mick thinks he's ready to go into the Zoo?"

"Ding, ding, ding!" she said. "Give the boy a prize."

"All of you can get fucking stuffed."

"Oh, come on, Mick. You know we're right," Roo said. "You don't need to worry about us thinking you're weak or anything. We know you're not."

"The fuck? I wasn't fucking worried about that before, but now I fucking am. Jesus."

Charles punched the Aussie in the arm. "He's just pulling your leg, Mick. Ignore the dummy."

"You're not ready yet, Mick," Booker said.

"I think I can be the judge of being ready or not," he retorted.

"You know what I think?" Reen didn't give anyone a chance to respond. "I think we've all been sitting in this building for too fucking long. Let's go get a drink."

"Think they'll still let us in after the stunt Roo pulled?" Mick asked.

Roo smacked him in the back of the head. "Fuck you, mate. It wasn't a stunt."

"Ouch." The Aboriginal made a big show of grabbing his head. "You shouldn't hit the invalid. For that, you get to buy my first coldie."

"That's a great idea, Mick. Make the Aussie asshole get everyone's first drink," Reen said. She hooked her arm through his uninjured one and walked out of the room.

"Ooh, are we calling him that now? The Aussie Asshole.

I like that, although I'm a little worried it could be put back on me," he said on his way out the door.

"Now, wait a minute. I never said I was buying anybody's drinks!"

"Bleddy brilliant! Let's hop to it before he changes his mind," Booker said and walked past Roo to follow Mick and Reen.

The Aussie looked at Charles, who merely shook his head and laughed as he followed the others out.

"Fuckin' a-holes," he muttered to the empty room.

"Roo!" Reen yelled from downstairs. "Waiting on your ginger ass!"

"I'm coming!"

"So soon? Who knew you'd be early to blow like that?" she quipped.

He joined them downstairs. "It's nice to know you're thinking of me."

She gave him the finger.

"Come on, people! The beers won't drink themselves," Mick said.

They walked through the camp to the Wateringhole. The sun was dipping below the horizon and flooded the sky with red and orange light.

"I hate the desert, but this is my favorite time of day," Reen said. "I mean, look at that sunset."

"It's the little things," the Aboriginal said.

They walked past a group of men seated around a bonfire they'd started in an aluminum trashcan.

"Look, the BOHICA wimps are at it again. This time, they had to recruit a gimp into their team!"

Charles caught Roo's shoulder and held him in place.

No one thought to grab Mick. He stormed toward the jeerer, grabbed the man by the front of the shirt, and hauled him away from the others.

"You think that's fucking funny, asshole? Huh?" he said through gritted teeth.

"What are you gonna do? Hit me?" The man sneered. He shoved Mick away from him.

The angry man punched him, but he used his casted arm. His opponent stumbled back into the sand. Mick clutched his arm.

"Ah, fuck. Look what you made me do! I broke my cast!" He frowned at the cracked plaster.

The man's friends stood, but Charles and Roo put themselves between them and their wounded teammate. Reen hauled the man he'd punched from the ground and dragged him back to the bonfire.

"Here's your trash. Take it out next time, don't just leave it lying around for someone else to do it for you."

Booker inspected the broken cast. "I think we should just cut it off."

"It's supposed to be on there for a couple more weeks," Mick protested.

"I thought you said you were fine. Besides, they gave you that new super-charged quick-fix stuff. That should count for something, right?"

"I don't know! I'm just going out of my bloody head sitting around with nothing to do."

The Brit reached for his knife, but Reen handed him her Bowie knife. "Here, use this."

"Um, no. Don't use that! Don't use anything. Do you have medical training?"

"Sure. I mean, field response training."

"Nope. I'm not here to be your guinea pig."

"Oh, stop bitching," she said. "Just let Booker cut your cast off."

"You'd be singing a different tune, little bird, if it was your arm in a cast and Booker was wielding a bloody large knife and threatening to poke around."

"Firstly, I don't appreciate that you just called me 'little bird.' Retaliation will be had for that," she said. "And secondly, Booker's got steady hands. I'm sure he won't cut you."

"It'll be fine," the Brit said. "Do you want me to do it? Or do you want to go to the infirmary and have to pay twenty grand or some shit like that to have them do it?"

With obvious reluctance, he held his arm out. Booker cut his cast off and tossed the two halves aside.

"See, that wasn't so bad, now was it?" Reen all but purred. She punched Mick in his left shoulder.

He ignored her and inspected his arm. The scar was puffy, a milky pink color, and about three inches long. "Huh. That's not as bad as I thought it was going to be. Do you think I'll get super-strength now? After all that space-age medicine?"

She rolled her eyes and walked on. The Brit snorted and patted him on the shoulder. "You can believe anything you want, but I don't think that's going to be a thing. It's made to speed up healing, not give you fucking super-powers."

"Sure smells fucking ripe. Jesus," Roo said.

"You're still buying me a beer."

Booker and Charles trailed the group as they continued on their way to the Wateringhole.

"What's on your mind?" the American asked.

"Huh? Oh. Just thinking that this isn't really a break. I think we need a change of scenery."

"Probably."

"Should we get out of here for a little bit?"

He shrugged and looked at his companion out of the corner of his eye.

The Brit sighed. "I know what you're thinking."

Charles grunted.

"You're thinking that going to Benin would be a change of scenery. I just don't know if we're equipped for that. We're just five mercenaries with guns. We aren't set up to rescue thirty girls."

"We could always see what Dan's got."

"Oh, sure. Go to Dan's and say, 'Hey, what do you have in your arsenal that'll help with rescuing schoolgirls?'"

"Sure. Why not?"

"It's ridiculous. Bleddy ridiculous." He sighed.

Charles opened the door to the Wateringhole and waved him through.

"I'll think about it," Booker said.

Charles followed him in and they joined Reen, Mick, and Roo at a table.

"Hey, Booker," Roo said, "do you think we have the equipment to make a video call?"

"Don't see why that would be an issue. You going to call your daughter?"

"Yeah. I thought it'd be nice to see her face, y'know?"

"Of course. After this, I'll see what I can do."

The connection wasn't the best Roo had ever seen, but it wasn't the worst and he wouldn't complain about it. His daughter's face filled the screen of the tablet—a little grainy, but he could still see her big smile and that was all he needed.

"Cassie! Hey, baby doll, how's it goin'?"

"Da-ad, how many times do I have to tell you? I'm not little! I'm almost a teenager!"

"Seems you'll have to tell your old man one more time."

"You're not old!"

"If you're old, then I'm older."

"Well, I guess you're old then."

"Hey! How's school been?"

"Fine."

"Just fine?" Roo leaned closer to the screen, pretending like that would help him see her better.

Cassie giggled and moved in closer too. "Yep!"

"Cassie, is something wrong?"

"Nope."

"You sure?"

"Strewth."

"Okay. I'd hate to find out you were lying to me and I'd have to come home and throw you in the pool."

Her laugh scattered through the connection and her image froze for a second but started moving again. "Dad, why would you throw me in the pool?"

"Because that's what happens to liars—your pants catch fire. Then, I'd have to come and put them out for you."

"That doesn't happen!"

"Sure, it does! It happened to me before. Your granddad had to throw me in the ocean because we didn't have a pool. I never lied after that."

"Do you want to see the project I made in school?"

"I'd love to."

Roo watched the shaky image on the screen as Cassie ran through the large house to the dining room. She showed him the model of a beehive she had put together. He listened as she explained the pollination process to him and how bees made honeycomb. As he did all too often when he spoke to her, he felt a pang that he couldn't be there to have her explain it to him in person.

"Hey, when I get back, do you want to get a real beehive?" he asked.

"Really? Can we do that?"

"Of course!"

"Dad! That would be totally awesome!"

He laughed. "Sure. They'd be your responsibility, though. Think you can handle that?"

"Yes. I can do it. Then maybe you'll see how grown up I am."

Movement caught his attention and he looked up from the tablet to see Reen leaning in the doorway with two beers in her hands.

"All right, Cassie. I'm sure you've got a big day planned of things to do. It's getting pretty late where I am."

"Bummer. Didn't you want to talk to Mum?"

"No, that's okay. You can tell her hello for me, though."

"When will I talk to you again?"

"Not sure, Cassie, but I'll try to make it as soon as possible, ok?"

"Okay. Love you, Dad!"

"Love you too, Cassie." Roo stared at the blank screen of the tablet.

Reen cleared her throat. "Who knew the Tin Man had a heart? And you didn't even need to follow a Yellow Brick Road."

"I feel bad, sometimes, you know? Not being there for everything."

"My dad was never around and look how I turned out."

"That's not exactly comforting."

"I'm sure she'll be fine. She has something I didn't have."

"What's that?"

"Her father's love. She knows you do everything for her, and that's what's important."

Roo nodded and she handed him a beer. He inclined his head and gulped half of it.

"Ah, fuck," he said.

"What?"

"We have to go rescue those girls."

"What made you change your mind?"

"They're all Cassie's age, or damn near it. If someone took her, I'd move heaven and earth to get to her. I can do that. Maybe these girls' parents can't, and if I was in their position, I sure as hell would want someone with the capabilities to do it for me."

Reen nodded.

"So, now we have to convince Booker to do it."

"Think we can do that?"

"Sure. He's a prick, but he's not an asshole. Besides, we can rope Charles into it. He can scowl Booker into submission."

She laughed. "Has he done that before?"

"Not really, but somehow, that bastard always manages to get his way."

She tapped their beer bottles together. "Sounds like a plan."

CHAPTER SIX

Harvesters Camp

Booker joined the other team leaders outside Franco's, waiting for the dispatchers to emerge and assign missions. The team needed a vacation, but they weren't going to get that. Nearly two weeks had passed since their last disastrous mission and Booker knew sitting around was no longer an option. They still had a couple of days before they had to reply to the President, but he hadn't raised it with the team as he wanted to see how well recovered Mick was. Besides, part of him really didn't want to agree to it.

"Booker!" Franco said when he exited the warehouse building and noticed the taller man. "Long time, no see. How's your guy?"

"Mick's doing a lot better. I think they gave him some sort of fancy medicine and he's healed up brilliantly."

"Great," the dispatcher said with a dismissive wave of his hand. "You ready to do a mission for me?"

"That is why I'm here."

"Right. I have a fauna capture and a flora gathering left. Which do you want?"

"Let's do flora."

"Sure. This one's pretty easy, as far as these things go. There are just a few plants that need to be harvested. Six to be precise. I'll send you the details."

"Sounds good. How soon do you need these back?"

"Oh, by the end of the day, if possible. Like I said, this one's easy. The glade isn't new and it's not deep in. I'm sure you and your team will be able to make it in and out in no time."

He sent the details to Booker's tablet. "Thanks, Franco. We'll get right on this."

The Brit left to round up the rest of the team for the mission. He walked in on Reen and Roo, predictably, having an argument while the other two teammates ignored them. Mick played with the parachute cord cat's cradle game he constantly fiddled with. Charles was whittling and the chunk of wood slowly took on the shape of a dog-like monster with horns.

Obviously, the team needed a vacation, but they couldn't do that right then. The mission was the next best thing. Sitting around was no longer an option.

"We've got another mission, people," he announced.

Reen stopped her argument with Roo to look at him. "Oh, thank fuck."

"You're lucky Booker showed up when he did," the Aussie said. "I was totally winning that argument."

She punched him in the shoulder.

"Hate to break it to you, bunj," Mick said, "but in what world were you winning that argument?"

"What's the mission?" Charles asked.

"Flora collecting. Thought we'd ease into working again."

"I'm not a fucking invalid," the Aboriginal protested. "We can do whatever. I'm totally fine."

Roo poked him in his right forearm and he tried to hide his wince. "Oh, bugger off."

"So, everyone, gear up. We've got to be moving. They're expecting this back tonight."

"And the flora is all plant, right?" Reen asked. "None of this carnivorous bullshit?"

"No mouths involved."

They quickly got their kits together and started toward the wall.

"Should we bring the Mule or the BTR?" Charles asked.

"I don't think so. We can do this on foot. The Mule is a lot of hassle to get over and around things and it ends up being faster walking," the Brit said. "Besides, the BTR is an animal magnet and we don't want that right now."

A group of men ran past them, hurriedly putting on armor and chambering cartridges.

"Well, that's odd," Charles said.

Another team sprinted past, yelling.

Roo snagged one of the last men. "Hey, mate, what's the big rush? What's going on?"

"The animals are storming the wall!" The merc shook him off and stumbled on.

Booker opened his mouth to speak but was interrupted by roars and snarls followed closely by the sound of the Ma Deuces at the top of the wall firing. They checked their weapons and raced toward the wall to join the other teams of mercs who now fanned out to form a line of defense.

The ground shook. The air was full of the sound of animals screaming and roaring. The noise battled with the flamethrowers and heavy artillery of the guards above.

"I wish we could see what the fuck was going on," Roo said.

A thunderous explosion preceded a veritable geyser of sand and blood.

"Looks like some of the bastards made it over the first wall," Booker said. "You might get to see what's going on sooner than you thought."

The guard at the Harvesters Camp gate turned and looked at the gathered crowd. "If anything makes it over, kill it. Don't let it get the fuck out of here," he yelled.

"No shit," Reen muttered. She stared at the top of the wall and bounced on the balls of her feet.

Booker looked around. "This is total shit. We can't all be here lined up like this. If this line doesn't hold, there isn't another defense." He paced back from the gathered crowd. "Hey, people!"

Several groups turned and looked at him. Another explosion detonated, followed by the distinct crack of cement.

"We can't all be standing here! We have to create different lines of defense. A third of you stay here, another third go to the center of camp and the last third to the end!"

Blank faces stared at him.

Charles walked up to Booker. He divided the crowd

with his hands as he yelled, "You, stay here. You, go to the center of camp, and the rest of you guard the perimeter!"

"What the fuck are you all waiting for?" Roo yelled. "Move! Move, move, move!"

"You heard the man," the guard at the door practically screamed and his voice cracked with tension. "Get going!"

People leapt into action, loosely following orders.

The Brit sighed. "It'll have to do. Come on, let's go get the BTR."

They ran back to Fiddler's Green to the armored vehicle they kept stored in a lean-to next to the building and climbed inside. Booker took the driver's seat, Mick took the gunner's cupola, while Charles, Roo, and Reen opened the top hatch and waited.

Booker positioned them on the main road leading out of the camp, facing the wall. A line of mercenaries formed up around them.

They waited, listening to the sounds of gunfire and explosions. Animals roared and screamed. They could barely make out the top of the wall from their position.

A giant lizard-like creature scaled the final barrier and dropped into the camp. It looked pre-historic, with its large jaws and crest of spikes. It roared and plowed through the humans. Two more followed it over the wall.

"Jesus," Roo said. "Those are gorgorexes."

"And it looks like the motherfuckers have learned how to blend in," Reen said. She pointed as one of the monster's black, iridescent scales shimmered and it turned the color of sand.

"Of course, the things are like fucking chameleons. Why wouldn't they be?"

The tell-tale wop of helicopters droned through the sound of the animals trying to force their way over the defenses and through the camp. The gorgorexes seemed to be the only remotely successful creatures but despite the lack of support, they wreaked havoc among the mercenaries.

"Looks like we've got company," Charles said.

Three Eurocopter Tigers swooped over the camp. They flew toward the gate and immediately started firing. The sound of their 30 mm Nexter turrets joined with the Ma Deuces that still worked to keep other Zoo animals back.

The gorgorexes raced into the maze of pole barns and low buildings that made up the Harvesters Camp. The move forced the helicopters closer to be more effective. The animals smashed through buildings and ripped apart anything that got in their way.

One of the helicopters got too close to the largest mutant. It leapt upward and bit the tail off the machine. The rotating blades hardly left a scratch on the scaly creature that was almost as long as the Tiger itself. It spiraled earthward and exploded. The remaining helicopters backed off but maintained their barrage.

The creatures raged through the camp, hurled men aside, and broke through the lines of defense as if they weren't there. The helicopters hounded them as they rampaged and tried to annihilate the invaders that plowed through buildings and flipped vehicles. One of the beasts ripped a roof off a building and gulped one of the people inside—all in less than thirty seconds.

"You guys ready?" Booker asked through the intercom system.

"Bring it on!" Mick yelled. He fired the Shipunov, and the shell struck one of the oncoming gorgorexes. The animal screamed and fell back a few paces but shook itself and resumed its charge.

"These buggers seem harder to kill than the last time!" the Brit muttered.

The mercenaries around the BTR opened fire. Grenades were thrown and even a few launched rocket launchers, but the animals pushed forward, determined to reach the greater Sahara Desert.

The mutant Mick had hit with the Shipunov raced right toward them. Charles slammed the top hatch closed as the creature ran over them. It tried to fling them aside on its way but the BTR only rocked on its suspension.

"Take that, you fugly bitch," Roo muttered.

"Not helping, Roo," Reen said.

Booker turned them to keep firing at the Zoo animals as they cut their way through the line of mercenaries. Men were hurled aside with bloody holes in the center of their bodies from the monsters' spikes. Those unlucky enough to have survived being impaled soon convulsed and began to foam at the mouth as the venom killed them.

One of the gorgorexes leapt upward and swiped at a Tiger that got too close. The helicopter pulled up out of its reach. The animal landed and raced into the open desert. The other two did the same. The remaining Tigers separated and followed their targets. Now that they were away from the confines of the camp, the attack helicopters used their 70mm missiles. The explosions hardly slowed the escaping beasts as they used their startling speed and agility to avoid the projectiles. Large plumes of smoke billowed into the clear sky but the escapees continued their headlong rush to put distance between them and the Zoo.

Roo threw the hatch open and watched the chase. The creatures' black scales shimmered while waves the color of sand rippled across the surface.

"Seems they haven't perfected the whole blending in bit quite yet."

The smallest of the three managed to disguise itself completely. He noticed it veer off in the opposite direction from the other animals. The Tigers remained with the still partially black mutants.

"Oh, shit. It's getting away!" Roo thumped the top of the armored vehicle. "Come on, get after it!"

Charles popped into the commander's seat beside Booker. "Looks like we're hunting this thing in the desert."

"Great," he said. "Hold on, everyone! This might be bumpy." He drove after the fleeing beast.

With no trees to hinder its movements, the gorgorex's muscular hind legs ate up the ground. Thankfully, the BTR's speed allowed them to keep the animal within sight. While it had worked out how to change color, its scales still glimmered in the hot sun.

The chameleon-like effect could also not hide the signs of its passage. Its huge claws left gouges in the sand as it ran. The tracks, coupled with relatively flat terrain, made it easy to follow the creature.

"It's a good thing I filled this up recently, huh?" Charles asked.

"Yeah, Charles. Congrats."

"I also threw in some supplies the other day. Just in case."

"For real?"

"Why not? I mean, we weren't really taking it into the Zoo because, well, it's an animal magnet. But I thought it would be good to have something in here. Just in case."

"Good thinking, Charles."

"Thanks."

"Good to see Americans can do something right."

"Hey!"

Booker laughed.

"Booker." Reen's voice came over the intercom. "Why aren't we gaining on this thing?"

"Working on it. It's pretty fast."

"We should be fucking faster!" Roo said. "It's running on two legs. We have eight fucking wheels and an over five-hundred BHP engine!"

"Thanks for the statistics, asshole. Still won't change the fact that I can't go any faster and it's already pretty far ahead of us!"

Several hours passed, and they still hadn't gained on their target.

"Do you think the others were killed?" Charles asked.

The Brit shrugged and white-knuckled the steering wheel. The terrain was getting harder to determine. The sun had reached the highest point in the sky and bleached everything out. Sand dunes rose like large mountains. Sudden valleys opened to them. They could no longer see the gorgorex, and its tracks became harder to identify.

"Fuck! We can't lose this thing. Mick!" Booker yelled.

"Yeah?"

"Can you see where it's gone? I'm going to need you to direct me soon."

"Sure thing, boss."

The Aboriginal gave directions while Booker drove them deeper into the Sahara.

"Looks like there's some sort of village coming up. Maybe two klicks away," Mick announced.

The driver slowed as they approached the collection of low huts. Smoke curled from the tiny village.

"Do you think they have food? I'm starving," Charles said.

"I thought you said you put rations back there?"

"Well, I did, but that doesn't mean I want to eat an MRE. Especially not when I can get a good home-cooked meal. Maybe they have goat stew? I've heard that's a pretty good thing here."

"You've heard? Where the hell have you heard that?"

"Around."

"Oh, around, huh?"

"Yeah."

They drove closer to the village. Booker cleared his throat. "Well, Charles, unfortunately, it doesn't look like you'll be getting any home cooking today."

"Ah, fudge."

The smoke they'd seen from a distance was not from cooking fires but from some of the huts burning.

"Looks like the gorgorex went through here," the Brit said.

He slowed the BTR and stopped outside the destroyed village. They got out of the vehicle and looked at the damage the creature had inflicted.

"This was the gorgorex, right?" he asked. He toed the

carcass of a goat. Its belly had been ripped open and its innards spilled into the sand.

Mick went farther into the village, avoiding the burning buildings and dead bodies of the dozen or so inhabitants. He inspected the ground and returned to the others.

"This definitely was the gorgorex."

"Shit," Booker said. "We have to catch up to this thing before it can do this again."

"Should we tell someone to…you know…come clean this up?" Reen asked.

"Probably. I'll see if we can get a signal," Charles said. He started walking back to the BTR.

"Okay," the Brit said. "Everyone, look for anything useful. Fuel, food, anything."

"We're going to pillage the village?" Mick asked. Then, he snickered. "That rhymed."

Roo laughed too.

"For real?" Reen scoffed. "A whole village has been slaughtered and destroyed and you're laughing at rhyming?"

"Just relieving the tension. Chill the fuck out," Mick said.

She started through the wreckage and the two Australians followed her lead.

Charles returned to Booker. "No signal."

"Bleddy hell, for real?"

He nodded.

"Fuck."

"What's the next move?"

The Brit squinted at the sun. It was starting to set. "Do

you think we should camp here or try to cover more ground to find the gorgorex?"

"I don't think we should go after it in the dark. It's a good thing we have Mick with us. We can't afford to get off track. Can you imagine if we started going in the wrong direction? We'd be lost in the middle of the Sahara Desert and a dangerous alien monster would be unleashed on the world."

"Charles, that's *exactly* what I'm trying not to bleddy imagine!"

"Right. Sorry."

"Okay. We'll keep going until Mick can't see anymore. Then we'll have to camp for the night and start off again at first light. Do you think he'd still be able to see the tracks if they're old?"

"I'm not the person to be asking that."

"Mick!"

The man rounded one of the smoldering buildings and jogged to where his two teammates stood.

"Do you think you'll be able to track the gorgorex, even if the trail is old?" Booker asked.

Mick squinted at the horizon. "Don't see why not. I mean, as long as there's not like a storm or something, we'll be golden."

"Perfect, let's round everyone up and head out. We still have maybe an hour of daylight left and we need to take advantage of it."

They found a table loaded with diesel and gas in plastic water and Coke bottles. The BTR was a hungry beast, but they managed to scrounge up what looked to be a couple of gallons of diesel between the bottles. Mick found some dried meat on a rack, but there wasn't much of use in the village.

They drove until the sun dipped below the horizon and the temperature dropped. In silence, they started a fire and ate MREs, watching the stars appear in the sky.

Off in the distance, they heard the lone gorgorex roar.

The next day, they started early after their quarry.

"The thing has to sleep, right?" Roo asked Reen.

"How the hell should I know? It's a fucking alien. I'm sure it doesn't ever act the way you'd think it should."

"Yeah, but it's still a bleddy giant lizard, in the end. Aren't those cold-blooded? I mean, won't it slow down in the cold?"

She whistled. "I'm impressed you'd know something like that. If it were only true, though. Cold-blooded creatures can keep moving in the cold, using the heat generated. They only go into torpor if they stop moving. Besides, if this bastard is some kind of dinosaur, then those were probably warm-blooded, or at least a hybrid version of life."

"Oh, fuck you."

"But you're right in that, traditionally, lizards are cold-blooded. But, again, I doubt there's anything traditional about the thing."

They spent the first half of the day with the only true evidence of the gorgorex being a slaughtered goat herd. There was no sign of the goatherder. The odds seemed to be diminishing—along with their previous confidence—

that they'd be able to catch up with the monster before it reached civilization.

"We're going to need to fuel up soon," Booker said to Reen, who had kicked Charles out of the commander's seat.

"You got any maps in here?"

The Brit handed her one.

"This is in Russian."

He shrugged.

"Okay. Well, I guess it doesn't really matter, does it?" She studied it to determine their position. It may have been in Russian, but it wasn't hard to figure out where the Zoo was and which direction they were headed in.

"We've made it pretty far. This thing sure covered a lot of ground in a short amount of time. But it looks like there's some sort of small town or village or something only about forty-eight klicks off. If the gorgorex holds this trajectory, we'll go right through it—or damn near it, at least."

"What village is it?" Booker asked.

"Again, the map is in fucking Russian, so we're out of luck of figuring that bit out. Do we have enough fuel to get us there? If it's big enough to make it onto a map, I'm sure it's big enough to have some sort of gas station."

Booker glanced at the gauge, which was dangerously near empty. He tightened his grip on the steering for a moment. "We should make it."

"Great," she said, leaned back in the seat, and folded her arms over her chest. "Wake me when something good happens."

"Mick, how're we looking?" he asked.

His teammate's bored voice came over the intercom. "Still good. Though I have to say, there's not much doing up here. I'm starting to go fucking blind looking at nothing but goddamn sand. After this is over, I never want to see the desert again."

"Unfortunately for you, your chosen job is right in the middle of the biggest desert in the world."

"Thanks for the fun fact, asshole."

"Here to please," he said with a laugh. "Oh, Reen said we should be coming upon civilization in about forty-eight klicks, so keep your eye out for that."

"You got it."

Booker drove in silence except for the sound of the BTR running and Reen's steady breaths. He started to zone out when he noticed her watching him. He glanced at her. "What?"

"Nothing. Just wondering what your deal is."

"What do you mean?"

"Trying to figure you out, Eustace."

"Don't call me that."

"Fine, *Booker*. What's your deal? Why mercenary work?"

"After the SAS, I needed something to put my energy toward. I'll be straight with you, Reen, the SAS was like the family I never had."

"So, you were chasing the comradery."

"And the money. Getting kicked out of the SAS wasn't exactly a lucrative thing."

"You got a girl at home?"

"No."

"A guy at home?"

He glared at her and she grinned. "Right. Didn't think

you were the type, but a person should never assume. Do you want someone waiting for you?"

"Do you?"

"Not really. Not right now, anyway. If I had someone at home, they'd expect timelines and promises I'm not willing to keep. The world is too big a place to be tied to one spot."

"Yeah, but a person likes to know there's a place they'll always have, I guess. Like Falmouth is to me."

"Why?"

"Why what?"

"Why Falmouth? I mean, no offense, but you don't have anyone at home and you don't talk about your family at all —so why is Falmouth so important to you?"

Booker couldn't think of a satisfactory answer, so he deflected. "What about you? Surely the great Serenity Nguyen has a place where she feels whole?"

"Honestly? I'm at my best when it's just me, my hog, and an open road."

"You drive a motorcycle?"

"You surprised?"

"No. I guess not."

They were quiet again.

"Land ho!" Mick said over the intercom to break the silence.

"We're not at sea, dipshit," Reen said.

"No, but I've always wanted to say that. We're coming up on a small fort or something."

They approached a low fort-like structure, the same color as the desert. There were several other buildings scattered around, each low and uninspiring. A short airstrip was off to the side of the fort and a prop plane stood beside it. Red, white, and green flags hung slack at each corner of the fort.

"Looks like we're in Niger," she said.

A Land Cruiser four-by-four in desert colors drove out to meet the BTR. Booker stopped and let the other vehicle approach.

"Everyone, be nice," he said.

"I'm always nice," Charles retorted. He opened the top hatch and climbed out.

A soldier got out of the Land Cruiser, his finger on the trigger of his machine gun. The bill of his dark green hat was pulled low over his face and he looked with narrowed eyes at the newcomers from under the shade this created.

"Hello!" Charles said, brightly.

"*Quel est votre but ici?*"

"Um, sorry. I...uh, I don't speak...French?"

The soldier repeated the question, this time brandishing his machine gun at him.

He held his hands up. "Woah there, buddy. English?"

"Who are you?" the soldier demanded.

"Right. My name is Charles. We aren't here to cause any trouble or anything, just passing through. We're out hunting."

"Hunting? What are you hunting?"

Charles hesitated, unsure if he should reveal that they were from the Zoo or not. "Do you have any fuel? We're running a bit low. We can pay you, of course."

The Niger soldier frowned.

"Mind telling us where this is?" the American asked.

"You have reached Madama."

"Great! Look, we'll just get some fuel from you and be

out of your hair in no time. I promise we won't make any trouble for you."

The soldier studied him and he tried to smile placatingly. After a minute or so, the man lowered his weapon, having decided he meant what he said. He got back in the Land Cruiser and waved them to follow.

"Think this is a good idea?" Booker asked.

"Don't see that it's a bad one," Reen said. "We'll be in and out. Don't want to be starting any wars with anybody."

"I don't know how Charles does it."

"Does what?"

"Diffuse situations like that."

"I don't think we'll ever really know. It's his superpower."

"Superpower?" Booker scoffed.

"What else do you want to call it?" she asked.

He sat with the question a moment. "Fine. It's his superpower. Just don't tell him I said that. We don't want him getting a big head."

She laughed.

The Land Cruiser led them into the old fort. Soldiers drilled in the courtyard.

"Seems we've found ourselves a garrison," Mick said.

"Let's just get in and get out and be fine," Charles said quietly.

"You nervous, wonder boy?" Roo asked.

"No."

The soldier who had spoken to Charles hopped out of the Land Cruiser again and directed Booker to park beside an old gasoline pump. They got out of the BTR.

"I am called Fernando," the soldier said, "And you all are?"

The American quickly made introductions.

"What brings you out here? You came from the desert, yes?"

"We are looking for something that was...lost," Charles said.

Fernando raised an eyebrow. "Lost?" He inspected the team standing in front of him. "What is BOHICA?" He asked, indicating the name painted on the side of the BTR.

"That's our company—the BOHICA Warriors," he explained.

"Ah, you are mercenaries then. You must come from the Zoo."

He didn't bother to respond to that.

"You promise you are not here to cause any trouble?"

"We'll be sweet as apple pie while we're here. Promise."

"I don't see the harm in giving you fuel for your journey, then."

"You got diesel?" Charles asked.

Fernando nodded and waved a hand vaguely at the pump. "You said you lost something? I suppose that would have to do with the giant animal that passed by here not long ago."

"You've seen it?" Roo asked, his enthusiasm thrusting his caution aside.

Fernando smiled. "Yes. We saw it. Whatever *it* is. I thought the soldier had lost his mind, but your presence here seems to confirm his story."

The soldier gave instructions in French and another man began bringing used plastic bottles filled with diesel.

Another stuck a funnel in the BTR's fuel tank and emptied the bottles into it one at a time.

"Doesn't that pump work?" Booker asked.

The soldier merely harrumphed and said nothing.

"What's with the empty Coke bottles filled with diesel? They had them at the last town, too," Charles asked Reen as the Brit handed over the fuel cans to be filled as well.

"You got me. That pump, though, looks old as shit. Maybe it doesn't work anymore?"

"I trust you'll be discreet about this?" Fernando asked as the last can was filled.

Booker nodded and handed a large wad of cash to the man. The soldier didn't bother to count the large sum but stuffed it in his pocket.

"Of course," Charles said to make sure the man understood Booker's nod.

"Right. Then be on your way."

They got back in the BTR and drove out of the fort. Mick picked up the trail of the gorgorex and they were on their way again as the sun began to set.

"That seemed too easy," Booker said.

"Were you expecting a fight?" Reen asked.

"No. But if I had soldiers and knew they were letting a random armored vehicle into my country, I'd be pissed."

"Well, maybe this country doesn't have your scruples? Who knows? Who cares? We got fuel enough to track down and kill this motherfucker. It's taking too fucking long."

"Won't argue with you there."

They drove until it was too dark for Mick to see the trail the mutant had left.

The next day went much like the day before. They drove and didn't run into any signs of life, still hot on the gorgorex's trail. They trusted Mick to keep them on track, and he was doing a good job—not that the others would have known the difference.

The sun was high in the sky and it was the fourth time the Aboriginal had made Booker stop so he could double-check the signs of the creature. Roo walked beside him, kicking at the sand.

"You know, mucking up the tracks of this thing isn't going to help us find it any fucking faster."

"Oh, right. Shit. Sorry."

"It's okay. I've got all we need. We're still heading in the right direction."

They trudged back toward the waiting BTR. The Aussie trailed behind his friend and tried to work out what the other man had seen in the sand. The closest thing to an animal track he could detect was the winding trail a snake made.

"How the fuck does he do it?" he muttered quietly. He squinted at the horizon in the direction Mick said the gorgorex was going before he turned and watched Mick disappear inside the BTR.

Charles suddenly appeared from the top hatch, his AK-47 aimed in his direction. "Roo! Run!" He opened fire.

Roo didn't take the time to look at what his teammate had seen. He sprinted toward the BTR.

The gorgorex roared behind him and the sound was far too close for his liking. He pushed his sprint to the limit.

The animal thumped behind him and he could practically feel its breath on him.

"Fuck, fuck, fuck, fuck!"

Reen flung the side door open and waved frantically at him. He took four more steps and launched himself toward the opening. The mutant roared behind him and he felt flicks of its saliva as he sailed toward the vehicle and his ears popped with the noise. He careened through the open door and she slammed it shut. Mick broke his fall on the hard metal floor. The second after she had shut the side door, the monster rammed into the side. The BTR tipped with the force of the strike but rocked back.

Their attacker screamed and shoved the armored vehicle again.

"Holy fucking shit, that was close." Roo gasped.

"You had us worried," Reen said and moved into position to begin firing on the monster that circled them.

"I've never seen you run so fast," Mick said.

"I never had to run so fast," he retorted, breathing heavily.

Charles patted him on the shoulder. "Glad you're still with us, buddy."

Roo shoved him away. "It'll take more than a fucking desert ambush to kill me."

The gorgorex screamed.

"I hate to break up the festivities I'm sure are happening, but we need to end this thing," Booker said over the intercom. "Now."

Mick returned to his position and aimed the Shipunov at the creature. The animal climbed on top of the BTR to roar and claw at the armor. It clung awkwardly to the barrel of the weapon. The man waited until a larger portion of its body was in front of the gun before he fired.

The shell knocked the mutant from the vehicle. It shrieked and blue blood gushed from the wound while its six, glowing orange eyes blazed at them. The enraged mutant lurched forward and Mick fired again.

Charles, Roo, and Reen added their rounds to the Shipunov's shells.

Booker backed the BTR so they had better room to maneuver. The animal stalked them, hissing and spitting. It didn't seem to care that one of its forelegs was missing and its blood splashed over the sand.

"Just die, you ugly bastard!" the Aussie yelled and held down the trigger on his AK-47.

Mick fired the Shipunov again.

The gorgorex took the hit in the center of its chest. It stumbled back with a violent screech. The animal wheeled and prepared to run into the desert.

"Don't let it get away!" Reen yelled through the intercom.

The Brit shoved the BTR into gear and the armored vehicle lunged forward. The wounded creature made it three steps before they plowed into it. It roared and fell, clawing and biting at the heavy vehicle, but didn't manage to scratch through the thick steel plates.

Charles handed Roo a grenade. "Care to do the honors?"

"Fuck, yeah."

He flung the cupola open, pulled the pin on the grenade, and lobbed it at the beast. He yanked the cupola closed again as the ordnance detonated and the shrapnel ripped a deeper hole in the animal's torso.

The American grasped his Remington, darted out of the cupola, and delivered a volley into their adversary's gaping wounds.

"He's still alive," he said as he dropped inside the BTR. "Hit it with the Shipunov."

It was too close to use the cannon, so Booker backed away until they reached the optimum position. Mick fired again and the 30 mm shell pounded the creature in what was left of its shattered chest. Blue blood sprayed out of the writhing monster as it collapsed onto the sand, then went still. Not trusting that it was dead, the Brit ran over it a couple of times, just to be sure.

They opened the cupola and climbed onto the roof. The gorgorex's eyes were glassy and no longer glowed. Its body steamed and the blood that poured out of it started to froth.

"That shit's nasty," the Aboriginal commented.

"Take that, motherfucker," Roo said and flipped the dead animal off with both fingers.

"I suppose we should call someone to clean up this mess," Charles said and rubbed the back of his neck.

"I'll see if I can get anyone to answer." Booker disappeared inside.

"This calls for a celebration," the Aussie said. He dropped into the vehicle but soon returned with the bag of dried meat they'd taken from the village a couple of days before.

Reen sniffed at the piece of meat, wrinkled her nose, and handed it back to him. "Yeah, I'm not going to eat that."

"Pussy."

He took a bite of the leathery-looking meat and chewed. The other three watched him carefully. His smug look was quickly replaced by one of disgust after he'd had it in his mouth for a few seconds. He turned his head and spat the mouthful out.

"Oh, fuck. Shit. That's disgusting. Don't eat that."

"I told you I wasn't," she said to the laughter of the others.

CHAPTER SEVEN

The Sahara Desert, Niger

"So, we have a bit of a problem," Charles said as he vaulted off the BTR to join the others who stood around the gorgorex.

"What is it now?" Booker asked.

"Still no signal."

"Well, shit. What the fuck are we supposed to do with the thing? We can't leave it here."

They stared at the corpse. Its blue blood continued to seep into the sand.

"Do you think it'll rot differently?" Reen asked.

"What do you mean?" Roo asked.

"I mean, in the Zoo, everything just gets absorbed back in. Out here, it's all earth material. It'll just sit here and rot."

"You don't think it'll, like, fuck with the ecosystem out here or something?" Mick asked. "I mean, you don't think its blood will activate and this'll become a mini-Zoo or something?"

They looked around at the empty desert.

"How the fuck should I know? I'm not a goddamn scientist," Booker said.

"I think it's a good question," she said. "We tracked it across almost a country and a half just to keep it from impacting the outside world. What if letting it bleed everywhere was a bad fucking idea?"

"I don't think you can say we're *letting* it bleed. It's just what's happening," the Brit said. "We shot the thing. Of course it's going to be bleeding."

"Should we put it on a tarp?" Charles asked.

"Where the fuck are we going to get a tarp, Boy Scout?" Roo asked. "We going to find a local goatherd and ask for one?"

His teammate didn't answer but returned to the BTR. He emerged a few seconds later holding a folded black tarp.

"Where the fuck did that thing come from?"

"I put it in there."

"Why?" Mick asked.

"Just in case."

"Jesus," Roo said. "I've gotta come up with a better nickname for you, mate. You really are a goddamn Boy Scout."

"Isn't that the point of a nickname? Isn't it supposed to describe the person?"

"Not my nicknames."

"I believe the word you're looking for, bunj, would be 'insult,'" Mick explained.

"Fuck you."

Charles unfolded the tarp.

"Okay. Wait. So, we wrap the thing up in the tarp, and then what?" Reen asked. "We just drag it through the desert back to the French Quarter? How the hell is that going to work?"

Booker looked at the map and frowned. "Well, we definitely don't have enough fuel to make it back to Madama—especially not dragging that bleddy overgrown lizard. No, I think our best bet is going…here."

"Where?" Charles asked.

"Hell if I know. This map is in Russian. But whatever this place is looks big enough, which means there are more people we can blend with and we're more likely to be able to get a signal or find a place to call someone to come deal with the gorgorex. Not to mention, they'll definitely have fuel."

"How far is it?" Reen asked.

"Far enough, maybe sixty klicks or so. I mean, we should have enough diesel to get us there, but only just."

"I don't like the sound of that," Roo protested.

"That's the best we can do right now. I'm not a fucking miracle worker. We can't teleport back to the Zoo."

"Jesus, mate, relax. I was just fuckin' around."

"Let's just figure out how to secure the gorgorex to the BTR."

The tarp wasn't large enough to cover the mutant. It would barely cover the torso and leave its muscular hindlegs and tail uncovered.

"Should we cut it up?" Mick asked as he inspected the large animal.

"I think that would defeat the purpose of us trying to keep its blood contained," Charles said. "Not to mention, we don't have proper hazmat suits to take care of that crap.

I don't know about you but being killed by a dead animal isn't high on my list of ways I want to go."

The gorgorex steamed and began to bloat in the beating sun.

Reen wrinkled her nose. "That shit's nasty."

"Well, I don't think we'll be able to do quite the bang-up job we'd want. We don't have the right equipment for it," Booker said. "So, let's just strap the wanker to the back and call it good. We'll do our best, obviously, but we might just have to accept that this one is going to be messy."

"I'm not sure dragging it on a tarp will work," Reen said. "The sand is too abrasive. Not to mention the sharp spikes that run practically the whole length of the thing's back. And then how would we get it onto the tarp without touching it?"

"Do you think it would be disturbed if we left it here?" Charles asked.

"What do you mean by disturbed?" Booker asked.

"You know, do you think anyone would mess with the body?"

"Are you suggesting we leave it here?"

"We can't really transport it, but if we made it to that city or town or whatever it is, we can call someone to come pick it up. It shouldn't be there for a long time. We can use the tarp to mark it and even bury it in the sand or something if we're worried about people touching it. There aren't really people out here, and besides, I don't think other animals will get into it."

"What makes you think other animals won't get into it?" Mick asked and kicked sand toward the massive head.

"Don't all animals have an instinct that tells them if something is a bigger predator or poisonous?"

"It's not the best plan," Booker pointed out.

"No, but do we have any better ideas?"

They stared at the dead animal. After a few minutes, the Brit heaved a sigh. "Fine. We'll do it that way."

They secured the tarp to the sand with stakes and did their best to cover the rest of the corpse with sand. Finally, they stepped back to look at their handiwork.

"Well, that looks like shit," Roo said and waved a hand at the half-covered creature.

"It's a disaster, but what can we do about it?"

"Now we know that none of you are murderers," Reen said.

The men stared at her.

"You clearly can't dispose of a body properly, and you would've been found out if you were."

"I think a human body is way different than a giant monster," Booker retorted.

"You saying you've hidden human bodies?" she asked with a wicked glint in her eye and a small smile.

"No! No. I just...I was just saying...you can't really compare the two!"

She laughed. "Don't get your knickers in a twist. I'm kidding. But seriously, this is a shitty job and the faster we get someone to come clean up this mess the better."

"No one wears fucking knickers anymore," he grumbled as he climbed back into the BTR.

"So, if we aren't going to drag the gorgorex, couldn't we just go back to Madama?" Mick asked.

"No. I still think it's better if we keep moving forward,"

the Brit said. He started the BTR and headed off into the desert toward their unknown destination.

"I know this place," Reen said as they drove toward the city.

"You do?" Booker asked.

"Yeah. It's Agadez. The US Military uses it as an airstrip for drones."

"Well, that's good, right?"

"Sure."

"I've got a signal," Charles said over the intercom system. "Who, exactly, should I call?"

"Shit. I didn't think about that," Booker said. "Who should we call? Do you think Prince would know? I guess we don't really have anyone's numbers. Perhaps we could call Shira?"

"Fuck that," Roo said. "Don't call that fanny."

"Okay. Then I think Prince is our best bet. He'll at least know who to get us in touch with."

"Got it. You want me to make the call or do you want to make it?" Charles asked.

The Brit thought about it for a minute. "You do it. I think he likes you better anyway."

His teammate didn't disagree with him and took the phone.

Prince answered on the second ring. "Hello?"

"Hey, Prince, we've got a bit of a situation over here."

"No niceties, eh? Who is this? The American one? I thought you'd be more for small talk. But it doesn't matter, I guess. Not in the grand scheme of things. Where the hell did you all disappear to? After the storming of the wall, no one could get ahold of you."

"Yeah. We went after one of the gorgorexes that escaped."

"No shit. We all sort of wondered what happened to the last one. Thought it was a lost cause. You get it?"

"Yeah, we killed it. But we can't get it back to the Zoo. We need an air team or someone better equipped to come haul it away."

"What does that have to do with me?"

"We didn't know who else to call."

Prince was silent for a minute.

"Hello?"

"Yeah, I'm still here. I think I know who can come get it off your hands. Just tell me where the body is and I'll have it taken care of."

"Thanks so—"

"You all are going to owe me for this."

"Maybe take it up with the people who did a crap job of collecting what escaped in the first place."

The Nigerian laughed. "Okay, big man. Just tell me where to send the team."

"Sixty klicks north-west of Agadez. I can have Booker send over more accurate coordinates. I'm sure he marked it."

"Shit. You guys went far."

"Yeah."

"Okay. Well, don't worry about it now. I'll take care of it."

"Thanks, Prince."

"Sure thing. Oh! Tell your British friend that I might want to work with you lot again."

"I'll pass it on. Bye." Charles ended the call before the man could request anything further from him. "Okay. It's all taken care of. Prince said he'd get a team to come get the body. I told him you'd send more accurate coordinates, Booker."

"Copy. I'll do that right now."

"What should we do now?" Mick asked. "Just go back?"

"You know," Charles said, "we're a heck of a lot closer to Benin than we were before."

"Your point being?" Booker asked.

"You're being difficult. You know what my point is. My point is that we are closer to being able to rescue those kidnapped girls."

"We should do it," Roo said.

"I thought you were against it," Reen reminded him but winked to also be sure he recalled their previous discussion on this very subject.

"I was," he answered. "But I changed my mind. I'm allowed to do that. I'm sophisticated like that."

She made a noise that seemed like she didn't believe Roo.

"I can," he insisted.

"Is everyone on board with the idea of doing a rescue mission?" the Brit asked.

Everyone said they were willing to do it.

"Okay. Let's do it, then. I'll call up the president and tell him we'll take the job—if he still needs us."

He found President Okonkuo's contact info and called

him but had to try the number twice before anyone picked up.

"*Oui?*" A man with a deep voice answered.

"Hello? I was given this information to call President Okonkuo."

There was a slight pause and he worried that the connection had been lost.

"You've reached President Okonkuo. Who do I have the pleasure of speaking with?" the president asked, his accent thick but still easy to understand.

"This is Booker, from the BOHICA Warriors Company. You got in touch with us in regard to some missing girls you needed rescued?"

Another short pause followed. "Yes. Good. I was worried I wouldn't hear from you. Have you decided about the job?"

"We'll do it for you. Though I do have to warn you that our team isn't necessarily equipped for a...finessed, shall we say, extraction. If you understand my meaning."

"You are telling me it will be bloody?"

"It's possible."

"I don't care about the insurgents. I just need the girls to be rescued. Of course, I need your promise that this will be done with the utmost discretion."

"Of course, sir."

"Many in my country are opposed to any meddling in this affair on the government's part, which is what I explained in my message to you. That being said, some are suspicious that I am sending for mercenaries. You can't cross into the country at Malanville. You would be coming from that direction, yes?"

"Yes."

"You will need to cross over the Niger River in the wilderness. You must not be caught doing this. And if you are, I won't recognize that you were working for me. Is that understood?"

"Yes, sir."

"Good. The last known location of the girls is in the WAP National Park Complex, the northwest side. I can get your information for payment at a later time. I've already been speaking with you for too long, I'm afraid."

"No problem, sir. We'll get on this right away."

"Thank you, Mr Booker, for doing this. I am greatly in your debt, and so are the girls and their families."

"Thank you, sir. And it's just Booker. Not Mr Booker. But I'd hold onto the thanks until we can actually deliver the girls to safety."

"I have every confidence in your team, Mr...uh, Booker, from what I've heard of you. *Adieu*." President Okonkuo disconnected the call before he could say anything more.

"All right, team, who's ready to go on safari?" he asked. "We've got a last known locale and we'll head there after we fill up here."

"Sounds like a plan," Mick said.

"Do we have more information than what was in the letter?" Charles asked.

"Unfortunately not. But hopefully, we'll be able to figure out more the closer we get."

"Let's go save some girls!" Roo whooped.

CHAPTER EIGHT

Niger River, Niger

It was dusk when they reached the bank of the Niger River. They'd navigated to avoid populated areas as much as possible.

They got out of the BTR to stare across the water. It was hazy, and the river itself was a deep, muddy-green color.

"How far across do you think that is?" Mick asked.

"Don't know. It looks manageable, though," Booker said.

"You think the BTR can handle it?"

Roo gave a strained laugh. "You chickenshit?"

"Don't see you jumping at the idea of getting across this thing."

The Aussie didn't answer.

"We'll make it all right," the Brit said.

"If not, you can all swim, right?" Reen asked and laughed.

Mick blanched and Roo slugged her in the arm.

She laughed harder. "Ever out-swim a crocodile?"

"Fuck you," he hissed.

"Relax," Charles said. "We'll be fine. This thing is built to swim like a Marine LAV."

"Enough dallying, people. We shouldn't sit here and wait to be discovered." Booker climbed into the BTR and the others followed him.

"You got this," the American said, having taken back his usual seat from Reen.

The other man nodded. "I know."

He drove the vehicle into the river.

"Mick," Reen said and nudged him with her elbow. "Mick, you can open your eyes now. Everything's fine."

He blinked at her. "We aren't sinking?"

She shook her head, opened the top hatch of the BTR, and stuck her head out. Water swirled around them. She watched the path they cut through it before she dropped down and pulled the hatch shut behind her.

"Everything's golden. Roo, you can let go of the seat now. Don't know what that would've done to save you."

Roo released his white-knuckle grip and gestured impatiently. "I'm fine."

"Whatever you say, pussy."

Booker navigated to the opposite side of the river without incident and they left the water ten minutes after they'd entered it.

"That wasn't so bad," Mick said when the vehicle lumbered up the bank.

"You never been in a fully amphibious vehicle before?" Reen asked.

He shook his head. "No way. I was okay jumping out of airplanes but never swimming across anything."

"Technically, we didn't swim across the river."

"I know that. You get what I'm saying."

"Everyone survive back there?" Charles asked through the intercom system.

"We had to talk Roo off a panic attack ledge, but everything's fine now," she said.

"Fuck you! That didn't happen!"

"It was pretty bad," she continued. "You should've seen it."

Charles and Booker laughed, making sure the intercom was on so the others could hear.

"You're going to pay for that," Roo said.

"Whatever you say, dipshit."

After crossing the Niger, he drove toward the W-Arly-Pendjari Complex—the WAP Complex—which was made up of three national parks: the Pendjari, the Arly, and the W National Parks. They straddled Benin, Burkina Faso, and Niger.

"How long is this going to take?" Charles asked.

"Maybe about five hours, give or take. It's about two-hundred klicks to the park from here. The roads are probably fucking awful, but the BTR will handle them just fine."

The American looked at the map they'd picked up in Agadez—luckily, it was in English or at least used Latin letters. "You said they were on the west side of the park?"

"That's where the president said the last known location was. The truth is, they don't really know. The park is a big place and 'the west side' isn't exactly a location."

"It's like a normal Zoo coordinate, I guess. We have

Mick, and he's some sort of tracking genius, so that'll help narrow things down. Besides, I'm sure there are rangers or other workers of the park who could maybe help us out."

"The president wanted us to be discreet."

"We will be. I just bet that those guys know a lot more than other people give them credit for. Besides, with a big enough bribe, I'm sure we could buy silence. We could even play the part of a nosy tourist."

"Okay, I get it. There are a lot of ways to get information without drawing a lot of attention."

They continued in silence. It was dark, but Booker still drove. They were only concerned about arriving at the WAP Complex. The BTR's headlights lit up the rough-hewn road as it rumbled over it.

"Now, here's the question," the Brit said, "do we continue into the park tonight or camp outside it?"

"I say we camp outside," Charles said. "We'll probably need all the light we can get to make sure we find those girls as quickly as possible. Besides, there might not be alien animals running around, but there are still wild animals."

"Yeah. You're right. Though you know they aren't just confined to the park, right?"

"I mean, yes, I know that. Of course, I know that. You get the drift of what I'm saying, though."

"I know what you're saying. Sounds like a good plan to me."

After another hour and a half of driving, they arrived on the east side of the park. They were on RNIE7, the only road into the reserve for a hundred kilometers.

"We're going in in the morning," Booker announced.

"We'll sleep the rest of the night here and then can move into the park and to the west side tomorrow. Mick, you're our best bet for being able to track those missing girls."

"You got it, bunj."

"Everyone okay with the plan?" the Brit asked.

"It's fine," Roo said. "Now shut the fuck up so we can get some sleep."

They started early the next day and soon passed signs indicating that they were entering the park. The sign was in French but it was easy to identify the name. The noise of the BTR sent a herd of black and brown korrigum sprinting away.

"It's kind of nice to see animals with the normal number of eyes and legs running around," Charles said as he watched them bound to a safe distance. "Those things aren't going to turn around and try to kill us."

It was the rainy season, and the park was green. Red dirt roads and tracks created by the animals crisscrossed through the entirety of the over seventeen thousand square kilometer park.

A troop of olive baboons clustered around a wild syringa tree stared at the armored vehicle as it drove past. They bared their teeth at the intrusion and screamed in annoyance.

"Even normal wildlife isn't that great," Booker said. "I wouldn't want to be pitted against one of those things without a weapon."

"Looks like we've got some company," Mick announced from his perch in the cupola.

An older man stepped into the path of the BTR. His long-sleeved collared shirt and matching pants looked like they had, at one time, been dark-green, but the sun had faded them to a soft olive. He stood his ground, not caring that the armored vehicle could easily run him over.

"Should we just go around him?" the Brit asked.

The stranger raised an old Model 1916 Berthier rifle and yelled something at them in what had to be the local language.

"Does anyone understand what he's saying?" Charles asked.

"Jesus, that rifle is falling apart," Mick said. "Look, the stock's fallen off and he's attached some piece of scrap wood in its place."

"I'll just drive around him," Booker said. He started to turn, but the man followed them and yelled louder.

"Cut the engine," Charles said.

Booker turned it off.

The man waved his gun threateningly at them, though he had to know that his rifle wouldn't damage the BTR. He yelled again, this time in a different language, *"Arrêtez votre véhicule."*

Reen heard that and flung open the top hatch.

"What are you doing?" Roo asked and attempted to stop her. "That psycho will probably shoot you!"

She shoved him away. "I'll be fine." She stood on the roof, her hands held up placatingly, and asked, *"Qu'est-ce que tu veux?"*

"Did you know she knew French?" the Aussie asked.

"Nope," Charles answered.

"What are we going to do with this guy?" Roo sputtered. "We can't have him snooping around. What's he doing out here anyway?"

"No," Booker said. "He's probably a park ranger and is just doing his job. He thinks we're the wankers snooping around."

"Strewth."

They all got out of the BTR and watched Reen speak to the man.

"What is your purpose here?" he asked in English, his accent thick. "If you think you can just barge in here and kill all the animals you want, then you are mistaken."

"We're not here for anything like that," Booker said. "We're not poachers."

"We are here looking for something, but we don't have any intention of harming wildlife," she confirmed and moved to stand beside the others.

The ranger inspected them with narrowed eyes, but he lowered his rifle. "What are you here for, then?"

Everyone glanced at the Brit. He stepped forward. "We're here because we heard there was a group of schoolgirls that was kidnapped. We've come to see if we can set them free."

"A rescue mission?"

"A rescue mission. Nothing more."

"My name is Ranger Achille Amadou," the man said, "I know this park better than anyone else, and I will offer you my assistance with this."

"Thank you, Achille. It will be very helpful to have

someone who already knows the territory for us to pull this off," Booker said and smiled.

"How did you hear about the girls?" Achille asked. "People don't usually bother themselves with what happens in Benin."

"We were in the general area and heard about it. We decided we had the right…skillset to offer assistance."

He nodded thoughtfully but he didn't seem to wholly buy the story. "Well, I suppose it's all the same outcome in the end. Do you have information on where the girls are?"

"Last we heard, they were in the western half of the park," Charles said.

"I have not been to the west in some weeks, so I haven't seen anything yet. The park is big and there aren't enough rangers to cover it. It is a thankless job and many young people are not interested in taking it.

"However, there are certain areas that seem to attract the less-than-desirables. I would guess that those holding the girls would be in one of them."

"Can you leave your territory to help out?" Booker asked.

"The entire W National Park is my territory," the ranger said with a laugh. "Or the Pendjari, or the Arly. We are all the same rangers, at least in the Beninese portion of the WAP."

"Good," Booker said. "Okay, Achille, welcome to the BOHICA Warriors! Come with us and we can see if we can find those missing girls."

They boarded the BTR and their new addition looked around curiously before Booker, following the ranger's directions, drove off the highway and deeper into the bush.

CHAPTER NINE

W National Park, WAP Complex, Benin

Achille knew several places in the western part of the park that would provide enough cover for a large group of people. With his direction, it narrowed down to where they would begin their search.

"How are you going to find the girls?" he asked as they drove deeper into the park.

"Mick here is our tracker extraordinaire," Reen said and clapped her teammate on the shoulder.

He shrugged her off. "I do all right."

"Don't be so fucking humble," Roo said. "You're fucking awesome at it."

"I, too, am a tracker," Achille said.

"Oh, really?"

"I like a challenge. I once tracked an injured wild dog through a rainstorm."

"Like a stray?" the Aussie asked.

"No. A West African wild dog. They are highly endangered. We aren't sure how many live in this part of Africa anymore. Under a hundred."

"No shit. Are they hunted?"

"Not necessarily. This one was just unlucky enough to get caught in a poacher's trap. It managed to escape, but we needed to track it down to be able to treat it and rehabilitate it."

"You have a lot of problems with poachers?" Reen asked.

Achille's mouth pressed into a firm line and he tightened his grip on his Berthier. "Yes. Poachers are the archenemy. My own cousin was killed by poachers."

"What do poachers want with people?" Mick asked.

"He was a park ranger, too. He tried to stop them from killing an elephant. So they killed him."

The Aboriginal shook his head. "Does that happen a lot?"

"Sadly, yes. That is another reason there aren't that many rangers anymore. The job is dangerous. I myself have been threatened with death several times in conflicts with poachers. This past year, a hundred rangers throughout Africa were killed in confrontations with poachers. Then, of course, there are the animals, too. Our job is very dangerous. What we are protecting does not realize that we are on the same side. A friend of mine was mauled by a lion he was trying to free from a poacher's trap. The tranquilizer wasn't strong enough. He released the lion but died of his injuries."

"He couldn't get medical help?" Reen asked.

He waved a hand. "The access we have to medical help

is mostly a joke. They could do nothing for him. He got an infection. That's what killed him, in the end."

There was something else in his voice, a deeper sorrow, but no one wanted to dig into that.

"Why do you still do it then?" Mick asked. "Don't you have a family that worries about you?"

"Not really. My wife and son have been dead a long time. I have a daughter. She lives in France, but I don't hear from her at all. I suppose I could call too, but I don't. After her mom died, Amabelle left and didn't look back. She went to Marseille," he said. "Not that I can blame her. A child needs parents who are present."

"Married to the job, huh?" Roo asked.

"It is more than a job to me. It is a choice to do the right thing. I have always dedicated myself to the protection of our native animals, and I will keep protecting them until I am taken from this life."

Mick whistled. "I have respect for that, mate. You're a better man than most." He shook hands with Achille, who gratefully inclined his head.

"So, these motherfuckers just come in here and kill the animals? For their pelts? Ivory?" Roo asked.

"Yes. There is, unfortunately, a lot of money in poaching. The forest elephants we have here, they are sought not only for their ivory but their meat. Elephant ivory can go for over two thousand American dollars per kilogram."

"Holy shit."

"The world is greedy," Achille said and his shoulders drooped toward his chest like he was folding in on himself. "People do not always understand what they are doing.

Though there are people who understand but still do nothing. Still consume. Those are the real villains."

Mick shook his head. "Let's not talk about this anymore," he said. "I want to know what it's like to spoor in Africa. I haven't had the chance to do much of that... well, not traditionally, anyway."

"The rainy season makes it more difficult. Tracks are washed away and guessing if a blade of grass is bent because of the rain or because a civet walked through is more challenging," The ranger shook his head and chuckled. "But I do enjoy the hunt and difficulty of it. It makes the success that much more rewarding."

"I was trained by my granddad in the traditional Aboriginal ways. He taught me to read the land and think like the animals I was tracking."

"He sounds like a smart man."

"He was."

"Here we go," Roo muttered to Reen, "they're going to nerd out about tracking."

She elbowed him in the arm. "Shut up. Let Mick have his moment. He missed talking about this shit."

"He can talk to me about it!" he insisted.

"Oh, really?" she asked, an eyebrow raised. "What do you know about tracking?"

"I mean, come on, it's not that fucking hard, right? You just follow animal tracks and shit."

"Uh-huh. You're a real tracker, Roo. All the times you've been able to successfully track something really backs you up."

"Whatever. So, he's better at tracking than I am. It's not like it's a contest."

Reen laughed. "No. I don't suppose it is. Which is good for you—you'd definitely lose."

"GFY," he retorted belligerently. "I'm letting Mick have this one. His ego needs him to be the expert at something."

"How very generous of you."

"I thought so."

"You're an asshole."

"Maybe. But you like it," he said.

She punched him in the arm so hard he fell out of the chair he'd sat in.

Mick and Achille looked over at them and the ranger frowned in confusion.

She shrugged. "He was just being his usual shit-head self. Don't let us disturb you."

CHAPTER TEN

W National Park, WAP Complex, Benin

Booker parked the BTR near the bank of the Pendjari River. They scrambled out and watched the muddy brown water cut through the dark-green scrub brush. Several hippos gathered in the center of the river, their small, round ears twitching bugs away. A pied kingfisher swooped and speared a small fish with its sharp beak.

"This is the farthest point in the Beninese portion of the park. Over there is Burkina Faso," Achille said, pointing across the river. "The Pendjari River is a natural border until it flows into the Niger to the north."

"Do you think they'd be somewhere in this area?" Booker asked.

"It is worth looking into and highly likely. There has been some strange activity over here recently—camera traps have been covered or destroyed. We just assumed it was poachers, but I suppose it could be the terrorists who stole the girls."

Mick and Achille split up and began looking for signs

that a large group of people had been through. They moved further into the bush. The others followed, their weapons at the ready.

An hour passed and Mick and Achille hadn't found anything. Roo squinted at the sun. He wasn't paying attention to where he was walking and tripped over a thick tuft of grass. A civet yowled and scrambled out of his way.

"What the fuck is that thing?"

"Looks like a weird sort of trash panda," Charles said.

"Trash panda?"

"Yeah. Racoon."

"That's a civet," Reen said and nodded toward the animal's black-and-white ringed tail as it disappeared into thicker undergrowth.

"How'd you know that?" Charles asked.

She shrugged. "Animal Planet."

"Do I have to remind you tossers that we aren't out for a Sunday stroll? Get serious," Booker said.

Roo made a motion of zipping his lips and throwing the key away. The Brit rolled his eyes and kept walking.

They resumed moving silently through the bush. Twice, Achille and Mick backtracked to be sure they hadn't missed anything. They spent another hour of fruitless searching. The sun beat down on them and everyone was starting to sweat.

"You know what would make this a hell of a lot easier?" the Aussie asked Reen in a harsh whisper.

She raised an eyebrow.

"A fucking drone. Can't we call up the hot-shot pres and ask for something like that?"

"He couldn't authorize his own army to go after the

schoolgirls. What makes you think he'd give you a goddamn drone to use?"

Charles shouldered his way past the duo and glared at them. She held her hands up in defeat and gave Roo a pointed look.

"I've got something over here," Mick called.

"What is it?" Booker asked.

He held up a scrap of plaid fabric. "Looks like this came from a skirt or something. And there are signs of smaller feet through here."

"Should we be talking so loud?" the American asked and peered in the surrounding trees and brush like the Ansaru terrorists would appear.

"This sign is old," Achille said. "Whoever passed through here did it several days ago."

"It was a pretty large group that passed through," Mick said. "Definitely more than thirty."

"If I'm remembering correctly, there is a plateau some forty kilometers from here that would provide a good natural barrier and protection."

"Wouldn't it have been patrolled at this point?" Roo asked.

"Not necessarily," the ranger explained. "There aren't as many rangers as there should be. The park is very large and there are whole sections that can go over a week without one of us moving through it. We do what we can."

"It's not your fault," Reen said.

"No, but something like this should not happen here in the park." He tightened his grip on his rifle and shook his head.

"Let's go back to the BTR and drive closer to that location you remember, Achille," Booker said. "We can move in on foot to check it out once we're closer."

They drove in silence, although it was thick with anticipation and adrenaline. Reen stretched and limbered up. Mick double-checked all his magazines were loaded and the FN-FAL he'd upgraded to was working properly. Roo did much the same thing.

"Do you want to use one of the AK's we have?" Mick asked Achille and broke the silence.

The older man glanced at the proffered weapon. He hesitated before he took it. "I don't know if I'd even know how to use this."

"You've taken great care of that rifle you've got there. I'm sure you can swing using this thing, bunj. I'll give you a quick crash course. The important thing is all in the aim with this. Just pull the trigger and let it fly. We don't really need to be doing any finessing."

Charles joined them in the main compartment and checked the medical stocks they had. He had supplemented the Russian's first aid kit with some of their own supplies. He'd put them in when they'd first acquired the BTR and hadn't checked them since. Once he was satisfied that everything was where it was supposed to be, he got out and looked around, his excess energy evident to the rest. He had to burn some of that, so he went prone to do some pushups, much to the amusement of Achille. The others didn't seem to notice it.

"What exactly is the game plan?" Roo asked.

"We won't know until we see how they're set up. We have to find them first."

"No shit. I'm just saying what kind of operation is this?

Is it a go in and eliminate everyone operation, or is it more of a take prisoners thing?"

Reen slammed the magazine for her Beretta home and put the pistol in her thigh holster. "I don't negotiate with terrorists."

"I don't think we can make that decision just yet," Charles said and turned into a seated position, his arms folded over his knees. "Let's see what we're up against first. But obviously, the goal is to get all the girls back— unharmed. It's likely there will be casualties."

Booker stopped. "I think we should move in on foot from here to have a geek around. I don't want to alert people to our presence by rumbling in or running into their camp accidentally."

He backed the BTR into some thick brush and under a huge tree. Mick and Achille looked around for signs of the missing girls. The others cut tree branches and other plants to better hide the armored vehicle.

"Okay. There's definitely something in the area," Mick said, his tone pitched low. "A big group of people. They aren't extremely close, but they're not that far away either —these tracks are pretty fresh. I'd say we're easily within a klick of them. Or at least near where heavy foot traffic is. There seems to be at least a small group that travels regularly through here."

"This is all recon," Booker said. "We aren't going to do anything unless our hand is absolutely forced. We need to be delicate about this extraction. We have to gather all the information first and then move in an informed way. There are more of them than there are of us."

The two trackers led the way through the brush and

meticulously checked the trail they followed. The sign became more obvious after they'd gone less than half a kilometer as if the people making the tracks had become careless and comfortable. Branches were broken and swaths of grass trampled. Boot prints became easy to distinguish in the soft, red earth.

They stayed low and as quiet as they could manage. Soon, voices could be heard—men talking and laughing.

Booker dropped to low-crawl forward and signaled the others to do the same. They snaked through the undergrowth, careful not to draw attention to themselves.

The team moved cautiously up a slight rise in the land and into a position that overlooked a large encampment.

Four firepits were in the center of the camp. Low grass hut-like structures had been erected and seemed to be used as housing. It was a more permanent camp than they had anticipated, which meant the insurgents were in this for the long haul. This wasn't some quick mission to raise cash.

Many young girls milled around, tied to one another with ropes in groups of five. Their school uniforms were dirty and most looked disheveled. They moved silently and tried to avoid the attention of the men.

The Ansaru insurgents wore drab green fatigue tops much like the ranger uniform Achille wore. Their pants and footwear were a hodgepodge of different styles and types. Most of them were armed with AK-47s.

A man with a red bandana tied to his left bicep snapped orders in French. A group of girls flinched and rushed to complete the task he'd asked of them—preparing a meal.

The longer they watched, the more it became obvious

that the girls were being used as servants. The man with the red bandana was obviously in charge. He gave orders and the men and girls listened to him.

"Try to count how many insurgents there are," Booker whispered into Reen's ear.

She nodded.

It started to grow dark and the evening meal was prepared. Bottles of alcohol were produced, and the men passed them around amidst laughter. The girls all sat silent and simply watched them. They weren't given any food to eat.

Halfway through the meal, a man approached the group of girls. He leered at them and swayed slightly while he studied them, then drew a knife.

The hidden BOHICA Warriors and Achille stiffened.

The man approached one cluster and untied one of them in the middle. He grasped her wrist and waved his knife threateningly at her before he dragged her toward one of the grass huts. She struggled and he backhanded her. The girl, no more than thirteen, crumpled. They could hear her sobs as the other men laughed. Her captor yanked her into the hut.

Charles gripped the back of Roo's shirt to hold the other man back. He pressed his elbow into his teammate's spine to immobilize him. Booker had hold of Reen, who trembled in fury. She, too, had tried to surge forward.

Several other girls were dragged away in the same fashion as the first.

The Brit retreated from their hiding place and the others followed. They moved silently all the way back to the BTR.

Roo picked up a rock and hurled it as hard as he could into the bush. "Those motherfuckers are going to pay!"

"I counted thirty hostiles and about fifty innocents," Charles said. He hadn't stopped scowling, and his hands were balled into fists.

"I counted the same," Reen said.

Booker ran a hand through his hair. "So did I. And it looked like there was at least one AK per insurgent."

"Those aren't great odds," Mick said.

"Fuck the odds." The Aussie's tone was wrathful. "We can do this. We're going to take those motherfuckin' sonsofbitches down."

"There are six of us," Achille said and his shoulders were slumped again. He sounded defeated.

Charles clapped the man on the back. "Yes, but we have the advantage."

"How? What advantage?" the ranger asked, raised an eyebrow, and looked at him with skepticism.

"We're the good guys. Not to mention, we're all very good at what we do."

"The BTR will help," Booker said. "We'll have to figure out a way to maneuver it close enough to be of use."

"We'll have to draw them away from the girls," Reen said. "We'll need a diversion."

"Maybe I could call for backup," Achille said and patted his walkie talkie. "The other rangers would willingly lend a hand. If I can raise them, that is. We don't have good communications here."

The Brit contemplated what the ranger said before he shook his head. "No. We can't risk them listening in, and uh..." he hesitated a moment, then plowed on. "We were told that they might be having some inside help. No insult is intended, but some of the rangers could be in on this. It's got to be just us."

He waited for the outburst of anger from the man, but instead, all he received was a sad, knowing smile.

"We need a way to put them all on guard but looking in the wrong direction," Mick said.

Roo held a grenade up. "What about this?"

"We can't throw a grenade at them," the Aboriginal said. "We don't want to hit the girls."

"No. We can detonate a grenade on the opposite side of their encampment. They'll be put on their guard and we'll have to make sure they think the attack is going to come from that direction."

"That's a good idea," Reen said. "However, I don't think a grenade exploding would quite do the trick."

"What then?"

"We can still do the grenade thing, but we have to draw them to a specific spot first. Which means one of us will be there, picking them off one-by-one. They'll just hear and see a lone shooter and they'll try to concentrate an attack in that way. Then the grenade can come in to hide the sound of the BTR coming from the opposite direction."

"What about the girls?" Achille asked. "And who will act as sniper?"

"I can do that," Mick volunteered.

"We can't get to the girls until the insurgents are sufficiently pre-occupied."

"They'll definitely still hear the BTR coming," Booker said. "Grenade or no grenade. They'll hear a large armored vehicle crashing through the brush, no doubt about it."

"It's obviously not perfect," she said, "but I don't see anyone else offering up any other valid ideas."

"So, if Mick is acting as sniper and diversion, and Booker is driving the BTR in, I think the rest of us should be on the ground, working on freeing the girls and getting them out of the crossfire," Charles said. "Someone can stay behind with Booker and operate the weapons system."

"I want to be on the ground," Reen said.

"Same."

Charles glanced at Achille and shook his head. "All right, fine. I'll stay behind with Booker and operate the BTR's guns."

"We can silently pick off the assholes who don't move toward the firefight," Roo said.

"Exactly."

"Let me play devil's advocate for a moment and just ask what if they don't behave in that way?" Mick asked.

She wrinkled her nose in confusion. "What do you mean?"

"We're expecting them to move and behave like soldiers would. They're insurgents—terrorists. They most likely don't have military training."

"Did you say they were Ansaru?" Achille asked.

"Yes," Booker answered.

He nodded. "Many of the Ansaru insurgents are ex-military. It is likely they will react as you think."

"No battle plan survives the first shot," Booker muttered. "But we have to have one."

"That guy who was running the show—the one with the bandana on his arm—seemed like a no-nonsense guy who keeps a tight ship," Reen said. "I bet he'd make sure his men were disciplined."

"This is the best plan we can come up with in the time limit and with our limited amount of intel and resources. We can make it work," the Brit said. "We have to."

"What are we waiting for?" Roo demanded. "Let's go kick some terrorist ass."

———

They maneuvered into position. Reen, Achille, and Roo hid in the scrub and waited for Mick's signal. Booker drove the BTR steadily closer as quietly as he could manage. Charles kept an eye out from the gunner's position.

The insurgents put the girls into the largest of the grass huts, still roped together. Only one man was left to guard the door while the rest clustered in the center of the camp. The man in charge addressed them. He spoke too quietly for anyone outside of his circle to hear.

Reen crept closer to the windowless back of the hut where the girls were kept, Achille directly behind her. She grasped the handle of her Bowie knife firmly and waited.

The rumble of the BTR's engine could be heard in the near distance. The men turned to look, and when they did, a shot rang out from the opposite direction. One man dropped to his knees, then collapsed face-first into the dirt. The insurgents stared at their fallen comrade as blood pooled around him. They recovered quickly from their shock and turned their attention toward the direction of the shot.

Mick took a deep breath, exhaled slowly, and squeezed

the trigger again. Another insurgent fell. The sniper immediately scrambled away to a point a little farther from
where he'd first fired. There was the roar of thirty—no,
twenty-eight now—AK-47s firing and round after round
pelted the area he had vacated seconds before.

After about twenty seconds, the gunfire ceased. He
waited another ten seconds and opened fire again to eliminate another of the men.

Roo added his firepower to Mick's assault. Reen used
the noise of the gunfire to cut a hole in the back of the hut.
She sawed away at it and soon, could see the wide-eyed
stares of the girls. Hastily, she smiled encouragement at
them and put a finger to her lips.

She reached through the opening she'd created and cut
the bonds of the nearest prisoner. Quickly, she pressed a
pocketknife into the girl's hand and motioned that she
should free the others while she got back to work to create
a large enough hole for them to escape through once they
cut themselves free.

The leader yelled something in French and the Ansarus
surged forward and out in an attempt to take cover but
also close in on their attackers.

Mick pulled the pin on his grenade and hurled it at the
oncoming terrorists. He hunkered down and blocked his
ears.

The grenade detonated, obliterated two of the targets,
and wounded several others.

Reen peeled back the thin side of the grass hut and
waved the girls through. They started to file out, and
Achille was there to lead them away.

"Hey!" a man roared. *"Ils s'en vont."*

"Ah, shit," Reen said. She motioned for the escapees to keep going and ran out the front to open fire on the terrorists, racing away from the hostages in an effort to draw the men's fire. Fortunately, it worked.

With a thunderous crash and a mechanical roar, the BTR plunged into the clearing and cut the men off from the girls. Booker fired the PKT coaxial machine gun at the men and the rounds plowed through their ranks.

Achille hauled the last girl through the wall and shoved her ahead. "Şişe," he hissed in Yoruba. "Run!" The sounds of the firefight faded behind them as they put distance between them and the camp.

Mick joined Roo and they moved forward to narrow the distance between them and their adversaries. The BTR's weapons system, combined with Mick and Roo's rounds, swiftly subdued the rebels.

The grass huts were shredded. Blood and body parts were strewn about the clearing. A few of the enemy were wounded but still alive, and they'd thrown their weapons down and held their hands high in surrender.

The two men surveyed the damage. Charles remained at the BTR's gun to cover the terrorists, but Booker hopped out to join the other two on the ground.

"What should we do with these motherfuckers?" Roo asked and waved his gun at the men who flinched and whimpered.

"Pathetic," Mick muttered. "They'll prey on a bunch of innocent girls, but when it comes down to it, they're all just fucking pussies. What a waste of humanity."

"I think we should tie them up and leave them here," Charles said. "I'm sure the rangers will find them eventually—if the animals don't first." As if on cue, in the distance, came the high-pitched cries of hyenas.

The men shifted uncomfortably. The leader, who was still alive, glared at the four men. He said something to them in his native tongue.

"Whatever that was, it didn't sound fucking nice," Mick said. "But you know what? Who gives a shit?"

They tied the men with the same rope they'd used on the girls and left them, back to back, in the center of the destroyed clearing. They turned to climb inside the BTR.

"Wait!" one of the terrorists cried in English. "You can't leave!"

Booker disappeared inside with Charles close on his heels.

"Looks like that's what we're doing, asshole," Mick said as he scrambled through the BTR's side door.

"If you didn't want this to happen, you should've fucking thought twice before kidnapping a bunch of fucking baby birds," Roo all but growled. "I hope the hyenas rip you apart." He slammed the door shut on the protests.

"Should we have left them there?" the Aboriginal asked.

His teammate glared at him. "What the fuck are you saying?"

"I mean, they're monsters, but does that mean we should leave them to the animals? That's pretty fucked up. Wouldn't that pull us to their level?"

"I wouldn't worry about it too much," Booker answered. "I doubt any animals will be in that clearing for a while yet. And when Achille gets in touch with his fellow rangers and we call the government or whoever to come get the girls, someone will come to take out the rest of the garbage."

"Let's go make sure the others got away safely," Charles said.

The Brit nodded and they drove away, leaving the struggling terrorists behind in a ring of destruction.

CHAPTER ELEVEN

W National Park, WAP Complex, Benin

Reen and Achille checked the girls to make sure none of them were injured. They were shaken, dirty, and hungry, but they were all in reasonable condition. Their mental state was not so good.

Achille had gotten hold of his chief ranger, who was sending a truck to pick up the remaining insurgents and clean the mess.

"How are they?" Mick asked as he slid out of the BTR once Booker had found where they'd gone.

Reen looked at the fifty girls who huddled together, her mouth set in a grim line. "They're traumatized but actually all right. Not all speak French that well, but from those who do, they told me that only a few were, uh…"

"Good," he said. "Not that part, I mean. But only a few, not all of them," he hastily added, realizing what he'd actually said.

She frowned but didn't seem angry at him, merely sad.

"When schoolgirls get kidnapped, they become 'jungle

wives.' Some get pregnant. Some stay with their kidnappers even after the others are released. Fucking sick world."

For once, he knew to simply remain silent.

"What's going on there?" he asked as he approached them and pointed to where Achille spoke to one of the older girls, who cried and waved her hands frantically.

"Beats me," Reen said and looked up as if grateful for the interruption to her dark thoughts.

Charles and Booker came out the back of the BTR holding packets of MREs.

"It's not much," the American said, "but it doesn't look like these kids have had anything to eat in a while. It might take some time still for us to get them out of the park. There probably isn't enough to go around, but it's better than nothing. Let's get them distributed."

"Somethings up with that one," Roo said and gestured at Achille and the girl.

"I'll find out what's up. You start feeding the girls," Reen said.

"What's happened?" she asked Achille.

He turned to them, concern etched across his face. "This is Numa. She says that one of their number was separated and taken away to a different location. She says she overheard some of the terrorists saying that she was being taken to Tahoua."

She frowned, leaned down to Numa's level, and grasped the girl's narrow shoulders. "We'll make sure someone knows about your friend," she said in English before shifting to French.

Numa wrapped her arms around her. *"Merci, m'dame."*

The girl yelled something in a local language, and the other girls suddenly broke out in choruses of thank you's— in French, in their tribal languages, and in English.

While the others tended to the girls, Booker stepped away to call the president on his sat phone, which surprisingly worked in the middle of the bush

President Okonkuo answered on the second ring. "Hello?"

"Mr. President, it's Booker."

"Please tell me you have good news for me."

"I have good news for you. We've managed to recover the girls—fifty of them. Though there seems to have been one girl removed from the others and taken to a place called Tahoua."

"A thousand thanks to you and your team, Booker. I am indebted to you. Benin is indebted to you. If there is any way I can be of assistance to you, please let me know."

"Of course. Thank you. It was the right thing to do, and we're happy we could help."

"You are still in the park?"

"Yes, sir."

"Good. If you will tell me your location, I will have a team meet you tomorrow to pick the girls up and deliver your payment. Is this agreeable to you?"

"Works for us, sir. Uh, we met a ranger here, Achille Amadou. He contacted his boss in the ranger headquarters in Pendjari Park, and that guy's sending a truck for the terrorists. Some of them are still alive. Captive, but alive."

"So, they know there were foreigners involved. Not good," the president said. "But no, you did well. I'm sorry to rain on your parade, as you say. This might work out, though. Rangers finding the girls. Good, good."

"Oh, and one more thing," President Okonkuo added, "is there a girl named Sophie Oladipupo there among the rescued girls?"

"Hang on, let me check," Booker said. He muffled the receiver against his chest. "Is there anyone named Sophie Oladipupo here?"

The girls shifted nervously. The movement reminded him of skittish foals.

Numa stepped forward again and whispered into Reen's ear.

"She says Sophie is the one who was taken," she said.

He nodded gravely. "Mr. President?"

"Yes?"

"I'm afraid that Sophie Oladipupo is not among the rescued girls. According to them, she was the one who was separated from the group and allegedly taken to Tahoua."

The man uttered a string of curses in his local language. "This is not good," he said when he reverted to English. "She is the daughter of Arnaud Oladipupo, a well-to-do businessman who just so happens to want my presidency. This will only fuel his fire."

"Can we help in any way?" Booker asked.

"I don't know," the president said with a sigh. "You have already done so much. You will be paid for your excellent work, but I think this might be where our business partnership comes to an end. Sophie is the child of a powerful man who will be able to do what it takes to get her back. Again, I thank you and your company for the service you have rendered for the country of Benin."

"It was no trouble at all," he said. "We were more than happy to help."

"When my people come to take the girls, I will have my messenger deliver your payment," President Okonkuo said. "Don't take this the wrong way, but I hope that I will not have future business dealings with you."

He laughed. "Don't worry, I understand what you are saying and the sentiment is the same."

They spent the night inside the park, sleeping in the BTR, and in the morning, a fleet of shiny, black Range Rovers arrived, all with the Benin crest on the side. The caravan followed an old beat-up pickup driven by a park ranger.

Emam, the messenger who had delivered the president's letter to BOHICA, stepped out of the first vehicle.

"Booker, I am glad to be seeing you again under these circumstances," he said and extended his hand.

"So am I," Booker said.

A medical team began assessing the girls. Once they were cleared, each was ushered toward the Range Rovers and safely closed inside.

"I was instructed by President Okonkuo to congratulate you on a job well done," Emam said.

"Thank you. We had some help, though. From one of the park rangers, Achille Amaduo."

"I will pass that on to the president and let him know."

"I already gave him the ranger's name, but we'd appreciate him getting a reminder."

The president's aide handed Booker a large, brown

paper package. He opened it to reveal stacks of West African CFA ten-thousand-franc notes inside.

"There are three hundred million francs in there or about five hundred thousand American dollars," Emam said. "The president felt that your team did an exceptional job. He wishes he could've given more."

The Brit ran his thumb along the edge of the crisp francs. "Well, we didn't deliver all the girls."

"You are referring to Sophie?"

"Yes."

"President Okonkuo does not blame you for this, nor does he hold it against your team. She was already missing from the group before you arrived. It is not your fault."

"You're sure we can't help?"

"No. We will handle everything else from here," he said firmly. "I was instructed to make sure your vehicle had fuel. There is a diesel fill station at Kandi. You can fill up there. The operator at the post has been given instructions to fill your vehicle and any spare containers you may have free of charge."

"A real filling station? Not just a bunch of plastic bottles filled with diesel?" he asked.

The aide gave a rueful smile, then said, "Yes, we do have black market fuel coming in from Nigeria, but no, this is an authorized filling station. The government has to use them, as I'm sure you can understand."

"Diesel's diesel, I guess," he said. "And thanks."

Emam inclined his head. "It is the least we can do. Benin is in your debt for the service you've rendered." He turned away and began giving instructions to the other soldiers who directed the abductees into the vehicles.

It took two hours to determine that none of the girls needed immediate medical attention. They were loaded safely inside the Range Rovers, and the team watched as the caravan drove away, leaving a cloud of red dust in their wake.

"Well," Reen said and stretched before she stood from the rock she'd sat on, "that's that."

"That's that," Booker echoed.

"What will you do now?" Mick asked Achille.

The ranger smiled. "I will continue to do what I've been doing for the last forty years—be a park ranger. Nothing has changed that. This trip was a momentary change of duty, but it was my honor to work alongside you and your team."

"We were glad to have you, mate," Mick said. He looked again at the beat-up Berthier rifle Achille carried again, having given back the AK. He adjusted his grip on his FN-FAL and after only a slight hesitation, extended the rifle to the other man. "I want you to have this."

Achille took a step back. "Oh, no. I couldn't."

"You could, and you will," he said. "You deserve it. Please, take it. It's the least we could do."

He took the rifle and tested its weight before he turned away from the group and looked through the sight. Finally, he looked at his benefactor and smiled. "This is much better than my Berthier."

The Aboriginal laughed. "No shit. Here, let me get you a box of ammunition for it." He climbed back into the BTR to retrieve it.

Booker was inside, counting the cash they'd received. "You gave your FN to Achille?"

"Yes. He needs a better weapon."

"Of course. I'm surprised that bleddy rifle he's been using hasn't completely fallen apart on him." He grabbed a small stack of franc notes and handed it to Mick. "Here. Put this in that box for him to find later."

"He won't like that we've paid him," he protested.

The Brit laughed. "I know. That's why I'm telling you to hide it. He may not like it, but he most likely needs it."

"He's going to split this with the rest of the rangers. He won't keep it for himself."

"You're probably right." He handed him another stack of bills. "In that case, we might as well give him more. We don't need the money as badly as the park rangers do."

Mick rearranged the two million francs under several boxes of 7.62x51 mm NATO rounds. Once he was satisfied that Achille wouldn't find the money right away, he returned to where the man waited and inspected the new rifle.

"Here you go," he said and handed him the metal carton of ammunition.

"Thank you so much. You do not know how this will help."

"I have a bit of an idea. I'm happy to do it."

"Can we drop you anywhere?" Booker asked the ranger. "We're headed to Kandi to refuel. Do you need to go in that direction?"

"Yes. If I could ride with you to my station, that would be great. It is on your way."

"Of course, you can," he said. "Okay, people, let's load up and move out. Our business here is done."

Achille directed them back to the highway, and the BTR

made its way toward the park entrance. More than a few vehicles pulled over and made way for them.

It took an hour to reach a small dirt road near the park entrance. Another five hundred meters in, they reached Achille's station, an unimpressive small, square building on stilts. A man in the same uniform as their guide stood at the railing and watched the armored vehicle stop below him. He was missing an arm, the sleeve rolled up and held closed with a safety pin.

"This is Jardin," Achille said after everyone got out to say their goodbyes. "He's a retired ranger, and I asked him to watch over the station while I was gone."

Charles shook hands, but he hung back, not saying much when Achille gave Mick and Reen a tour of his station.

"What is it?" Booker asked his friend

"Huh?"

"What's the matter? You look all sullen."

"I'm just thinking about that other girl."

"The Sophie bird?"

"Yes."

"There's no way we could've prevented her from being taken. Who knows when that happened?"

"I know that, but I just wish we were going after her too. I'd like to be able to wrap this whole thing up neatly."

"I get what you're saying, but the president seemed very clear that he didn't want us involved. She's apparently the daughter of some high-up politician and powerful businessman. I'm sure she won't be missing for long."

The American remained silent. He unfolded the map they'd used and looked for Tahoua. "Looks like we'll be passing right through that area on our way back to the Zoo."

"Charles," Booker warned.

"What? I'm not saying we tear the town apart looking for her," he said. "But it wouldn't hurt anything if we just looked around for a little bit. Nothing too serious. And if we find any intel, we can decide what to do with it."

The Brit sighed. "We'll have to see what the others think."

His teammate grinned.

"Don't go getting your hopes up," he warned. "I would love to rescue her, but we don't want to meddle in a political rivalry when we've been told to stay out."

Achille led Reen, Mick, and Roo out of the station and back to the BTR where Booker said, "Thanks again for your help."

"Of course, it was my duty and my honor."

They all shook hands with the weathered ranger. Mick pulled him into a hug and smacked him solidly on the back.

"Take care of yourself, Achille," he said. "If you ever need anything, give us a call."

He smiled at them. "I will. It was a pleasure working with a team of such honor and caliber as yourselves. That situation could have gone far worse than it did. Those girls are on their way to their homes thanks to you."

"Thanks to you, too," Reen said. "It was a team effort."

They climbed into the BTR and each of them waved goodbye to him as they went. He stood in the middle of the road and watched them drive out of the park.

CHAPTER TWELVE

Outside of Tahoua, Niger

Booker drove past a field of date palms. The trees lined up in perfect little rows. A herd of mangy stray dogs ran amongst them and a few barefooted boys stopped and stared as the armored vehicle rumbled past.

"So, about this missing girl," Charles said.

"What about her?" Reen asked.

"We should go rescue her," Roo said.

"That's why we're headed through Tahoua," the big man said. "Booker said we could go rescue the girl."

"No," Booker said. "I didn't say anything about rescuing her. I said when we're in town we can just sort of geek around. Nothing too in-depth. We aren't authorized to do anything. Besides, we aren't really equipped to start a war with some insurgents. I, of course, want to help if we can. But I just don't know what we can do."

"Can you think of any better reason to start a war with some insurgents?" Charles asked.

The Brit pinched the bridge of his nose. "You're giving me a fucking headache."

"As much as I'd love to do something like that, I don't think it's that great of an idea," Mick said. "Not that we've made heaps of great decisions lately. But this is definitely out there. Especially since Mr President wanted us to keep our noses out of it."

"Oh, shove off," Roo said. "I know you're just dying to show off your great fucking tracking skills."

"I don't need to show off a goddamn thing. I'm just not too keen on the idea of busting through a town looking for a girl where the only detail we know is her name. That's shit to go off of."

"Mick's right. We don't even know what she looks like," Reen said. "Still…"

"Do you think Achille could find out for us?" Charles asked.

"How would Achille know more information about the missing bird than we do?" Mick asked.

"I mean, he is from the place," the American said. "Maybe he knows her."

"Don't be a wanker, Charles. He's from the same fucking country as the girl. That doesn't mean they're neighbors," Booker pointed out.

"You don't know that."

"Okay. Fine. It's *highly* unlikely that the missing girl is neighbors with a park ranger."

"Didn't the pres say she was the daughter of some political figure?" Reen asked.

"A businessman," the Brit clarified.

"I'm sure her father has the means to rescue her, then," Mick said.

"If he had the means, why hasn't he done it all ready?" Charles asked.

"Seems to me," Roo said, "that the prick doesn't care. So, she's out there all alone and no one is going to rescue her."

Everyone sat with that information for a few minutes as they drove closer to Tahoua.

An old school bus with a poor rendering of the Malbaza FC team—the closest football club to Tahoua—on the side trundled up beside the BTR. Bags and packages were piled high on the top of the bus. A few young men sat on the strapped-down baggage. The bus itself was over-crowded with people, and they all stared out the grimy windows.

The driver honked a few times, pressed on the gas, and cut in front of them. The whole thing swayed dangerously on the rough dirt road but remained upright and careened toward the town.

"So much for keeping a low profile," Booker muttered.

"I didn't realize that's what our goal was," Charles responded.

"It's always better to not draw attention."

Before they entered Tahoua, they drove beneath the arched necks of two giant, orange metal camels with *Bienvenue Tahoua* painted on them.

"Seems like a friendly enough place," the American commented.

Booker eased into the traffic of the city. People stared and soon, there was the familiar whine of police sirens. Two motorcycles with flashing lights pulled in front of the

BTR while an old Honda-turned-police-vehicle penned them in from behind.

He started to pull over, but it wasn't fast enough for the officers. "*Arrêtez-vous! Arrêtez-vous!*" blasted through the loudspeaker of the car.

"Reen, what's he saying?" Booker asked.

"Pull over."

"I am fucking pulling over," he grumbled. He shut the ignition off.

"*Sortir du véhicule!*" This was yelled by one of the motorcycle cops who banged on the side of the armored vehicle. "*Sortir du véhicule!*"

All the policemen were armed with Ak-47s. There were four of them in total, and one stood off to the side, talking into a radio.

"Everyone behave," the Brit said and looked pointedly at Roo.

His teammate glared at him. "I always fucking behave."

They climbed out of the BTR and held their hands up placatingly. They attempted to look non-threatening, but it was unnatural for them. The best they could do was stand tall in a straight line in front of the armored vehicle.

Immediately, the police aimed their guns at them and began yelling in French.

Reen said something and the policeman with the radio stepped forward. "What is your purpose here?" he asked. His accent was thick and his English halting. He scowled at them under his black beret. A bead of sweat rolled down his face. The short-sleeved black uniform he wore had three stripes on the left arm, signifying his higher rank to the other three officers.

"We're just driving through," Booker said. "That's all. We will fuel up, maybe get some rations, and be on our way."

The policeman looked over the rim of his reflective Aviator-style sunglasses. "You have no business bringing a military vehicle through Tahoua."

"We don't have business," Roo said. "We're just passing by."

Charles elbowed him in the side.

The Aussie ignored him and continued, "We could have business here, though."

The policeman stepped up to him and leaned over the shorter man. "Are you threatening me?"

He folded his arms over his chest. "Seems to me, bucko, that you're the one threatening people."

"Forgive him," Reen said, "he's a little slow." She followed this statement up with something in French.

The policeman stepped away from him and smiled lasciviously at her. He said something to her in French and she grinned. Her teammate balled his hands into fists and Charles pinched the flesh above his elbow to hold him in place.

"Stop being so fudging difficult," the American muttered.

Roo shook him off. "Fuck off."

"Where are you heading?" the policeman asked and reverted to English.

"We're going back to Libya," Booker said.

"Back to Libya? When did you come through?"

"A few days ago."

"What business do you have in Libya?"

"Our own."

The policeman's scowl deepened. One of the junior officers stepped closer and said something in a low voice. "Do you have papers?"

The Brit nodded.

"We will look through your papers. You can fuel up and be on your way first thing in the morning."

"First thing in the morning? Now, wait a minute. We were just trying to drive through," Booker protested.

The policeman smiled a humorless smile that seemed more like a baring of teeth. "Your plans are now changed. Welcome to Tahoua. We will escort you to *d'hôtel*."

He turned away from the team and spoke to his underlings. The officer who was a passenger in the police car climbed into the BTR. "Elon here is going to drive you. We don't want to risk you getting lost."

Roo was about to protest again but Charles slung an arm around his neck and hauled him into the vehicle. He elbowed him in the ribs and shoved the larger man off of him.

"What the fuck, Charles?"

"Behave."

"I'm not some fucking dog you can just drag around, asshole. I can be sensible."

"Then be sensible."

"These fuckers are acting skittish," the Aussie said, lowered his voice, and glanced toward the front where Booker and the policeman, Elon, sat.

"I know that," his teammate said. "But we don't want to upset them. Driving through here was a mistake."

"I thought you wanted to find the girl? You backing out on that?"

"No! I just think we didn't go about this in a smart way."

Reen settled herself next to Roo and patted his leg. "You're letting your gingerness get ahold of you."

"Fuck you."

Mick huffed. "How are we supposed to get anything done with these wankers breathing down our necks?"

"Very carefully," she said. She glanced out one of the gun ports at the police car behind them.

They lurched forward and drove through town. People stared as they passed.

"Everyone seems kind of subdued," she said.

"What do you mean?" the American asked.

She waved a hand. "I mean, this is a pretty big town. It seems like it's a bit of a trading center. So why isn't there more action? Everyone seems to be keeping their heads down. Trying not to be noticed."

"You catching all that through the gun port?" Mick asked.

"Yes, dipshit. It's called being observant."

"I wonder if they were tipped off," Charles said.

"If they were, that means there is more going on than some insurgents kidnapping a girl," Reen said.

"What makes you say that?" the Aboriginal asked.

"Think about it. Why did they separate this one girl from the fifty others they had? Besides, they were just camped out there. What were they waiting for? A ransom? With a camp that permanent? They knew no one was coming to rescue the girls. Why not just keep this Sophie chick with the others?"

"Maybe it wasn't the insurgents," Charles said. "It's possible her businessman father has enemies who wanted her specifically."

"Bingo."

"It's all speculation," Mick said. "We don't know shit about anything in this situation. And sitting around here asking questions we don't know the answers to isn't going to help."

They sat in silence for a few minutes. The police escort took several winding turns through the town and then stopped in front of a long, low building the color of buttermilk. *Hotel* was painted on the side in tall, blue letters.

The policemen dismounted from their motorcycles and the other got out of the car. He banged on the side of the BTR again.

Reen flung open one of the side doors and hopped out. She folded her arms over her chest and stared at the policeman.

He took his sunglasses off. "We have already called ahead and arranged a room for you. You don't have to worry about anything like that," he said in French.

"Do we have to stay in the hotel room?" she asked.

The policeman smiled. "No. Of course not. We aren't holding you prisoner or anything. You will, of course, have to leave to refuel and get supplies. I will give you a list of the best places to accomplish this." He passed her a scribbled note on an old napkin.

She put it in her pocket and didn't say anything else as the others got out.

A clerk from the hotel came out of the office and showed them the room the police had arranged for them.

The hotel was only one room deep and had eight rooms, each connected by a covered walkway and ending in the office. The clerk wore a bright orange fez-like cap and only spoke French. He explained to Reen that they still had to pay for the room, even though the police had booked the rooms.

"Who is in charge in this town?" Roo asked the lead policeman.

He frowned. "What do you mean?"

"I mean, who has you on his bankroll? Who are you protecting?"

"I don't know what you're talking about."

"We just came from Benin," he pressed and ignored Charles' throat-clearing attempts to get him to shut up.

"Nice place."

"Yeah. We heard about a kidnapping while we were there."

The policeman said nothing.

"You hear anything about that over here?"

"We would like you to all be gone first thing. Tahoua is a peaceful town and we wouldn't want to disturb that," the man replied calmly.

He returned to his car and drove away. The two motor-cycles followed in his wake.

"This is all sitting sideways with me," Booker muttered.

"No shit," Mick said.

They opened the door to the room. It was dark inside and smelled like molding carpet. Roo walked in first and looked around.

"Well, this is a shithole," he said.

There were two queen-sized beds separated by a nightstand. The beds had twin divots where previous people had slept. A shade-less lamp stood on the nightstand. A yellow-brown stain spread from a crack on the opposite wall from the door.

"Those motherfucking assholes," Reen muttered. "I blame you, Roo."

"Me? What the fuck for?"

"You were a dick and provoked them."

"Something tells me this had little to do with Roo," Booker said. He kicked the corner of one of the beds. The whole frame shifted and something small and rat-like darted from under it to the safety of the other bed. "Let's go get something to eat and refuel. This clearly wasn't the best idea. I know we were going to try to find the girl, but I think it might be in our best interest to lay low and get out of here before we start a war."

"I kind of doubt those jokers would be able to stop us," Charles said.

"Maybe. You're probably right, but it would be an awful lot of work. I just want to get back to the Zoo and back to normal."

"I'm fucking famished," Mick said. "Let's go get some grub. I thought I saw some sort of a market a few blocks back."

They grabbed their weapons from the BTR.

"Do you think it's a good idea to be fully armed like this?" Charles asked as he checked his Remington.

"Do you think it's a good idea not to be?" Booker countered.

"Mick, where's your FN?" Roo asked.

Mick shrugged and pushed his hands into the pockets

of his fatigues. "I gave it to Achille. He needed it heaps more than I did. I'll get another from Dan when we get back."

The American went back to the armored vehicle and retrieved one of the extra AK-47s. He passed it to Mick, who slung it over his back.

They made their way to the open-air market. There were piles of dry goods and other food. Sun-bleached canvas stretched over PVC pipes provided some shade. The tents were weighted down with large rocks. Locals milled around doing their shopping. Tahoua was large but it wasn't much of a tourist town, and the five BOHICA Warriors stood out.

One vendor was selling freshly grilled chicken on skewers with charred peppers and other vegetables. He cooked it on a large, flat piece of metal that was suspended over an open flame. Behind him, in slatted wood crates, were the chickens.

Charles gave the skewers a sniff, immediately bought a dozen, and passed them around.

"We should get some of these guys to come to the Zoo," Roo said around a mouthful of grilled chicken. "This shit is good. They'd make a killing at the Harvesters Camp."

Mick watched the people around them. Everyone was clearly aware of the strangers but did their best to avoid looking at them. "Something's not right," he muttered.

The American nodded. "I'm getting a weird feeling."

A group of children jogged past and their laughter ceased when they noticed the unfamiliar group. Charles smiled, and the kids darted away between buildings.

"We should look around for the girl," Roo said. He

stared at the surrounding buildings. The sun was setting and they were backlight by the blood-red sky.

Booker shook his head. "No. I don't think that's a good idea. There's something sideways going on in this town, and I sure as fuck don't feel like figuring it out. It's not worth dying over. Not today."

"It's too damn quiet," Mick said. "There are a lot of people living here. This is a big market. Why is it so fucking quiet?"

They picked up a few loaves of dense bread from one of the vendors and some dried beef from another. The transactions were civil but not friendly.

A policeman approached them. He was younger than the others who had pulled them over originally. He stopped a few feet from them and started speaking in rapid-fire French. Reen answered him.

"No gun," the policeman said, pointing at their weapons.

Booker folded his arms and stared at the younger man. "We aren't causing any trouble. We're just moving through."

The policeman fidgeted with his sidearm. The Brit raised an eyebrow and the younger man's gaze darted around the area. The locals pretended not to watch the interaction. He took a step away from them.

"*Ne pose pas de problème,*" he said in a gruff voice.

The left side of Booker's mouth twitched upward. He didn't need to speak French to understand the cop. He raised both hands, palms out, and said, "No, no problems."

He nodded and walked away.

"Too bad the others weren't such pussies," Roo muttered.

They wandered back through the town. The few people who were on the streets moved to the opposite side when they walked past. People closed shutters and windows and conversations stopped.

"Something really isn't fucking right," Mick said.

The others nodded their agreement.

They arrived at the hotel without incident.

Reen stopped short of entering the room. She patted the sides of her curly mohawk. "You know what? I'm going to sleep in the BTR."

"Don't want to bunk with us?" Roo asked and waggled his eyebrows.

She looked at the inky sky. "No, dipshit. I'm worried about the other pests that are in there."

"I think I'm with Reen," Mick said.

"Me too." Charles nodded emphatically.

Booker shook his head and closed the door. "The room's all yours if you want it, Roo."

"Fuck that noise. I don't want to stay there either."

The BTR was parked in the dirt on the opposite side of the road from the hotel as the paving stone parking lot wasn't large enough to accommodate it. They walked toward the vehicle and froze when they heard the unmistakable sound of a grenade launcher firing. All of them instinctively ducked as a streak of white light and smoke trailed after the RPG as it streaked into the side of the armored vehicle. The BTR was swallowed in an explosion of dirt and flame.

They hit the ground. Charles flung an arm around Reen and shielded her from the explosion with his broad back.

"Jesus," Roo said and gaped at the burning hulk of their ride. "Fuck."

"Get off me, Charles," Reen hissed and shoved him away. "I appreciate the gesture, but I can take care of my fucking self."

People from the surrounding buildings stumbled out to look. The hotel clerk came out and screamed something in French. In the distance came the whine of sirens.

"Really fucking brilliant," Booker said. "Just great."

"Where's Mick?" Charles asked and dusted himself off.

They looked around but didn't see him. Their weapons were raised, and they looked at the surroundings for signs of another attack.

"He was right beside me," Roo said. "There's no way he was near the BTR when that thing hit."

They walked carefully toward the vehicle, but there were no other signs of hostility. The acrid smell of burning rubber made their eyes water.

"Fuckin' a," Reen muttered. She kicked dirt toward it.

"There's no way this thing is going to run without a complete overhaul," Charles said. "Maybe more."

"A million dollars down the drain," the Aussie said bitterly.

"We need to find Mick," Booker said. "And a new ride."

"What do you think happened to him?" Roo asked. He fingered his weapon as he glared at the tops of the surrounding buildings, trying to see where the RPG had come from.

"I don't know," Charles said. "I'm sure he's fine, wherever he is. No one approached us, and he wasn't close enough to the blast to get caught."

"Maybe he caught sight of the fucker who did this," Reen said.

"You think he would've said something," Booker said.

"Shit. What do we do now?"

Three police cars and an ambulance screamed down the street. They halted in front of the wreckage.

"Is anyone hurt?" the policeman asked—it was the same man who had escorted them to the hotel. He didn't seem pleased to be interacting with the BOHICA Warriors again.

"No," Roo answered. "But we would like to know who the fuck did this. We weren't disruptive. We weren't doing anything wrong. We were going to leave in the morning, just like you asked."

"What are you implying?"

"I'm implying, motherfucker, that you know the wanker who did this."

Charles pulled him away from the policeman. "Come on, let's go see if we can spot where Mick ran off to."

"We're going to need another vehicle," Booker said to the policeman. He didn't apologize for his teammate's outburst.

The official folded his arms over his chest and muttered something in French. From the expression on his face, it was very likely that he was cursing.

The other two men walked away from the scene. They looked in the surrounding alleys and tried to question some of the locals, but no one could tell them anything about Mick or the RPG shooter.

"Someone sure doesn't want us the fuck around," Roo said.

"Well, if they didn't want us around, they shouldn't have marooned us here without a ride."

"You know what I mean."

"We clearly weren't in there."

"True, but still."

The duo returned to the market. It was still open, but it seemed to be transitioning into more of a bar and dinner market than groceries and goods. Strings of outdoor lights were being put up in anticipation of sundown.

The vendor with the chickens was packing up his booth when the two walked past and he arranged a tarp over the remaining chickens. The crates were stacked in the bed of a dusty old Toyota pickup.

"Excuse me, sir," Charles said.

The old man turned and smiled. He only had four teeth.

"Does this thing run?" the American asked and pointed at the pickup.

The man's brow furrowed, and he said, *"Je ne parle pas anglais."* He waved at another vendor from across the aisle —a woman in a hot-pink dress and red headscarf. She came over with an indulgent smile. She looked at the two strangers and her gaze lingered for a few moments longer on Charles.

Charles smiled. "I'm sorry, we don't know French. Do you speak English?"

"Yes, I do. How can I help?"

"I wanted to know if that pickup worked."

The woman conveyed the question to the old man.

"He said it does. What do you want with it?"

"Would he consider selling it?"

The man looked at the vehicle, then back at the two men.

"He wants to know what you want it for."

"Our vehicle...broke down. We just need a way to get back home."

The man and woman talked for a while. He waved his hands around and the woman answered him patiently.

"This doesn't look too promising," Roo muttered. "We need to get back and find Mick."

"Just hang on a second," Charles said.

The woman turned back to them. "He might consider it. If the price is right. He asks that you come back tomorrow."

"Thank you," he said and smiled again.

They walked away. "Do you think that POS truck would work?" the Aussie asked.

His teammate shrugged. "Sure. I mean, it's not the best, but it's better than anything we have right now. I don't know about you, but I'd rather avoid walking across the Sahara if at all possible."

By the time they returned to the hotel, the police had gone. Reen and Booker stood outside the room. The BTR still smoldered and filled the still air with a rancid stench.

"Any luck?" Booker asked.

They shook their heads.

"No," Charles said, "but we did scope out a potential vehicle."

"What the fuck?" Roo muttered. He looked over Reen's shoulder as Mick strolled up to them. "Where the fuck have you been?"

"Worried about me?" he asked with a grin.

"Where the fuck were you?" He repeated the question.

"When that RPG hit, I ran in the direction it came from. I wanted to catch the bastard who did it."

"What'd you find?" Booker asked.

"I found the gunner but decided not to engage," Mick said. "I followed the prick back to his hideout. I have a feeling that our mystery gunner is part of the gang who has that missing girl. I think the building he went back to is their headquarters and where they have the hostage."

"Show us," Booker said.

They followed him through a labyrinth of alleys. The stone and stucco walls of the houses they passed radiated heat even though the sun had set. He led them to a building that was the same as all the others—one-story, red stone, with a flat roof. There was a light inside but what appeared to be bedsheets had been tacked to the windows. The only difference between it and the neighboring buildings was the two armed guards. One was seated on a barrel next to the front door with an FM 24/29 light machine gun across his lap. The other stood on the roof of the building and walked the perimeter slowly, a matching machine gun in his hands.

They stayed out of sight and watched the structure for half an hour. No one entered and no one came out.

The Brit motioned in the direction of the hotel and they slipped away.

"You're probably right, Mick," he said once they'd returned.

They stood in the center of the unsavory room.

"I know I'm right," Mick said.

"What are we going to do about it?" Roo asked. "Those motherfuckers need to pay."

"We can't do anything about it right now," Reen said. "We need better light to scope it all out."

"She's right. We'll have to do it in the morning. The best thing we can do right now is get some sleep," Booker agreed.

She sighed and looked at the beds again. "Again, this place is a total shithole."

"It could be a lot worse." Charles tried to sound cheerful.

"Fuck your optimism, Charles," Roo snapped.

"I'll take first watch," the Brit said.

The others arranged themselves as comfortably as possible. Reen got extra towels from the hotel clerk that smelled clean enough and spread them on one of the beds. Roo took the other bed and Charles and Mick tried to get comfortable on the floor. Booker set himself up outside the door.

They started early the next day as none of them had slept well the night before.

"I think I got fucking fleas sleeping in that goddamn room," Roo muttered and scratched his ankle.

Reen ignored him.

They lay stretched on their stomachs on the roof of a building catty-corner to the one Mick had identified the night before and had been there for almost two hours. The sun was creeping into the sky, and the day was heating up.

Booker, Mick, and Charles went to the market. It was open, though there were hardly any people up and about yet. A few round tables were set up on the sidewalk. They were occupied by old men smoking, playing chess, and drinking espresso.

"We're going to need a technical," the Brit said. "We'll most likely need to make a fast escape."

"I've already got something in mind," Charles responded.

He approached the same vendor. The old man had emptied the crates of chickens from the bed of the pickup and he decided that was a good sign.

The young woman from the night before was there. She saw him and smiled.

Quickly, she approached him and handed him a steaming mug off coffee. "This is for you," she said. Her hair was out of the turban it had been in the night before, and she tossed the long braids over her shoulder.

"Thanks," he said.

"Who are your friends?" she asked and nodded toward Booker and Mick. "What happened to the short redheaded one who was with you yesterday?"

"He's still around," he said with a shrug. "These are some more of my friends."

"How many friends do you have?" she asked and batted her eyelashes.

He smiled and changed the subject. "You mind translating again…"

"Eugenia."

"You mind translating again, Eugenia?"

She pressed her lips together, then smiled. "Of course!"

They moved across to the old man and she spoke to him for a few moments. "Marcus said if he's going to sell you the truck, he needs to be properly compensated. He knows it's not much, but it does work. He uses it to transport his goods. He'd need enough to replace it."

Booker still had the money President Okonkuo gave them, and they used this to bargain with the old man—or, more correctly, with Eugenia.

"He could be trying to give the damn thing away and we wouldn't know," Mick muttered as she spoke to Marcus about the truck.

"Well, we're sort of at their mercy, aren't we?"

"And it really works?" Charles asked her again.

She nodded and smiled. "Would you like to see?" she asked.

He nodded.

Marcus climbed into the cab and started the vehicle. The engine turned right away and although there was a strange rattling noise, it seemed to work fine.

Charles popped the hood and examined the engine.

"What is the bottom line he'll take for this?" Booker asked and took control of the negotiations while his teammate inspected the pickup.

"What are you offering first, and I'll tell you if that's his bottom line or if you need to go higher," Eugenia said. Her voice had a harder edge to it, and he realized she would rather have talked to Charles.

"A million of these West African franks work for Marcus?" he asked.

Charles slammed the hood shut and wiped his hands on his fatigues.

"How is it?" Mick asked.

"It'll do."

"Four million," Eugenia said after speaking with Marcus. "Four million and he won't say anything either. We're assuming you want this transaction to be…how do you say, under the table? Yes?"

Booker narrowed his eyes at her. She smiled. "That's four and a half thousand dollars for something that looks twenty years old if it's a day."

She simply stared at him, the same smile plastered on her face.

"Bugger all. Fine." He finally gave in, pulled the money out, and counted the bills into the man's weathered palm. Marcus grinned and handed the keys to Charles.

The American saluted the old man and swung himself into the cab of the truck, rocking it with his weight. He looked too big for the small vehicle. Mick climbed into the bed and Booker got in the cab.

They drove the pickup through back alleys and side streets and tried to avoid the main thoroughfare. Fortunately, they blended in better with the battered pickup.

"You think they'll tip someone off?" Charles asked.

"Probably," Booker said. "Hopefully, the extra cash at least delays that inevitability."

Mick pressed the back window open. "So, what exactly is the plan? We don't have the BTR to work as cavalry now. I'm not too great at this urban warfare shit."

"Hopefully, Roo and Reen were able to find out some useful intel," the Brit said. "We'll go from there."

"This is probably a bloody fucking stupid idea, huh?"

"Probably."

"It's going to be a shit show," Mick said.

"Most likely," Charles said.

"But we've gotta do it."

His teammates both nodded.

"Ah, WTF," he said and turned to press his back against the cab. He tilted his head back and squinted at the clear, blue sky. "There are worse ways to go. Might as well die being a fucking hero."

"You're not going to die," the American said.

"You don't know that. It's okay, bunj. No biggie. I made my peace with dying a long time ago. And again, if I have to go, this is the way to do it."

"Positive thoughts, Mick," Booker said. "Positive thoughts."

Charles parked several blocks away from the building. He wasn't worried about concealing the truck since it blended in with all the other vehicles parked along the street.

Reen ran into them after they'd walked a block. "There you are," she said. "Come on. We've got to make our move soon."

"Why?" Booker asked.

"It looks like they're preparing to leave. It just started. I think our entry into this buttfuck of a town spooked them and now, they're clearing out."

"You got any good news?" Mick asked.

"Sure. There are only six of them."

"Well, those odds aren't bad," Charles said.

She shook her head. "Nope. We should be able to do it. The problem is, they definitely have more firepower than we do."

"Have you seen the girl?" Booker asked.

"Only glimpses of her. She's more woman than girl, though. Definitely in her late teens."

"Do they have her tied up or something?" Mick asked.

"Again, we haven't been able to catch a really good look at her, but she didn't seem to be with them by choice."

"Their change in location will probably help us," Booker said. "It'll be easier to get the girl when they're on the move than holed up."

"Were you able to secure a good technical?" Reen asked.

"An old beat-up Toyota pickup."

"Well, I guess that's better than nothing."

They climbed to the rooftop again and watched the activity in the house below. Four men walked repeatedly from the building to a dust-covered black Land Rover Defender, carrying boxes which they strapped to the luggage carrier. An older model Jeep was parked behind it.

"There are six of them?" Booker asked.

Roo nodded. "Two more are inside, guarding the girl. Poor little bird. I hope none of those sick fucks have hurt her."

"These guys seem different than the assholes in the park," Reen said.

"What makes you say that?" the Brit asked.

"They seem...cleaner. More professional. These guys act like bouncers or well-paid bodyguards for some tycoon, not desperate, scrabbling insurgents."

"Does that look like bulletproof glass to you?" Booker asked.

Charles squinted at the Defender. "I can't tell. It's possible."

"So, what's the plan, boss?" Roo asked.

"We wait for them to all get onto the road. It is most likely that they'll take the back routes. We get them in a tight alley and neutralize the vehicle."

"How do you propose we neutralize the vehicle?" Reen asked.

"Find a way to take out the tires."

She nodded. "I can do that. Get them in a tight alley and I can blow their tires out."

"We don't want to get the girl caught in the crossfire," Mick said.

"We'll do our best not to, but there's no telling what those wankers will do," Booker pointed out.

"What alley are we going to use?" Charles asked.

"There's a good one about three blocks away," Mick interjected. He described the route to the others.

"Okay. Charles and I will get the pickup. You guys stay here and then tail that truck. The town isn't really set up for a high-speed chase so you should be able to accomplish this. Reen, you're good to blow out the tires?"

She gave him a thumbs-up.

He and Charles left them on the roof.

The men below seemed to have loaded all their supplies. Two slid into the front and started the Land Rover. The other two stood guard, their FM 24/29s at the ready.

The last two men came out carrying a young woman between them. She was blindfolded and appeared to be gagged. Her hair was in an unruly afro and she still wore her school uniform. Her legs dragged along the ground as the men hauled her none too gently toward the waiting vehicle.

"Christ," Roo growled. "I'm going to kill these fuckers. Did they knock her out?"

"I don't think so," Reen said. "She just doesn't seem to be cooperating."

They rushed off the roof, hung back, and watched as the men loaded the girl into the car. When she got closer to the vehicle, she stopped being limp and thrashed against her captors. She kicked and fought like a wildcat, but the men were much larger than her and easily muscled her into the back seat.

The remaining two men got into the Jeep and followed the Defender.

"We'll have to take them out before we can get to the girl," Mick said.

"I can do that," Roo said.

"How?" she asked.

He shrugged. "I'll think of something."

"Okay, well, Mick and I will stay on the Defender," she said. "I'll stay directly behind. Once they get closer to the alley, I'll take out the rear tires."

"Make sure they don't see you," the Aussie warned.

"No shit, Sherlock. Same goes for you. This is probably our one chance—we can't fuck it up."

The Land Rover lurched forward and Mick loped away and disappeared into the maze of buildings. Reen started off at a jog and kept the two vehicles within sight. She knew she wasn't exactly being subtle, but she didn't necessarily care.

Roo ran through an alley. He was glad the vehicles

weren't moving quickly. The kidnappers didn't seem to be worried about being followed. It was possible that the location change was routine. He needed to come up with a way to separate the two vehicles from one another before they reached the alley.

He jogged past a tuk-tuk, then stopped. The three-wheeled covered scooter was unoccupied. Its driver stood a few feet away, pissing against the wall of a building with his back to the vehicle. A trailer had been attached and was stacked high with a leaning tower of empty crates. The Aussie looked around hastily before he ducked quickly into the small cab. The keys dangled from the ignition. He started it and pressed the gas to the floor. The vehicle coughed, lurched, and wobbled down the road.

The owner screamed at him and sprinted to catch up. He attempted to get into it, but he shoved him away.

"Sorry, mate! I just need to use this for a minute. I'll bring it back!"

The man yelled and waved his arms but stopped his pursuit.

"Sorry!" Roo called back again.

"*Ohu ezi!*" The man stopped in the middle of the street, his fist raised at the thief's retreating back.

He drove the three-wheeled scooter faster than it should've gone. Whenever he took a corner, the whole vehicle tilted. Crates from the stack fell off and splintered behind him.

Roo stopped at one of the cross streets. He looked around the corner to see if he was in the right place. Mick appeared beside him.

"Where the fuck did you get this thing?"

"Unimportant. Where are they?"

"Should be coming around the corner soon. There was a bit of a mishap with a small herd of goats."

He laughed. "You let someone's goat herd free?"

"They were already free. I just...guided them in a different direction. What's the plan with this thing?"

"Roadblock."

"Ah. For the Jeep?"

"Yeah. Is Reen close?"

"I'm assuming so. I lost track of her."

"Mr Tracker losing someone?"

"I wasn't tracking her. I just lost sight of her. But she's on it, I know."

"Watching her take out the tires is going to be fun. Think she can do it?"

"I don't see why the hell not."

The low rumble as tires crunched over loose gravel alerted them to the convoy's approach.

"Here they come," Mick said.

The Defender drove past and Roo accelerated. The tuk-tuk lurched forward and crossed the alley before the secondary vehicle could follow. The Jeep's brakes squealed and he launched himself from the scooter as the Jeep collided with the stacked crates. Metal and wood crunched with the impact.

Mick fired two rounds. One hit the driver of the Jeep in the head, and the other buried itself in the passenger's shoulder. The Aussie heaved the injured man out of the Jeep and slammed his elbow into the man's face. A crunch of cartilage and bone confirmed that the man's nose had been broken. He hurled him into the side of a building and climbed into the vehicle, unbuckled the corpse, and shoved it out the other side as Mick opened the opposite door.

The Land Rover had slowed and stopped. Two of the guards leaned out the open windows and fired.

"Ah, shit." Mick threw the Jeep into reverse to disentangle it from the wreckage and swung into the alley to avoid the gunfire.

Reen sprinted around the corner of a building and skidded to a stop behind a parked vehicle. She fired at the Land Rover, which precipitated indistinct yelling as the machine-gun fire stopped. It surged forward and kicked up a cloud of dust. Her two teammates stopped beside her. She scrambled in and stood in the back seat of the Jeep. The soft top was off, and she braced herself against the roll bar.

"How close are we to the alley?" she asked.

"Nearly there," Mick said. "Hold on!"

They followed their quarry around a sharp corner. The left side of the back bumper collided with a wall.

Reen grabbed the roll bar to keep from falling over. "Jesus! Watch it!"

"Sorry!"

She sighted down her M492 and took a few steadying breaths. The two vehicles were almost at the end of the narrow side street. The kidnappers leaned out the windows again and fired.

"Roo!" she yelled.

"On it," He said and returned fire to catch one of the abductors. The man's body went limp and fell halfway out of the window. The other jerked inside.

Her focus now unhindered, she aimed for the right rear

tire and pulled the trigger. The round struck the back bumper and she cursed and fired again. The second round found its mark and the tire began to shred and thick chunks of rubber peeled away. The Defender fishtailed but the driver managed to pull it straight again. She sighted the other tire.

Charles and Booker made an appearance at the far end of the street in the old Toyota to block the only exit. The Brit made no effort to slow as they hurtled toward the kidnappers.

Reen fired again and the other rear tire met the same fate. The rims dug into the earth and the rear of the vehicle skidded sideways. It careened into one of the buildings and the rear windshield shattered.

One of the occupants immediately fired his machine gun through the broken windshield. Mick and Roo ducked and she dropped onto the rear seat. The Aboriginal pressed the accelerator and rammed into the back of the Defender.

Charles and Booker had stopped and flung themselves out of the Toyota to approach the front of the vehicle in a running crouch. The American fired at the front windshield and obliterated it. He quickly fired again and hit the driver.

Booker ripped open the front passenger door and dragged the body out. The remaining kidnapper grabbed the girl, who sat bound in the back seat, and yanked her out of the car by her hair. He screamed at the BOHICA Warriors, used her as a human shield, and aimed his pistol at her head. The man had left the machine gun in the Land Rover and was bleeding from shards of glass. It also looked like he'd hit his head when Mick crashed into them.

The young woman's eyes were wide but not from fear. She trembled with anger, her nostrils flared, and chewed on the gag. The blindfold they'd put on her had fallen loose and hung around her neck. Her hands were tied together in front of her and the man had one arm roughly around her hips, pinning her against his front.

The team closed in on him. He continued to scream in French and pressed the barrel of the gun into her temple.

"Easy does it," Booker said. They had him surrounded in a half-circle, their weapons all aimed at him. "Reen, tell him if he lets her go, we won't kill him."

She conveyed the message and stared down her gun at the man.

He shook his head, then his hostage.

"No go, boss," she said. "I don't think he's as afraid of us as whoever wanted the girl kidnapped."

"Try again," he said.

They inched closer and the man shook the girl again. His threat was evident, and they stopped moving. Reen spoke in a level voice to the man. He sneered and spat a glob of saliva and blood in her direction.

"Well, that's just rude," she said.

"What's the game plan here, Booker?" Roo asked.

"Anyone got a clean shot at him?"

"No," they all said.

He stepped closer and the man yelled. He pressed his back against the wall and shook his captive roughly again.

"We have to get her away from him somehow," the Brit said.

"Or we need to get him away from the wall," Charles added.

"Any suggestions?" He gritted his teeth.

The young woman came up with the solution for them. She brought her tied hands down and back and caught the man in the groin. He cursed and his grasp loosened enough for her to continue the motion and drop to the ground, kick out, and wriggle awkwardly forward.

Her captor didn't have any time to retaliate or catch her again. Mick, Roo, Booker, and Reen fired simultaneously while Charles flung himself forward and hauled the young woman toward him to shield her.

The dead man dropped to his knees and from there, face-first into the dirt of the road, his brains and blood sprayed on the wall behind him.

The American rolled off the girl and helped her to her feet. He untied the gag.

"Who the hell are you guys?" she asked.

He untied her hands and she pulled her wrists from his grasp and folded her arms over her chest.

"We're your rescuers," Booker said. "You're welcome, by the way."

Mick nudged him with his elbow and raised an eyebrow. He waved him off.

"Are you Sophie Oladipupo?" Reen asked.

"Yes. And you are?" she said in flawless English, although with a hint of an accent like that from some expensive Swiss boarding school.

"I'm Reen. This is Booker, Charles, Roo, and Mick," she said and pointed to each of them in turn. "We're called the BOHICA Warriors."

Sophie pursed her lips and studied each of them. "Who hired you?"

"President Okonkuo," Booker said.

"That's bullshit," she said with a humorless laugh.

"What makes you say that?" Charles asked.

She turned and gave him a scathing look. "Because President Okonkuo wouldn't do anything to help my father. My father is an asshole who tries to undermine the president any chance he gets." Her shoulders slumped a little and she looked less defiant. "But I guess that doesn't matter. Thank you, by the way, for rescuing me."

"Did those motherfuckers hurt you?" Roo asked.

"No. I'm fine. Just in need of a shower and a comb," she said and patted her hair self-consciously before she pinched the bridge of her nose. Finally, she adjusted the small gold ring of her septum piercing.

"Well, I guess we should get you returned to your father. Which way's the police station?" Booker asked.

Sophie stepped back and fear flashed briefly in her eyes before she could mask it. "No way. Please don't take me to the police."

Mick frowned. "What's wrong? Don't you want to go home?"

She shook her head. "No! You can't make me go home. Just give me some money and I'll hole up someplace."

Reen folded her arms over her chest. "Sophie, do you know who kidnapped you?"

The girl looked at the ground. She stepped away from the pooling blood of the dead man and the step brought her closer to the woman.

"Sophie?" she asked and moved toward her.

"I'm sure your pops is waiting for you," Roo said. "If my

daughter were missing, I wouldn't rest until I got you back."

"You're a good father then. Mine isn't so great. In fact, he's the one who wanted me kidnapped. Those assholes? Yeah, working on my father's dime. And the real exciting part? They were going to fucking kill me. Just waiting for the go-ahead."

"Why would he do something like that?" Charles asked, his hands in fists.

"Because my father is a grade-A prick who only thinks about himself and propelling his political career forward. He was going to have me murdered so he could pin it on President Okonkuo and get him kicked out of office. Then, my father would take his place. Having a kidnapped and murdered daughter really goes a long way for that sympathy vote."

"That can't possibly be true," the Aussie sputtered.

The others stared at her. Sophie gave them a tired smile. "Better believe it."

"I'm sure your father loves you," Reen said tentatively.

Sophie waved her hand in the air. The gesture was tired as if she was used to making it. "Please, don't try to tell me what my father is like. You don't even know the bastard. But I do. His heart shut off to any emotion long ago. No. I am only a pawn to him."

"I'm sorry," Booker said. "Fathers can be shitty."

She considered him for a moment after that comment, then shook her head again. "You can't make me go back. Thank you for rescuing me and all, but you might as well have left me with those imbeciles if you're just going to return me to my father."

"We won't make you do anything you don't want to," Charles said.

"You have a right to choose," Reen added.

"Well," Roo said, "you're safe now. We won't let anything happen to you, little bird. You can come with us."

Sophie frowned at the "little bird" comment.

Booker also frowned. He grabbed the Aussie's arm and pulled him away from the young woman. "We've got to be moving on from this spot. We weren't exactly subtle. I'm honestly surprised the police haven't showed up by now," he said. "But first, we need to discuss something. Give us a second, Sophie."

She nodded.

The others gathered in a tight circle.

"We have to take her with us," Roo said.

The Brit heaved a sigh. "I know she's ignited all your protective instincts, Roo, but we can't take her with us!"

"Why not?" Reen asked.

"Yeah, why not?" Mick echoed.

"Because!"

"Because isn't an answer, Booker," Charles said.

"Because the Zoo is dangerous. More dangerous than here for her and she's a civilian—worse! She's a *schoolgirl*."

"She seems capable enough," Reen said. "I don't think she'd freak out. And she can be with us until we figure out a safer place for her."

"Why are you so against this?" Mick asked. "What's your deal?"

"I don't have a deal!" Booker protested.

The Aboriginal shook his head. "You're acting weird, mate."

"Mick's right," Charles said. "What's wrong? Did you get injured or something?"

"Bugger off! I'm bleddy fine. Better than fine. I'm fucking perfect."

"Then shut the fuck up. You've been out-voted, Booker," Reen said. "The girl comes with us."

In the distance came the whine of emergency vehicles.

"We've gotta get moving," Charles said.

"So, I can come with you?" Sophie asked. "I promise I'll stay out of the way. I'm very level-headed and good in an emergency. I took first aid last semester."

"Christ," Booker muttered.

Roo grinned at Sophie. "Stick by me, little bird. Ignore the British asshole. He's in a mood."

Charles started the Toyota pickup. It coughed to life and whined. Black smoke started leaking from under the hood. "It's burning oil now. We won't make it far in this thing."

The Brit swung himself into the passenger seat. Everyone else climbed into the bed of the truck. "There's a small airport on the other side of Tahoua. We can get us a flight out of here from there."

"Sounds like a plan."

CHAPTER THIRTEEN

The Zoo - Thor

The demiwolf pack didn't have any luck getting over the wall. They didn't even get close. The rounds from the Ma Deuces, combined with the flamethrowers, were enough to hold them at bay. That didn't mean they hadn't tried. Two of the pack died. Half of the beta's face was burned off. She'd mostly regenerated, although the fur along the puffy scar hadn't returned, leaving the right side of her face bone-white.

Thor hadn't attacked the wall with the same fervor as the others. He had desperately wanted to get over. Something he didn't understand drove him. But he'd been there before and he knew there wasn't anything there for him other than Charles. He had sat off to the side while all the Zoo animals flung themselves at the big barrier. It was confusing. The Zoo part of him urged an attack on the wall, but the part that Charles had influenced—the introduction of humanity and taming of his less-wild parts—told him it wasn't a smart idea.

He watched the gorgorexes easily scale the thick cement and disappear over the top. Several other lizard-like animals succeeded in making it over, and even one of the black-and-orange striped cats made it. They were quickly cut down on the other side—out of sight but not out of hearing.

The pack noticed that he didn't didn't try to get over, and this labeled him as an "other," something never good in a pack society. This had pushed him to the fringes again, almost an afterthought. The alpha tolerated him, although Thor knew that could change at any moment. He was already the omega of the group, but the position was strictly enforced on him once again.

Now that the attempt on the wall was over, the pack jogged in large circles around their territory in the jungle. They returned to their usual routine boredom of waiting for something exciting to happen, like coming across a human or the hunt for the next meal.

The alpha stopped at the watering hole for a drink. Thor sat and waited for the others to drink, although he was thirsty. He panted and his long purple tongue lolled out of his mouth.

Most of the pack was finished drinking their fill. Only two remained at the watering hole, and he assumed it would now be acceptable within their social fabric for him to take his turn.

He approached the edge of the shallow pool and dipped his head to drink. His tongue had barely touched the water when the one on his left snarled and pounced. He struggled under it. When the older animal opened his jaws and clamped them around his neck, he went submissive and froze. After a few seconds, the demiwolf stepped off him with a dismissive sniff and went back to drinking.

Thor remained in the dirt, waiting for the others to finish.

A bright blue butterfly flitted above the water. It landed in the mud next to his nose. He watched its long tongue uncurl and test the ground. Its wings fluttered and shimmered and he watched it in fascination for several seconds, and that distracted him from his growing thirst.

The butterfly moved closer to his snout. He could smell its distinctive scent. It smelled like everything else in the Zoo—earthy and metallic.

He lunged for it, crunched it up, and ate it.

Thor stood and looked at the pack. They watched him and waited. He took his time drinking.

When he was finished, the alpha wheeled away and trotted into the jungle, the pack on his tail. Thor easily kept pace. He'd grown considerably since entering the Zoo. While he was the youngest of the demiwolf pack, he wasn't the smallest—not anymore—and hadn't shown signs of slowing his growth. At the rate he was growing, he would soon be as large as the leader himself. He was almost as big as the beta.

The alpha didn't feel threatened by him. Not yet. However, he began to pay closer attention to the younger animal.

Thor needed food again. He vaguely remembered when his meals used to be delivered by people and put in a large dish. Now, he killed for what he ate.

The pack shared their feelings of hunger as well. They were all connected to the alpha and operated on the same wavelength, it seemed. If one of the pack was hungry or thirsty, the rest of the pack would be too.

It was time for a hunt.

The demiwolf pack's food of choice were small, six-legged gazelle-like creatures. They were tender and surprisingly filling, despite their size. The animals' only protection against attack were their sharp fangs. These were used mostly as tools for extracting the light-pink moss they preferred to eat from the bark of silver-leafed trees, but they were equally as effective in piercing a predator's hide.

The pack ghosted through the jungle, looking for their prey. The alpha led the way and howled occasionally to keep them oriented. They weren't worried that the howls would give them away. Stealth was not their trademark, and the Zoo was full of howls, roars, and snarls. Animals constantly fought and called to one another.

Their hunger pressed them faster and deeper into the Zoo where the leader knew a large copse of the silver-leafed trees was.

Anticipation thrummed through Thor's veins. He opened his mouth slightly and tasted the air. He let his tongue hang out of his mouth as he loped along. It might have helped—or might not have—but he located their prey before any of the others. Strands of saliva hung from his jowls. His teeth practically ached with the anticipation of burying into the velvety flesh of the small gazelle-like creatures.

The pack slowed and stopped. Working as an instinctive unit, they spread out and stalked forward to surround the copse of silver-leafed trees.

The prey was hard to identify. Their short hair was a mottled green-and-brown that aided them in blending in. They stood no more than three feet at the shoulder and pranced on soft black hooves that barely made a sound on the spongy jungle floor.

Five gazelles grazed amongst the trees. Each was focused on a separate tree at a time. It would approach the trunk, pierce the thick black bark with its fangs, and peel the layer back in thin strips. The goal of their careful stripping was the cotton-candy-pink moss that grew on the underside of the bark. It clung like a thin layer of crushed velvet to the black outer layer. When a gazelle uncovered a patch of moss, it used its bright blue tongue to lick it off.

The prey was oblivious to the impending danger as the demiwolves crept forward, spread out, and surrounded them. Thor was excited and hungry, and that combination made hunting infinitely harder. With his attention on the prey, he let his relative inexperience with hunting show when he stood on a root and it cracked beneath him.

The gazelles' small, round ears swiveled and pricked. Their chests rose and fell rapidly as their heart rates sped up.

The pack leader growled, and with their approach discovered, he charged forward. The creatures bolted, and this was where the demiwolves' hunting methods paid off. One of the animals, in its panic to get away from the alpha, ran into one of the others in the pack. The predator snarled as he pounced and sank his teeth into the hindquarter of the nearest prey. It bleated and kicked out but it was a pointless effort. He released it for a moment, then bit down at the base of its neck and pinned it to the earth while it scrabbled. The demiwolf smothered it while it pressed the willowy creature to the ground so the angle of its neck cut off the air supply and the sharp teeth sank deeper and deeper. It would soon still.

The remaining four bolted, but the rest of the pack were ready as well and hedged them in. They forced their quarry into a tight ring at the center of their closing circle. One of the small animals tried to break free and lunged toward a gap in the predator circle between Thor and the beta.

He beat her to prevent the animal's escape. The terrified creature coiled and sprang in an effort to leap over the demiwolves' head. He jumped, intercepted it, and thrust the smaller animal back with his superior weight and strength. When he landed on top of it, the other members of his pack moved in, not wanting to wait any longer.

The clearing was filled with the harried squeals of the prey but in minutes, there was silence. This was swiftly replaced by the sounds of the predators devouring their prey.

Thor understood that he was supposed to wait until the alpha and the rest ate their fill first. The gazelle in his jaws was not his kill, but the pack's. Despite this knowledge, he was running out of patience and his stomach felt hollow. He needed to eat.

Hunger overcame his caution and he snarled when one of the others moved in to take his kill, and he pulled it back. The demiwolf growled a warning at him and bared its bloody teeth.

Undeterred, he ripped off a chunk of tender belly and the blood, fats, and flesh filled his senses.

His pack mate pounced on him, intending to pin the younger demiwolf and put him back in his place. Thor kicked his opponent off him. He was larger and heavier and he put the advantage to good use.

When he managed to get a mouthful of ruff fur, he heaved and shook his head and, by extension, the other animal. It uttered a sharp whine and he released it. The demiwolf's blood warred in his mouth with the gazelle's.

The rest of the pack watched the interaction but none of the others intervened.

Thor started eating. The defeated pack mate sat and waited for him to finish.

The alpha observed him through it all. His nostrils flared and his hackles half-rose. The youngster was clearly coming into his own and the leader felt, in the back of his mind, that he would be able to challenge him before too long. He wasn't sure, though, if he would do it. The younger demiwolf seemed to have no interest in being the dominant of the pack, but the alpha knew that things could change. In a few more weeks, Thor would get bigger and stronger, even to the point of being equal with the beta.

He looked at the mutilated beta. She showed signs of lagging. Even the Zoo's healing properties hadn't helped her much. It seemed like the Zoo had decided it was her time and was letting her injuries weaken her to the point where she could be eliminated. The alpha knew Thor would be able to challenge her and most likely win against her.

Once he'd eaten his fill, Thor let the other demiwolf finish off the carcass. The alpha stared at him and he returned it. He wasn't as scared of him as he had been when he'd first joined the pack. He could sense a shift happening. When the leader bared his teeth, he knew the alpha could sense it too.

Thor looked at the rest of the pack, but they paid no attention to what he was doing. He huffed out a breath of air and looked at the jungle canopy. Several monkeys swung across the space and the ever-expanding vines that tangled in the branches and slithered down the thick tree trunks.

He tilted his head back farther and howled. A split second, later the pack leader howled as well and his cry drowned out Thor's as the entire pack joined in.

CHAPTER FOURTEEN

Fiddler's Green, Harvesters Camp

"We've already had this conversation, and I don't want to have it again. You cannot tell the president I'm here," Sophie insisted and folded her arms over her chest. She leaned away from the table and propped her heavy boots on it. The girl was no longer in her school uniform. She had roughly the same waist-size as Reen and wore some of her fatigues. The pant legs were rolled up because the woman was four inches taller than Sophie's 5'7".

Booker narrowed his eyes at her from across the table. "We can't keep you here! Now we've become the kidnappers!"

"Jesus, mate," Roo said and settled into the chair next to Sophie. "Fucking relax. We didn't kidnap her. We saved her and she came willingly. We aren't going to let anything happen to the little bird."

"Stop calling me that," she snapped.

He ignored her and focused on the other man. "If her

old man really is trying to kill her, then alerting the president would only put her in harm's way."

"Roo's right," Mick said.

"I don't think the president is corrupt," the Brit started but stopped when she held a hand up.

"I don't think he is, either," she said. "But my father is a bastard, and he has eyes and ears everywhere. He would find out."

"The safest place for her is here," Charles said.

Booker threw his hands up. "You too?"

"For fuck's sake, Booker, what the hell crawled up your ass? It's fine! We're keeping the girl protected with us until we can figure out something better to do," Reen said.

"I see you've all turned against me."

Roo shoved his chair dramatically from the table and looked under it.

"What are you doing?" the Brit asked.

"I'm looking for your balls," he said. "Seems to me you've lost them somewhere."

The other man stood and walked out of the room. "*Re'th kyjyewgh hwi.*"

"What does that mean?" Sophie asked after he'd gone.

Reen shrugged. "Who fucking knows? Probably not anything nice."

"Is he always such an asshole?"

"No," Charles said. "That seems to be a more recent development."

She frowned. "If it's really too much trouble, I can go somewhere else. If you just help me catch a plane ride, I have some friends in Switzerland who would gladly give me a place to stay until I figure things out."

"No way," Roo said. "You're safest with us."

"Booker will come around. He's just been on edge and probably needs some sleep. He's not a bad guy," Charles assured her.

Sophie nodded.

"In the meantime," Reen said, "we should get you some clothes that fit properly."

"This is fine."

"No. It's a little too obvious that those aren't yours. If you're going to blend in with us, you'll have to look like you were meant to be here," Mick said.

"Do you think Dan has any clothes?" Roo asked.

"I don't see why he wouldn't," Charles said. "He has everything."

Booker stopped them before they left the room. "Where are you going?"

"We're going to Dan's," Reen said. "Sophie needs better fitting clothes."

"And I need a new weapon," Mick said. "The AK doesn't have all the finesse I want."

"Fine. Let's go."

"You're coming?" Sophie asked.

He looked at her over his shoulder as he led the way down the stairs. "Sure am, Teasy."

The girl mumbled a string of rapid-fire French and Reen laughed but didn't bother translating for the men.

"What's it mean?" Charles asked Booker as they walked.

"What?"

"What you just called Sophie."

"Oh. Right. Just a bit of fun. A Cornish term, mostly

used for annoyances or irritable people. Usually, it's directed at children."

His teammate frowned. "That's not very nice."

"Get the hell over it," he retorted. "It's not like I was insulting her. It's a good-natured thing. Endearing."

Charles didn't seem completely convinced but let it go.

Dan stood outside his armory warehouse smoking a cigarette when they walked up to him.

"Well, look what the cat dragged in! We thought you were all dead, which would've been a shame," he said. He looked at each of them before his gaze lingered on Sophie.

Booker shifted to effectively block his view of her. "Here we are."

The man laughed, clapped him on the shoulder, and dragged him toward the building. The others followed. "I see you've picked up an extra tagalong."

He chose not to respond.

"I got that package you were waiting for," Dan said. "That why you dropped by?"

"Yes. We also need a few sets of clothes and a new FN-FAL."

The supplier nodded. He looked at Sophie again. She stepped forward to give him a better view and ignored Booker's frown. "Lighten up, Brit. Jesus," he said. "Give me a minute." He turned and disappeared into the rows of shelving that gleamed with weaponry, armor, and other miscellaneous items. He soon returned with a new rifle for Mick, a stack of black fatigues and t-shirts for Sophie, and a large cardboard package for Booker.

The girl pulled a shirt from the top and held it against

her. "This'll work. But you don't happen to have anything in green? That's definitely more my color."

He laughed. "Does it look like I operate a fucking Macys? What you see there is what you get."

"I was kidding. This'll do fine." She held up a pair of fatigues. They seemed to be the perfect length. "Thanks. How'd you guess my size?"

"It's a gift," he said.

"Watch it," Roo growled.

Dan held his hands up. "Someone control the leprechaun. I mean no harm. You asked me to outfit her and that's what I did."

"I'm not a fucking leprechaun! I'm not even fucking Irish, you bloody great thunder-ass."

Reen slugged him in the shoulder. "Take it down like five notches, tough guy."

"You register that you've got a minor on board now?" the supplier asked.

Booker cut the cardboard box open with his Fairbairn-Sykes. "I didn't realize you were one to play by the rules," he said.

"I'm not a minor," Sophie said. "I'm eighteen."

Dan snorted. "Right. So, not a minor."

"What did you get?" Mick asked Booker.

The Brit pulled a black canvas jumpsuit from the box and tossed it at Mick. He unfolded it and whistled. There were loops for a utility belt and *BOHICA* was embroidered in light gray letters on the shoulder.

"It was supposed to be a surprise," he said. He shrugged, then grasped the back of his neck. "If you guys don't like them, I can always send them back."

Roo rifled through the box and found a uniform in his size. "This is fucking tight, mate." He shucked his shirt off and quickly dropped his pants to step into the new uniform. He zipped the front up and made a slow spin. "Fucking awesome."

Mick followed suit and changed too.

"Does this look like a fucking locker room to you?" Dan protested.

Booker grinned and handed the other two teammates theirs. When Charles stripped down to his boxer briefs, the Brit noticed that Sophie tried to look anywhere but at him.

Reen whipped her shirt over her head.

"Now, wait a minute!" Dan protested.

She winked at him. "Just be grateful I put a sports bra on today."

Booker pulled another uniform out of the box and handed it to the younger woman.

Sophie blinked at him.

"I ordered a few extra," he said. "This one looks like your size. It'll help you blend in."

She grinned and reached for the hem of her shirt.

He grasped her wrist. "It might be better if you changed into it when we're back at the building."

"Everyone else is wearing theirs."

"I'm not," he said and cleared his throat. "I'll put mine on when we get back too."

"You shy, Booker?" Roo asked.

"No."

The Aussie flexed in the uniform. "What do you think, Sophie?" He struck a bodybuilder pose.

She laughed. "I think you look like an idiot flexing like

that." She nudged Booker with her elbow and held the uniform close to her chest. "Thanks."

He smiled. "Don't mention it, Teasy."

"Hey, I was just starting to like you. I don't need you to come up with an obnoxious nickname."

"I don't think you have a choice in the matter."

"Fine. I'll just have to come up with one for you."

"Go on ahead. I don't nickname easily."

"Isn't Booker a nickname?" she asked.

The Brit pursed his lips. "It's more of a moniker, actually." He grabbed the nearly empty box and started walking out of Dan's.

Sophie jogged a few steps to catch up, brushed past him, and her shoulder skimmed his arm. She walked backward in front of him. "You aren't going to fool me with your fancy-sounding words. Moniker means the same thing as nickname, and you know it."

He smiled. "Smart-ass."

"No," she said and tossed her head so her curls bounced, "just smart."

Roo and Mick walked on either side of her and drew her attention away from Booker. He followed a few paces behind them and listened to her laughing at what they were saying.

Charles and Reen walked on either side of him.

"Careful, Booker," she said.

"What?"

"You know what."

He shook his head. "I don't know what you're talking about."

"She's a kid."

"She's eighteen."

She raised an eyebrow.

"You heard her!" he sputtered. He looked at Charles for support, but the big man simply gave the woman a knowing look over his head.

"You two are ridiculous. Bleddy ridiculous."

The big man clapped him on the shoulder. "She is pretty, though."

Booker glared at him and he grinned in response. "Ah, fuck the both of you."

Reen laughed. "But in all seriousness, Booker, just remember where we are."

"As if I could fucking forget. Besides, I don't need any of your cryptic messages. I'm not Roo. I won't jump just anything that moves. You should be lecturing him."

"Nah," Charles said, "look at him. He's acting like she's his kid sister."

Roo flung an arm over Sophie's shoulders and looked at the three of them. "What's wrong? Why are you all walking so slowly? Let's get back and have something to eat. I'm fucking starved."

"Let's go feed the beast before he throws a hissy fit," Booker said and lengthened his stride as if to get away from Reen and Charles' attention. The other two easily kept pace with him, however.

CHAPTER FIFTEEN

Cotonou, Benin

Arnaud Oladipupo sat in his wildebeest leather chair, his back to his large wooden desk. He looked out of his seventh-story window at the city below. The sun was setting, and he paused to admire the way the dying light glistened on the large cube of ice in the tumbler of bourbon he nursed. In all honesty, he didn't like bourbon all that much. He preferred *ogogoro*, although the stuff could be, literally, deadly. It was his love of Western culture that kept him importing the expensive bourbon.

He spun away from the view and looked at the papers spread over his desk—maps of Benin and Niger, with two particular locations circled in bright red ink and high-lighted. The highlighting was done by his assistant, Angelique, who wanted to be sure he knew exactly where to look. Arnaud would've thought it an impertinence if he didn't really need it. He had always been useless when it came to maps and directions and left that to other people. His talents lay elsewhere.

He leaned closer to inspect the highlighted portions—the WAP Complex and Tahoua. "How hard is it," he muttered to the empty office, "to keep a group of school-girls hidden? It's not rocket science. What *abrutis*."

Someone knocked tentatively on his door. Angelique had already left for the day, which meant it could only be one person—Okafor, his witless aide.

"Come in," he commanded in English. He went to university in South Africa and it was where he learned English, so he still had the South African accent. He insisted that everyone in his office practice speaking English, not French, and certainly not Fon, Benin's primary tribal language. Most of his businesses were concentrated in English-speaking countries.

Arnaud took a sip of the bourbon and swished it between his teeth before he swallowed. He waited for the aide to come in.

When he was about to repeat the command, Okafor opened the door and entered slowly. He glared at him. The young man always stood hunched like he was afraid of being noticed. The way he walked reminded his boss of small prey animals because he never really walked anywhere like a normal person. He skittered as if he were afraid someone would pick him up by the scruff of the neck at any moment and toss him out a window. The only reason he kept Okafor around was because the kid was a computer genius.

"What is it?" Arnaud asked. He shuffled the papers on his desk and hoped he would hurry up.

The young man opened his mouth, but he interrupted

brusquely. "It had better be good news about those bastard mercenaries I wanted taken care of."

Okafor pursed his lips and a tremor went through him.

"Oh, for fuck's sake, what is it now?"

"It's the mercenaries, sir," he said. "They've gotten away."

Arnaud slammed the tumbler down on the desk and sloshed amber liquid onto the map. His aide rushed forward to clean it, but he held a hand up.

"What else?" he asked. "If that's it, then that's not all bad. Hopefully, they've gone back to where they came from. It was bad enough that they had to free all those schoolgirls. If my intel is correct, then that asshole of a president hired them. It's no matter, as long as they don't come back. I still have the Sophie part of the plan."

Okafor winced.

"I still have the Sophie plan in motion, do I not?" he asked, his dark eyebrows furrowed.

"About that, sir. You see, the mercenaries got away, but it's also suspected that they took Sophie with them."

"What did you say?"

"Sophie is gone, sir."

"What happened to the mercenaries who were supposed to handle her?"

"Dead, sir."

"Dead? All of them?"

"Now, yes. One of them survived, but he just died of his injuries."

Arnaud hurled the tumbler at his head. The young man ducked, and the glass shattered against the door.

"Who the fuck are these men? I hired the best of the best! This should not have happened!"

"No, sir. Of course not."

"You are useless! Do you know nothing?"

Okafor shook his head. "The only thing we know is that they were seen leaving with Sophie. Our people asked around and it seems they, too, are mercenaries. From the Zoo."

"The Zoo?"

"Yes, sir. The big alien experiment site in the Sahara."

"I know what the fucking Zoo is, Okafor. Do you think I'm stupid?"

"No, sir! Of course not!"

Arnaud looked around his desk for something else to throw at his hapless aide but he didn't find anything. Angelique had stopped replacing his paperweights after he'd shattered the fifteenth one against the wall. The woman had grown too comfortable in her position. The young man seemed to know that he had nothing more to throw and relaxed a little.

"Enough fucking around," he said. "Get me the one who never fails. He'll fix this for me. He'll put everything to rights."

"Yes, sir. Right away," Okafor said and hurried quickly out of the room.

He looked at the portrait of himself and his daughter that he'd commissioned the year before and glared at Sophie's image. The painter had captured the matching look in the father's and daughter's eyes—intelligent and mocking. He was struck again by her beauty—she'd inherited her mother's high cheekbones and soft curves. Her brilliance and tenacity she got from his side of the family.

Sophie was the result of a fling with an inconsequential zouk singer when he was traveling abroad. He'd met her mother in a cigar-smoke-filled bar in the middle of a typhoon. Their love affair lasted as long as the typhoon but unfortunately, that was all the time needed to create a daughter.

Arnaud would have made Sophie disappear like he had her mother but he realized what having a beautiful young daughter would do for his public image. Fathers of beautiful daughters had more appeal.

The idea to have her kidnapped had occurred to him after a bourbon-soaked dream and after the bastard President Okonkuo was re-elected. Having a beautiful, kidnapped daughter had worked wonders for his public image. People couldn't get enough of the tragedy.

He looked out his window and smiled, his lips thinning over his teeth so the expression was more snarl than smile. "Having a beautiful dead daughter will be even better."

CHAPTER SIXTEEN

Fiddlers Green, Harvesters Camp

Charles sat on the flatbed of the Mule, whittling. The vehicle barely took up any space in the lean-to now that the BTR was gone.

The two women were nearby. Reen was teaching Sophie how to throw a knife. Mick and Roo watched and critiqued the women's form until she challenged them.

"Charles," she said, "you judge the competition."

"I'm not that great yet, Reen," Sophie protested. "Maybe we should wait a few days until I'm proficient."

"No way. We'll do this now. I'll make up for your lack of skill," she assured her.

"We'll go easy on you, little bird," Roo said.

She gave him the V sign, something he now regretted teaching her. "First, I told you not to call me that. Second, not a chance in hell, old man. I'm not a sore loser. Besides, how am I really going to get any better if you coddle me?"

"She has a point," Mick said.

"Okay. Well, fair warning, we're now going to wipe the floor with you."

"Roo, can you throw a knife?" Charles asked.

The Aussie held his hand out and Sophie passed him one of the stainless-steel throwing knives Reen was training her with. He studied what they were using as target practice—a picture of Sophie's father taped to a square of plywood. She'd found the image online and convinced Dan to print it for her.

Roo hurled the knife toward the target and it embedded itself in the middle of Arnaud Oladipupo's right ear. He frowned.

Charles laughed and set his whittling aside. "This is going to be good. Let's say, winning team is the first to get to twelve blades right between the jerk's eyes."

"What does the winner get?" Reen asked.

"Winners get bragging rights," Mick said. "Losers do the dishes for the week."

"Just the dining table dishes or the pots and pans used to make meals, too?" Sophie asked.

"Everything."

"Sounds good to me," Reen agreed.

The four competitors shook hands on it.

The Aboriginal drew a line in the sand and stepped back from it. "Ladies first," he said and bowed theatrically toward them.

Sophie threw three knives at the target. One hit Arnaud in the jugular and the other two in his cheek. Reen stepped up to the line and flicked her three knives one after the other. They flipped through the air and stuck, vibrating, in the space between his eyes. Her partner clapped and high-fived her. Mick looked amused and Roo had begun to turn a splotchy red.

"Lighten up," Charles said and nudged him with the toe of his combat boot. "It's just dirty dishes."

Mick got two knives to hit their mark, and Roo got one.

"You act like we're already fucking losing," the Aussie said to Charles.

The big man waved a hand at the board where Reen hit her target all three times again. Sophie's knives were getting closer.

Mick landed two more on his next turn. Roo's knives hit across Arnaud's eyeballs.

"That should fucking count," he said. "I'm so close."

"Close isn't on the mark," Reen protested.

"Look, the blade is practically in the bridge of his nose!"

"Charles is the judge," Reen said. "Let him decide."

Charles pulled a muttering Roo away from the board. He shook his head. "No go, Aussie."

"For fuck's sake! You Yanks are ganging up on us! This whole thing is rigged."

"Yeah, Roo, we started this as an elaborate ploy to get you to do the dishes. Fucking relax. If you can't handle losing, then you can give up now and we won't mention it...much," she said.

"Also, I'm Beninese, not American," Sophie added.

"Don't be such a sook," Mick said. "We've not lost yet."

"No, but you're about to," Reen snarked.

Sophie stepped up to the line and prepared herself. She gripped the handle of the blade, pulled back, and threw. The knife somersaulted through the air and stuck on the tip of Arnaud's nose.

Booker came around the side of the building in time to watch her throw. He stood next to Charles as she threw her second knife, which stuck in Arnaud's left eye.

"Try holding it further down the handle," he said, "and just with the tips of your fingers like you're tilting someone's chin upwards."

She gave him a Sphinx-like stare that he couldn't decipher but did as he instructed. Her knife sailed forward and struck the target right between the eyes. She whooped and jumped up and down.

"Thanks!"

"Don't mention it," he said.

"Yeah, thanks, asshole," Roo said.

"What?"

"We're in the middle of a little healthy competition," Reen explained. She found the target with all three knives again.

Mick's knife found the target all three times, and two of Roo's hit.

"We're at a tie," Charles said. "Only two more each."

Reen jerked her head toward the target. The paper was almost falling off. "Go for it, kid."

Sophie started to grip the knife the same way she had been but then changed her mind and held it the way Booker told her. Her first knife impaled Arnaud's cheek. The other two struck the mark.

She squealed and jumped up and down. Reen laughed and they high-fived.

"Ah, shit," Roo muttered.

Mick shook their hands. "Nicely done."

"What did you win?" Booker asked.

"Bragging rights," Sophie said.

"And those two idiots get to do all the dishes for the week," Reen added.

He laughed. "Birds are tricky. You should've known better than to challenge Reen, Roo. And it seems Teasy has a knack for winning, too. Brilliant."

"I didn't challenge her," the Aussie blustered. "Do you think I'm a bogan? She challenged us!"

"And you accepted."

Mick ripped the picture of Arnaud off the target board. He balled it up and tossed it at Reen, who caught it. "All in good fun. Now, who wants to get something to eat? I'm so hungry I could eat a whole 'roo."

His teammate flipped him off.

"You know I mean the animal, you wanker."

Sophie wrinkled her nose. "You eat kangaroo?"

"Sure. Why not?"

"You'd think they'd be too…stringy for that."

"Nah, it's not so bad. Throw a steak on the barbie. The stuff's great with A-1 actually. It seems Americans can do something right. Roos make great jerky, too."

"Gross."

"A-1 originated in the UK, actually," Booker said.

"He's right," Sophie said and halted Roo before he could protest. "I learned about it when I studied global corporations."

"You studied global corporations? What kind of school did you go to?" Reen asked.

"My father is a businessman. It looked good to have his daughter be groomed to supposedly take over his empire. Now, I thought we were going to get something to eat?"

They left Fiddler's Green and headed toward the Wateringhole.

"You've got a good eye," Reen said. "I think tomorrow, we'll take you out shooting."

"That would be tight," she said.

Sophie dropped a piece of paper in front of Booker. They were seated around the table eating a simple breakfast of scrambled eggs, bacon, and toast.

He picked the paper up and looked at it. "What is this?"

"That's a grocery list."

"What for?"

"For groceries."

"No shit, Teasy. Why the hell are you giving it to me?"

"Because the food is shit, and if I'm going to be your chef, I'll need better ingredients."

"You can cook?" Roo asked around a mouthful of egg.

She frowned at him. "Don't talk with your mouth full. It's disgusting and rude. Also, yes, I can cook. What made you think I couldn't?"

He opened his still-full mouth to answer, but she raised an eyebrow and he settled for shrugging.

"No one's asking you to be a chef," Reen said.

"I know that. But I'd like to contribute somehow. Not to mention I still owe you a lot for rescuing me. I'm not half-bad at cooking, and I figured it's probably all you'd let me do at this point."

"Don't fucking argue with her," Mick said. "Just do what she wants. If she's shit, then who cares? Anything will be better than that microwave shit those wankers at the Wateringhole can come up with."

"Thanks for the vote of confidence," Sophie said.

He winked at her. "No problem, babes."

Booker folded the list and put it in his pocket. "I'll see what I can do, but don't expect any gourmet shit."

She smiled. "I have faith in you, Booker." She turned toward Charles and Reen. "Now, when do I get that shooting lesson?"

"Right after this," he said.

"What are you giving her to use?" the Brit asked.

"Thought we'd pick up an M16 from Dan," Reen answered.

"The recoil isn't bad and she'll be able to handle it," Roo agreed.

"Before you protest about spending the money," the woman said. "I'll pay for it."

Booker waved a hand in the air. "It doesn't matter who pays for it. We can take it out of the BOHICA budget."

"Mick, you coming?" Sophie asked before heading out the door.

He shook his head. "No. I'll stay around here. Someone has to do the dishes, after all."

"Right, mate, sorry about that. I'll get it next time," Roo said and ducked hastily out of the room.

"You bet your ass you will!" his friend called after him.

"You ever shoot a rifle before?" Charles asked Sophie as they walked to Dan's.

"Sure. Nothing big. My dad let me shoot a pistol a couple of times, but that's about the extent of it. I've seen lots of weapons fired."

"Seeing and doing are two different things."

"I know that."

"You'll do great," Reen said.

"How do you know?"

"You picked up the knife-throwing fast enough. Throwing a knife and shooting a rifle are, obviously, two hugely different things, but your aim is good, and that'll help."

"I'm a quick study."

"Where are we taking her to shoot?" Roo asked.

"There's that range out behind the Wateringhole," Charles suggested.

"I never understood why they put that thing there," Reen said.

"Why?" Roo asked.

"Alcohol and precision shooting don't mix."

"At least they're shooting at targets," the American pointed out, "and not each other."

"I guess. Still doesn't bode well."

"It's early enough in the morning that we should have it all to ourselves," Roo said.

They stopped outside Dan's.

"I'll go in and get the rifle," Charles said. "You guys can wait here."

The others nodded. They placed themselves between the open door and Sophie as Charles disappeared inside.

Sophie frowned at them. "What are you doing?"

"Waiting," Roo said.

"Not that. Why are you standing in front of me so people can't see me from the door?"

Reen cracked her neck. "We just figure it's better to keep you under wraps."

"We're standing in the middle of the pathway," she pointed out.

"Yeah, but there's no one around."

"The fucker has a big mouth on him," Roo added.

"Who?"

"Dan. The wanker gossips like an old bird in a Woolworths queue."

The girl pursed her lips but let the matter drop. Charles soon returned with an M16 and a carton of 5.56mm cartridges.

"Let's roll," he said.

The range was empty as Roo had predicted. It was a walled-in tract of sand about two hundred meters long. At the farthest end were three cut-outs of six-legged panther derivatives. Closer in were crates stacked at varying heights and distances.

"Looks like Swiss cheese," Reen commented and nodded at the hole-ridden targets.

"It'll work," Charles said.

They spent the next hour giving Sophie a crash-course on safe weapons handling. She didn't need pointers on how to aim and easily hit all the targets.

"This is a lot easier than the knives," she said. She managed to blast the head off one of the panthers.

"Nicely done, little...uh, Sophie," Roo said and hastily changed what he had originally intended to say when he saw the volcano starting to erupt in her eyes.

"Why do you think it's easier?" Reen asked.

Sophie narrowed her eyes as she glared at Roo, then

flipped the safety on and handed the M16 to Charles. "Maybe because I'm not going through the work of making the weapon move. All you do is aim and pull the trigger with that thing."

"How do you think you'd do under pressure?" the Aussie asked.

"What do you mean?"

"He means, how would you perform when there are blood-thirsty animals charging you?" Charles asked.

"How am I supposed to know that? The only way would be to put me in a field test. I'm cool under pressure —you guys saw that."

"I have a feeling you'd do just fine, Sophie."

"You have a feeling?"

Reen groaned. "Don't get the asswipe started on how he thinks he's psychic."

"You're psychic?"

"Sort of. The whole Demopoulis clan has a touch of the intuition."

"You make it sound like a disease," the woman muttered sharply. She looped an arm around Sophie's shoulders. "Let's go see if Mick and Booker got up to any trouble while we were away."

The two men trailed behind them.

"They seem to be getting along great," Roo said.

Charles nodded. "Reen's good with greenhorns."

"How do you think she'd do in the Zoo?"

"I don't know. I suppose she'd be fine. But you can never tell with civilians. And she really is so young."

"How old were you when you enlisted?"

"About her age, actually."

"How would you have done?"

"Honestly? I would've fudging lost it. What about you?"

"If we're being honest, I probably would've shit my pants. But then kept going."

Charles laughed.

"Do you think Booker'll let her come?" Roo asked.

The American shook his head. "No way."

"We need to go on mission. I don't like the idea of leaving her behind with the fucking creeps this place is crawling with."

"I don't like the idea of that either."

"I'll ask Booker. If we bother him enough, we can wear the wanker down. If not, then we just vote on it."

Booker was practicing his own knife-throwing when they got back. Mick sat in the shade watching.

"You not trying to challenge Booker, Mick?" Reen asked.

He laughed. "No fucking way. The man's a machine. He'd even have your ass beat, Reen."

"But she's so good," Sophie protested.

The woman laughed. "Knife-throwing is not my specialty, Sophie."

Booker threw four knives in rapid succession. They landed a hairsbreadth from each other and vibrated in the plywood.

"See," she said. "I definitely couldn't do that."

"You could if you practiced," Booker replied.

"Probably, but I don't want to practice that."

She and Sophie disappeared inside. Mick and Charles soon followed.

Roo pulled the knives from the target and handed them to the Brit. "I was thinking…" he started.

He sighed and sent a knife rocketing through the air. "That's never a good sign. Out with it."

"We need to go on a mission soon," he continued. "Cash flow needs to happen. So, when we do, we can't just leave Sophie here. Who knows what the motherfuckers in this goddamn place would do to her if we weren't here?"

The other man frowned and threw another knife.

"So," he continued, "I was thinking we should take her with us."

"No fucking way. You must be out of your goddamn mind, Roo."

"I'm serious!"

"So am I."

"Look, she's capable. We've seen how she is under pressure. She practically saved her fucking self! And she's got great fucking aim. I mean, she's a real menace. Strewth."

"I don't like it."

"Neither do I, but I like it more than leaving her here."

"No, I mean, I don't like that she's sort of become part of the team."

"What the fuck?"

"Look, nothing against her, I just…I don't think it's right to be putting a civilian in danger like this. We shouldn't've brought her to the Zoo. She's not ex-military. She's a schoolgirl, for God's sake!"

"Look, mate, I hear you, but I also know that she's way fucking safer with us than back in Benin. I mean, look what her shit of a father tried to do to her. No. She's safest with us."

Booker sent his final knife sailing toward the target. "I'll think about it."

When they walked inside and up the stairs to the kitchen, Sophie was busy sorting through the groceries he managed to procure.

She grinned at him when he walked in. "Thanks, *loutre!*"

Reen laughed.

"What did you just call me?"

"*Loutre.* Otter. I'm trying out new *monikers* for you," Sophie said. "What do you think?"

"I think not, Teasy. Try again."

"Yeah, maybe not. Otters are too cute and furry. We'll see."

"Jesus," he muttered.

Charles patted him on the shoulder and carried the M16 into the armory. He followed him.

"How'd she do with that thing?"

"Great, actually."

"Yeah?"

"Yeah. She's a real natural, it seems."

The Brit grunted. He folded his arms over his chest and leaned against the wall, glanced into the hall, then shut the door and resumed his position.

"What is it?" his companion asked.

"How do you feel about her being here?"

"What do you mean?"

"It's sitting a bit sideways with me that she's a civilian— not to mention a schoolgirl—and she's here with us in one of the most dangerous places in the world."

"She's perfectly safe with us."

"You aren't answering the question."

Charles turned toward Booker and mirrored his stance on the opposite wall. "I think you're being paranoid."

"Do you?"

"I just said I did. Look, I get it. It's not ideal to have her here. She's untrained and young. But she's made great friends with Reen, and she would never let anything happen to her."

"Which puts Reen at risk. Like she told you when you were all over trying to protect her."

The American nodded and said, "Point taken. But right now, I think being here with us is the safest place she could possibly be. Her own father had her kidnapped to try to gain political control."

"I don't want anything to happen to her, either."

"None of us do, but nothing is a guarantee."

"You aren't making this any better, Charles."

"I don't know what you want from me, Booker. No one's safety is guaranteed. We'll do everything in our power to keep her safe, and I think that's enough."

Charles left him in the armory. He still leaned against the wall. Reen and Sophie walked past the door, laughing together.

He finally pushed away from the wall and left Fiddler's Green to Dan's where he bought a set of newer body armor for Sophie.

"If she's going to stay, I'm going to fucking look after her," he muttered to himself as he brought the armor back to their house.

When he walked in, the whole building smelled familiar and homey. Sophie glanced over her shoulder when he entered the kitchen. She'd tied her springy hair into two buns on the top of her head. It made her look even younger, and he felt another pang of regret and unease.

He put the set of armor on the table.

"What's that?" Sophie asked.

"It's body armor. For you."

"Really? What for?"

"If we go on a mission, we can't leave you here."

She turned fully to face him. "You mean, I could go with you on a mission?"

Booker frowned at the excitement in her voice. "It's not a fucking picnic."

"I know that. I know. I'm just…surprised."

"Why?"

"You seem like such a hard-ass. I didn't realize you'd want me with you guys."

"It's not a matter of *want*. It's more of a necessity."

Sophie waved her hand in the air. "Technicalities."

"What are you making?" he asked and changed the subject.

Her smile widened. "Beef Wellington."

He blinked at her.

"I thought you'd like it," she said. She lifted one shoulder, dropped it, and turned her back on him.

Booker was almost out of the room when her voice stopped him.

"If you hate it, do me a favor and pretend, okay?"

He smiled, although she couldn't see because their backs were to one another. "Got it, Teasy."

CHAPTER SEVENTEEN

Fiddler's Green, Harvesters Camp

"I'm sick and fucking tired of sitting around all goddamn day," Roo said. "Booker, we need a mission."

"I wish you'd shut up about it already," he retorted.

"He's right, there's nothing doing around here," Mick said.

"If you're worried about me, you don't have to be," Sophie said. "I've been training with Reen and Roo and they say I'm ready."

"Don't get ahead of yourself, kid. I said you were competent. Being competent and being ready aren't the same things," Reen said.

"Oh, shut the fuck up, Reen," Roo said. "You're not helping our case."

She held her hands up.

"We can do something easy," Charles said.

"You too, Charles?" Booker asked.

"Yes. I didn't come all the way over to Africa to sit on my hands."

"Are you all set on this?"

"Yes," they answered in unison.

"Fine. Fine. I'll go to Franco's and pick something up. Don't get too excited, though. If we have to take Teasy with us, I'm picking something really fucking easy."

"Fine by me," Mick said. The others echoed their agreement. Except for Sophie herself, who folded her arms over her chest and glared at him. He was unfazed by her dirty look.

He was one of the last team leaders to arrive at Franco's. The wiry dispatcher saw him immediately and waved him over.

"Booker! I thought you were dead or moved on to greener pastures," he said.

"Well, here I am."

"What happened to you?"

"We chased down that fucking gorgorex that escaped. Then got a little sidetracked down near Niger, but we're back now."

"Rumor has it you picked up another member."

"People need to mind their own fucking business."

"Right," Franco said. "What do you want? Flora or fauna?"

"Flora. And nothing too strenuous. We're easing ourselves back in."

"Sure, sure. But you know nothing is ever easy."

"And how would you know that?" he asked. Insulting the man who handed jobs out wasn't the best idea, but it didn't seem to bother Franco.

"True. I prefer to get my hands dirty in other ways," he

conceded. "I have a flower collecting job. Nothing much. Only twenty-five."

"We'll take it."

"Sending you the details now. Good luck. See you tonight."

Booker returned to Fiddler's Green, running through the intel Franco sent him about the mission.

"Did you get something?" Charles asked when he walked up to the building.

"Yeah. Let's gear up and get ready to head out."

They gathered on the first floor of the building. Everyone wore the uniforms he had bought. The others had packs, but Sophie only carried her weapon, an extra magazine, and a Bowie knife borrowed from Reen.

The Brit handed Sophie a small square of metal. She looked at the letters and numbers punched into its surface. "Are you fucking kidding me?"

He smiled.

"What is it?" Reen asked.

The girl thrust the ID tag toward her. She glanced at it and started laughing.

"I can't believe you did that," Sophie said.

"I don't see the big deal. Besides, you're here to hide, right? I couldn't possibly give them your real name."

The others snickered at the tag before she tucked it into one of the hip pockets. Booker had registered her as Teasy Loutre.

"The mission is straightforward. We're looking for some flowers. They're apparently round and a blue or blue-purple color. It should be a pretty easy plant to spot since it grows in a ring around the center of the Zoo at this specific distance from the center, too, roughly twelve klicks in. The leaves of the bushes are green with red spots."

"Carnivorous?" Mick asked.

"Harmless as your average rose bush," he said. "Well, as long as you don't ingest the stuff. It's poisonous and will melt your insides right out of your body."

"Melt your insides?" Sophie asked, her eyes round.

"Just don't eat it," he said. "Okay. Everyone ready? Let's go."

The newest team member dropped her carefree act and began to pay careful attention to everything that happened around her. She stuck close behind Reen as they walked through the first gate. The guard barely gave them a glance.

The walls had lighter patches of re-poured concrete. In some places, the wall hadn't been repaired completely and boards were drilled in place.

Booker stopped before entering the third and final wall.

"Okay, this is it. Get your heads on straight, and keep alert," he said ostensibly to everyone but it was obvious he was speaking specifically to Sophie.

They walked across the scorched sand and into the shade of the jungle. She stared at the dark canopy that closed in around them.

"It looks so…alive. Like it's breathing," she whispered.

"Keep pace with me," Reen told her. "We'll jog staggered like this and evenly spaced because it helps with mobility and is a good formation to watch for enemies."

"Tell us if we need to slow down," Charles said. He and Booker were leading the group. Mick and Roo acted as Tail End Charlies.

"I'll be fine," she said. "But thank you."

"Don't feel embarrassed asking for it. Seriously," Booker said.

"She's not an idiot, Booker," Reen interjected. "She'll say something."

They jogged through the jungle. Sophie stared at everything they passed.

"I've never seen so many crazy colors all in one place. It's like a trip," she said.

"It is pretty wild," the other woman agreed.

"Do the plants really eat people?"

Reen nodded.

"Jesus," she muttered.

Booker held up a hand balled in a fist and everyone stopped. Sophie tightened her grip on the M16 and took a calming breath. Reen raised a brow and she nodded in return.

Ahead of them, they caught flashes of bright blue amongst the green foliage. A komodo dragon-like animal thumped out of the ferns toward them. It hissed and flicked a long, forked tongue to taste the air. Charles and Booker opened fire.

The large lizard continued its approach. Reen stepped farther to the side to get a clear shot without hitting Charles—who was also firing twelve-gauge slugs into it— and fired her M492. After she inhaled a calming breath through her nose, Sophie followed Reen's example.

Roo and Mick watched their six while the other two men poured shot after shot into the mutant lizard.

With a final gurgling roar, it collapsed. Its yellow blood soaked rapidly into the ground.

"How many times did we hit it?" Sophie asked.

Booker and Charles started jogging again. "Looks like that one took twenty rounds."

They made their way deeper into the Zoo. Her arms tired from carrying the M16, but she didn't complain. She might not have a lot of upper body strength, but she easily kept pace with the rest of the BOHICA Warriors because she had the advantage of being eighteen and had been on the cross-country team at her school.

There were no more mishaps with any larger predators. Monkey-like creatures occasionally threw tree nuts and various sticks at the passing humans from the canopy, but they didn't engage further.

The Brit kept glancing over his shoulder to check on Sophie.

"Focus, man," Charles said.

"I just want to make sure she's doing fine."

"Relax. She's great. Plus, she's by Reen, and Reen won't let anything happen to her, that's for darn sure."

"Yeah, you're right. I know."

"What do these flowers look like again? Like that?" Charles asked a few minutes later and pointed to a glade ahead where blue spherical flowers were spread.

"Yep. Just like that," Booker said.

The plants weren't dense but there were enough of them to be able to tell that they grew at an even distance from each other.

"These are some frustrated wankers," Roo said.

"What?" Charles asked.

"I mean, look at the poor bastards. All's I see are blue balls," he said and he and Mick dissolved into laughter.

"Fucking children," Reen muttered.

The American frowned at the two Australians. "That wasn't even funny."

"Is there a certain way we're supposed to pick these?" Sophie asked Booker and ignored the others.

"Clipped an inch below the flower. Mick, Roo, you keep watch. We'll pair up and fill a couple of sample containers. Sophie, you're with me," he said. He passed her a clear synthetic sample container and gave Charles an identical cylinder. Once he'd retrieved two pairs of scissors from his pack, he handed one to Reen.

"Hold that open for me," he said and nodded at the sample container.

Sophie unscrewed the lid and slid it off. He started clipping the round, fuzzy blue flowers from the bush. She positioned the container beneath the flowers he cut to catch them.

After only a minute or so, she noticed how careful he was to avoid touching the flowers. "I thought you said they were only poisonous if you eat them."

"One can never be too careful in the Zoo. Things tend to evolve rather quickly here—and all with the intent of better killing a man."

She was quiet for the rest of the time. Her gaze darted around, and she turned her head toward any sound.

"Mick and Roo have our backs," Booker said.

"I know that. Just…a person can never be too careful, I guess. Besides, an extra set of eyes occasionally isn't going to hurt anything."

"You nervous, Teasy?"

Sophie snapped the lid shut on the full container and screwed it on tightly. "I'm not relaxed."

"You're smart not to be."

"Specimens collected," Charles said and shut the lid on his sample container. "We're done."

"So are we," Booker said. "Let's get these back to Franco and get paid."

They were three klicks from the wall when a vine whipped out, wound around Sophie's right knee, and dragged her upwards. She screeched once and dropped her rifle but didn't make a sound after the initial shock.

"Fuck!" Reen yelled. She looked up her sight at the vine but didn't have a good shot as the girl was in the way.

"I don't have a shot!" Charles said.

"We'll get you down in a second!" Roo yelled.

"Shit, bugger, fuck," Booker said. "I don't have a goddamn shot, either."

Sophie was being hauled higher and higher and farther out of reach from the others. "Okay, Sophie, if you get any higher, the fall is going to be much worse," she muttered. She looked up at the dark treetops where the vine seemed to be taking her. Others snaked downward. Some of them had round mouths lined with several rows of teeth that looked like they could shred her with ease.

She drew Reen's Bowie knife from the sheath strapped to her thigh and levered herself upward by tightening her abdominal muscles and sliced at the vine that held her by the knee. The knife buried a quarter of the way into the creeper. A bright red blood-like substance oozed out and the whole plant shuddered. The others started to drop faster.

Panic threatened but she pushed it back and hacked again, then once more. The vine snapped with a wet, tearing sound and she plummeted toward the jungle floor.

"I got her!" Charles yelled. He dropped his Remington and held his arms out as he stepped into her path.

She flailed as she fell and dropped the knife.

The American grunted and his knees wobbled somewhat when he caught her. She made an *oomph* noise and grasped his uniform, her fingernails biting into his shoulders.

"Nice catch!" Mick said.

"Are you okay?" Roo asked and all but ripped her out of the other man's arms.

"I'm fine." She pushed away from him. "Let me go."

"Nice knife work," Reen said. Color had begun to return to her face.

"Thank you, Charles," Sophie said.

"Don't mention it."

The girl smiled. She picked the knife up from where it fell and wiped it on some fern leaves. Her hands shook, and she tried desperately to hide it. While she was deeply shaken at how close she'd come to becoming plant food, she was damned if she would show it. She took a couple of deep breaths, made an effort to smile, and looked up.

Booker looked at her with concern in his eyes and he opened his mouth to speak, but she waved him off. "Let's get going," she said brusquely

Reen and Roo took up positions on either side of her. Mick and Charles led the way, and Booker brought up the rear. One of the six-legged panther-like animals darted across their path but it didn't engage.

Sophie remained alert and watchful, even after the wall was in plain sight and the trees thinned. She didn't fully relax again until they were safely in the first wall on their way out of the Zoo.

"Are you okay?" Booker asked her when they were through the walls.

"I'm fine," she said.

"Come on, let's get back," Reen said and looped an arm over her shoulders. "I'll cook tonight."

The Brit looked reluctant to let the others go back to Fiddler's Green without him, but after only a moment's hesitation, he turned and marched toward Franco's to hand the samples over.

When he joined the others, he walked into the dining room where Roo argued with Mick and Charles while Reen cooked dinner. Sophie wasn't in the room.

"How'd we do?" the Aussie asked.

"We got a large enough amount that Franco raised it to thirty."

"The cheap bastard."

"Sophie did well," Charles said. He frowned. "I wasn't too happy about the whole vine-snagging thing, but she handled it really well."

"Yeah, that was a fucking mess." Mick shook his head.

"I'm glad it wasn't worse," Roo muttered.

"Speaking of, where is Sophie?" Booker asked.

"She said she was going to go freshen up," the Aussie said. "I still don't understand what the fuck that means when women say that. Reen, what does that mean?"

She gave him a sharp look over her shoulder. "Do I look like a person who'd say that?"

"Worth a shot." He shrugged.

Booker left the dining room to put his weapons away. He unzipped the uniform and rolled it down to his waist so he stood in shirtsleeves and half the jumpsuit. He locked the gun case and turned to find Sophie standing behind him.

"Sophie! How long have you been there?"

"Not long," she said. "Reen sent me to find you."

"She did?"

"Well, she said no one was eating until everyone was there, and no one wanted to move so I elected to go find you myself." She smiled at him but her smile faded the longer he stared wordlessly at her. "What the hell is it? Do I have something on my face?"

He shook his head and stepped closer and grasped her wrists gently. "You sure you're okay?"

She smiled. "I promise I'm fine, Booker. I could use a deep tissue massage, though. Know where a girl can get one of those around here?"

Booker coughed and released her to grip the back of his neck.

"I mean, obviously, I'm a little sore from the fall," she said. "And I know there aren't any massage places around here. Only joking."

He studied her quickly and told himself he was checking for more obvious signs of injury.

Sophie shifted her weight. She opened her mouth to say something else but was interrupted by Roo yelling from down the hall, "Jesus Christ, can we hurry the fuck up so I can eat before I've gone and shoved it of old age?"

Booker shook his head. "Uh, sorry."

"What are you apologizing for? Come on, *mon cheri*," she said and headed to the door. She looked over her shoulder and sent a wicked grin his way, having shaken off her earlier embarrassment. "Reen cooked up some sausages, and there's nothing more satisfying than a good sausage."

He watched the sway of Sophie's hips as she walked out the door.

What did she mean by that? A good sausage? Was that a double entendre?

"She's fucking eighteen," he muttered to himself, feeling guilty and perverted for even wondering. "Fuckin' a. I'm eleven years older than her. Keep it professional. That's all this is. Be a goddamn professional."

"Are you coming, Booker?" she called from down the hall.

"Ah, shit."

CHAPTER EIGHTEEN

The Zoo - Thor

A restless energy settled over the demiwolf pack. They snapped at each other and jostled through the dense jungle foliage.

Something in the air made them uneasy. Thor couldn't tell exactly what it was, but he could feel where it came from and that was where they were heading.

The alpha remained in the lead and his long legs ate the ground relentlessly as he pelted through the jungle toward their destination.

The uneasiness gave way to an overwhelming feeling of hatred and the need to attack. It made Thor bare his teeth and growl low in his throat. The other demiwolves around him responded with throaty rumbles of their own.

Their leader howled and the others took up the hunting cry.

Thor saw red, and the whole demiwolf pack surged forward. They were all affected by the injection of pure rage and adrenaline the Zoo gave them as it urged them toward their prey.

He could smell what they hunted now—people. There were at least three humans ahead. Everything in his being told him the humans had damaged the Zoo in some way.

His pack mates howled and barked and made no effort to sneak up on their intended prey.

The humans clustered in a small clearing and the predators moved in to hedge off any escape.

A flare lit up the night in a shower of blinding red. It illuminated the trees and the shadows of the demiwolf pack that circled the trio of humans.

Thor's eyes glowed the same color as the flare. His hackles rose and he growled low in his throat. Saliva dripped from his jaws and his body thrummed with excitement.

The alpha snarled and lunged forward, snapping. One of the humans stumbled back, the weapon in his hand went off, and the alpha yelped sharply.

The pack launched themselves forward.

Thor bit deeply into one of the man's legs. His jaws closed and the femur snapped. The human screamed and tried to shove him off but his bulk and horns prevented the person wresting himself free. Another demiwolf ripped into the man's throat and his struggles ceased.

The sweet coppery taste sent a spike of adrenaline through him and he released his hold of the human and licked his lips. He looked over the dead man as the others began to feed on the kill. For a brief moment, an image of Charles flashed through his mind. This person looked almost like the big black man, but he knew it wasn't him.

The Zoo swelled stronger inside him and he wondered what he'd do if he saw Charles again. He didn't think he'd attack, but he wasn't sure. Humans were the enemy. Even if a few had shown him kindness, it didn't mean he'd return the favor.

One of the men tried to drag himself away from the attacking pack, but the animals didn't let him get far. He stabbed uselessly to try to fend off the onslaught. One of his arms was torn off before a demiwolf ripped his throat out.

The three bodies were quickly devoured. The creatures fought over the sweet meat and lapped up the blood greedily. The alpha uttered a triumphant howl.

Thor didn't join in. He had focused on the burbling flow of blood from the wound in the alpha's hind leg. It was a ragged hole as big around as Thor's snout and was the only mark the humans had managed to inflict on the pack.

The beta nosed up to the leader and tried to lick his wound. He snarled and snapped at her and she slunk away.

Despite his wound, he still sprinted through the jungle. The others followed him. Thor sensed the mood amongst the large predators shifting. The alpha was weaker and would grow more vulnerable as the days passed. The desire to challenge him strengthened in the younger demiwolf's mind.

The pack stopped to drink. Another pack member snapped at Thor to keep him from drinking, but he snarled in return. He growled and bared his teeth until the other animal backed down.

The beta watched the interaction happen. She approached him with her head down.

He tracked her approach while he lapped lazily at the muddy water. The beta bared her teeth and he returned the gesture.

The others gathered in a loose circle and yipped nervously as she closed the distance between herself and the younger demiwolf.

She pounced on him, pinned him beneath her, and grasped one of his black horns. He twisted beneath her and managed to bite where her foreleg met her chest. She yelped and released her hold on his horn.

They circled one another, huffing and growling. The beta rose on her hind legs and bore down on him. Their horns smacked together and he didn't move under the assault. She reared for another blow. He drove himself up into a lunge, his hind legs pulsing with power, and when their horns collided, his opponent stumbled back a step. Thor took advantage of the other demiwolf's instability. He rammed into her and thrust his full weight behind the movement.

At a loud snapping noise, the beta screamed. He had broken half of her left horn. The remaining portion was split down the center, all the way to her skull. The flesh parted and blood bubbled up. The beta howled again but still tried to fight him, even though she was severely weakened.

Thor lunged forward and bit into the side of her neck and shook his head, jerking the slightly smaller demiwolf around.

She snarled and struggled against him, but he didn't let

her regain any ground. He deliberately released her and rammed his horns into her side. Ribs cracked and a shard of bone sliced into one of her lungs.

He pinned her beneath him and ripped her savagely to shreds. She fought until her heart stopped beating.

The pack watched him kill the beta and finally looked to see the alpha's reaction.

Their leader squared up opposite Thor and stared menacingly at the younger demiwolf. He returned the alpha's stare. He didn't submit, but he held himself in a relaxed and unchallenging way. Even with the injury he had, the animal was still strong.

The alpha stepped toward him and waited for him to close the distance. Thor complied and the larger demiwolf growled once and touched noses with him. He acknowledged Thor as the new beta.

With pack formalities completed, the leader wheeled and ran into the woods. The rest of the pack followed closely behind.

The dead beta's body began to melt into the Zoo floor.

As he followed on the alpha's heels, he felt the pack shift behind him and adjust to the change in hierarchy. No one issued a challenging growl.

He looked at the alpha's wound again. It constantly reopened and blood still dripped from it and matted the fur of his hind leg, but the leader barely limped.

CHAPTER NINETEEN

Sahara Coalition Sector, The Zoo

The van that pulled into the Sahara Coalition base was covered in a layer of dust. It was large and white with no discernible markings on the outside. The guard at the entrance stopped it and asked for papers.

The driver handed over a stack of ID cards for himself and the eight men with him. The guard leafed through, then frowned.

"I'm sorry, sir, I need more than just one name."

The man turned his head and looked at the sentry, his eyes hidden by the dark sunglasses he wore. To the guard, the men looked like nothing particularly special. They wore drab olive fatigues and were armed to the teeth with semi-automatic rifles and other state-of-the-art weaponry he couldn't see all that clearly from the driver's open window.

"The name is Jam. That's all you need to know."

He passed the IDs back. "I'm sorry, but that's not really how this works."

The man called Jam smiled at the guard. It triggered a chill that rippled up and down his spine.

"Listen, kid, I appreciate that you're doing your job, but, please, stay the fuck out of my way and I won't cause any trouble for you."

He looked hastily over his shoulder to where his partner tried to pick up a video signal to chat with his girlfriend at home. When he couldn't catch the man's eye, he turned to the van full of mercenaries.

"Where are you from?"

"It doesn't matter where I'm from," Jam said. "These boys are from Benin."

The guard nodded. "Okay. Fine. Go on through, but don't kick up any trouble."

The merc grinned again and the sentry didn't need to see his eyes to know the smile didn't reach them.

"Smart move, kid."

Jam drove through the well-organized Sahara Coalition sector. Soldiers and mercenaries marched in groups, each focused on reaching their destination. No one paid attention to the van—it wasn't that unusual a sight.

He stopped in front of a square two-story building. The word *Hotel* was painted on the side in six different languages.

The other mercenaries waited in the van while he walked up the three steps and went inside.

A young man with a turban sat on a barstool behind the front desk. He scrutinized the new arrival.

Jam didn't remove his sunglasses. "I have a reservation," he said.

The clerk tried to place his accent but couldn't. He

could've been from Nigeria, but he didn't think so. "Name?" he asked.

"Jam."

"Here it is. You ordered the whole second floor?"

"That's what it says, doesn't it?"

"Yes. First name, sir?"

"Jam."

"You are Jam…Jam?"

"No. Just Jam."

He looked up from his ledger book and took in the stranger's appearance. He was used to people carrying weapons into the hotel so it didn't bother him. In fact, he had an AK-47 under the desk, just in case. The way this man carried himself was what freaked him out.

"Sure thing," he said. "Just sign here, please, and I can get you your keys. Will you need help with any baggage?"

"No." Jam signed on the line the clerk indicated. He simply put an 'x' down.

The clerk watched him and the other mercenaries haul their luggage in from the van. He noticed seven crates of ammunition and twelve gun cases—and that was only what was in plain sight. He didn't doubt that there were more weapons hidden in the black canvas bags. While he was curious about the apparent lack of armor the men had between them, he assumed they would buy that later.

The leader had a room to himself. When the last of his bags were brought in, he shut and locked the door. The rest of the team loitered in the hall and allocated the remaining rooms between them. They occasionally cast glances toward the closed door but it didn't re-open.

Once the accommodations were settled, they left in search of food.

One of the mercenaries stopped short of knocking on the door.

"Leave him, Anton," another man whispered. "He's shitty company."

Anton shrugged and followed his companion down the stairs. "I just thought I'd be polite."

"Who cares?" another mercenary said. "I'll be happy to get this job done and be rid of the cocksucker."

"He freaks me the fuck out," Anton agreed.

"It's ironic, isn't it?" another asked.

"What?"

"That his name means peace."

"I wouldn't say that to his fucking face."

"Do you think I'm an idiot?"

The eight men stopped in front of the clerk's desk. "Where can we get something to eat?"

"If you go down three streets and make a left, there's a tavern. They have great food. I especially love the cous-cous-stuffed bell peppers."

"Thanks."

The mercenaries were almost out the door when the clerk called for them to stop.

"If you're looking for jobs," he said, "the tavern is also a good place to make connections."

Anton waved at the clerk. "Sure. Thanks. We'll keep that in mind."

The young man watched them leave. He usually got great tips for telling new blood where to find jobs. These mercenaries, however, hadn't cared at all, and he wondered if they already had jobs lined up. He supposed it was possible, but it didn't happen very often.

Half an hour after the team left, Jam received a call. He stared at the number on his phone and answered it after the fourth ring without saying a word.

"Hello?" a man's voice asked, hesitatingly. "Hello? Jam, you there?"

He grunted.

"Jesus, man, why don't you say anything?"

The merc didn't reply.

"Fine. You made it all right? You're getting into position?"

"We will be ready soon."

"Excellent! And you know what to do?"

"Yes."

"Great. I can count on you with this, right, Jam?"

"Yes."

"Good. Don't fuck it up, or there'll be hell to pay."

Jam simply hung up. He'd heard enough. With a sigh, he stretched his lanky body out on the hard bed, closed his eyes, and fell asleep.

CHAPTER TWENTY

Wateringhole, Harvesters Camp

Roo slammed his empty pint glass onto the table. He dragged the back of his hand across his mouth and wiped away any remaining foam. "How long was that?"

"Ten seconds," Reen answered. "Not bad."

"Beat that, motherfucker," he said and belched.

Sophie wrinkled her nose. "Gross."

"I'm a red-blooded male, sweetheart. Get used to it."

Mick grabbed a full pint glass and raised it toward his friend. "Okay, captain dickhead, I can beat that time."

"Like hell you can, you wanker. But let's see you try."

The Aboriginal nodded at Reen and she got ready to start her stopwatch again. He grasped the pint and threw it back.

"How long was that?" he asked after he slammed his empty glass down.

"Nine point five. Looks like we have a winner."

"Fuck yeah, motherfucker! I told you!" he shouted.

Roo folded his arms over his chest. "Oh, get the fuck over yourself. It's not that great."

"Aw, don't be a sore loser, ginger," Reen said. "Now get your ass over to the bar and get us all another round. It's on you."

Booker and Charles returned to the table as he walked away.

"He lose?" the big man asked as he sat beside Mick.

"Yeah. Thought he could beat me, the tosser. He should've known better."

"Does he ever know when to back down?" the woman asked.

Mick laughed. "Good point. How was pool?"

"Good," Charles said.

"Who won?" Sophie asked Booker.

"I did, of course."

"I don't see what's so *of course* about you winning at pool," Charles said. "I gave you a run for your money."

"But I still kicked your ass."

"Good to know you're not a sore winner." She nudged Booker with her elbow. The jarring made him spill a little beer down the front of his shirt. "Oops. Sorry."

"You're not."

"No, I'm not. Serves you right for being mean to Charles."

"I wasn't being mean."

"You weren't being nice."

"All in the name of good sporting, Teasy."

Roo returned with a pitcher of beer and an unfamiliar man in tow.

"Who are you?" Charles asked.

The man, who wore light olive-and-brown fatigues with a bright orange scarf tied around his neck, gave a slight bow. "My name is Andreas."

"Found this guy staring at us from the bar, so I decided to invite the fucker over. He said he has something important to say. Spill it."

Andreas looked around the table of mercenaries and his gaze lingered for a few seconds longer on Sophie. She tilted her chin defiantly and returned his stare. He focused on Booker, who glared at him.

"I come from Côte d'Ivoire," he said in thickly accented English. "We need your help." The man glanced around the Wateringhole. No one paid attention to them, but he still seemed nervous. "Is there anywhere more private we can speak?"

Reen asked him something in French, and he answered, looking relieved. Sophie joined the conversation and the three of them spoke for a few minutes.

Roo's eyes glazed over. "Jesus, it's like we aren't even here."

"I guess we all really need to learn fucking French," Mick said.

"Okay, let's take this back to home base," Reen said and pushed up from the table.

"We practically just got here," the Aussie protested.

"This could be important," she responded firmly.

"It *is* important," Andreas said.

"Okay." The Brit held a hand up to silence Roo's objections. "Let's go."

They remained on the first floor of the building. The visitor didn't seem to mind or question them standing in the nearly empty room. Booker decided they needed a conference table but standing in a circle would have to do for now.

"What help do you need?" he asked.

"I have been sent by the Azaud family to ask your help in returning their son, I'nsan. He came to the Zoo to seek his fortune and now, he and his team are in trouble," Andreas said. "We ask that you go in and rescue I'nsan and see him safely returned to his kingdom."

"His kingdom? Is he a prince?" Reen asked.

"Yes."

"I know some Baoulé princes, but I don't think I've ever met this I'nsan," Sophie said.

Andreas nodded. "I have also been told to offer you a reward if you are able to accomplish the task of bringing I'nsan out of the Zoo."

"We can't guarantee that he isn't dead already," Booker said.

"I don't think his family expects that of you. They know of the dangers. They just want him home. If he is alive, the reward will be larger."

"How much?" Reen asked.

"I'nsan's mother is ready to pay a million American dollars for the return of her son."

"We'll have to think about it for a little bit," the Brit said.

"I understand, but there is not much time. One of the members of the prince's team managed to escape and return to the Sahara Coalition. That is how we knew that I'nsan needed help. They are trapped in a swamp."

"Give us a minute."

Andreas nodded and stepped outside.

"When did we become Search and Rescue?" Charles asked. "Not that I'm saying we shouldn't do it. I'm just wondering."

"We are getting a bit of a reputation," Reen pointed out.

"The Ivory Coast and Benin have a good relationship," Sophie interjected. "It's possible the president caught wind of this and gave your names as reliable. This I'nsan Azaud's family must be pretty high up and very rich to be offering such a large reward for a third son."

"How do you know he's the third son?" Charles asked.

"In Baoulé tradition, the third child is always called I'nsan."

Booker was quiet while he considered what he'd heard.

"Well, I think we should do it, obviously," Mick said.

"I don't know for sure," Roo said. "If we decide to do this, we should also get some two-second frogs while we're rescuing this bastard. You know, in case the Zoo's already gobbled him up."

"Why don't you know for sure?" Mick asked.

"Because, who are these people? I mean, really? Are we going to run head-first into the Zoo on some rescue mission that just fell out of the fucking sky and into our laps? It seems a little too good to be true if you ask me. The reward is high. And it's like Sophie said, all for a third son."

"I don't think it should matter when the poor bastard was born," Reen said.

"I know, but something is a little strange to me here. It smells off."

"I think we should do it," Sophie said. "I mean, there are a ton of kingdoms in the Ivory Coast. I've gone to a few political events with my father there but not all of them. I was away at school. I don't necessarily recognize the name Azaud but that doesn't really mean anything. I think we should go rescue the prince."

"Does everyone want to rescue the prince and his team?" Booker asked.

"I'm in," Charles said. The others echoed his response, although Roo was quiet.

"Roo?" Booker prompted.

"This seems legit to you, Sophie?"

She nodded.

"Okay. Let's go save a goddamn prince."

The Brit called Andreas inside. "We'll help. Where was the last known location of the prince?"

"He was near the border of the Sahara Coalition and the French Quarter. Roughly speaking. The man who escaped and brought the news couldn't remember exactly where," the man explained. "He was...greatly distressed. I have a map with me that will show where he thought they were."

"Great, thanks. You can tell the family we'll start the search right away," Booker said. "Give me the map."

He opened a briefcase and withdrew a map that he handed over. After another small bow, he left Fiddler's Green.

"Should we take the bus to the Sahara Coalition and cut through that way?" Mick asked.

"We don't have the BTR, so we won't be able to cover the ground that fast," Roo said.

"The BTR did a shit job in the swamp, not that it matters now," Booker said morosely. "You guys get the kits together. I'm going to go to Dan's and see if he's heard of a new swamp popping up."

"Sounds like a plan," Sophie said.

Booker frowned at her.

"What?"

"Nothing."

"I'm coming with you guys," the girl said.

"Of course, you are," Reen said. "There's no way we're leaving you here."

"While I'm at Dan's, I'll see if he got the armor I asked for," Booker said.

"You're getting us new armor?" Charles asked.

The Brit nodded. "Yeah, perfect timing too. Now, let's get a move on. The longer we sit around talking, the slimmer the chances of saving the Baoulé prince. Like Roo said, that's even if he hasn't become Zoo-food by now, which is probably the case."

Dan's was uncharacteristically empty. Booker approached the table the supplier did his deals on and waited.

"Hello?" he called.

A distant crashing sound was immediately followed by a string of curses. Dan appeared from the back of the large room, wiping grease-streaked palms on his fatigues, but only succeeded in spreading the grime everywhere. He frowned at his hands and shrugged.

"Booker, sorry about that. I left someone at the front here but obviously, the motherfucker decided to take his leave. He won't be coming back and if he thinks he is, he has another think coming. What can I do for you?"

"Do you have that armor I asked for?"

"Yeah. It's right here." He picked up a box that was near the table, opened it, and hauled out one of the armor sets and passed it to Booker to examine. It was all a single piece made up of hard synthetic plates held together with spandex-like material. The supplier set a helmet on the table. It had a full facemask and tapered to a point like a speed skater's helmet.

"And this is the good stuff?" Booker asked while he stretched the surprisingly thin and pliable material.

"Don't insult me, Brit. Of course, it's the good shit."

"How does it do with poisons?"

"Great. Just don't go marinating in a vat of something."

"Obviously not." He pulled his tablet out and transferred money to Dan from the BOHICA Warriors account.

"Was there anything else?" the other man asked.

"Yeah, actually, there was. You hear anything about a new swamp?"

Dan glanced around, but they were still the only ones in the building. "Yeah. Down by the Sahara Coalition side. Not so deep, too. I heard it was about ten, maybe a dozen klicks in. Shrinking fast. Why? You trying to go after some more swamp critters?"

"Something like that. Thanks, Dan."

"No problem."

He returned to Fiddler's Green with the information and the new armor. They pulled it on over the BOHICA uniforms.

"This is a little...uh, tight," Charles said. He tugged at the material that hugged him.

Reen laughed. "Look at you, Charles. You can be black Superman, now."

"I never wanted to be a superhero," he retorted.

"Never?" Sophie asked.

"Nope. I just wanted to be a Marine."

"Well, that's a sort of superhero," she countered. "Plus, you did a pretty great job of saving my ass, which is also superhero-like."

He smiled and looked away in embarrassment.

"Will this protect us from anything?" Roo asked. "It seems like pretty flimsy shit."

"It's the best," Booker confirmed and adjusted the fit of the armor on his shoulders. He rolled them and stretched experimentally. The armor was tight but it still allowed full range of motion.

"Time's a wastin'," Mick said and dropped into a deep knee-bend to test the suit. "Let's get this fucking show on the road."

"Did we decide to take the bus to the Sahara Coalition?" the Brit asked.

"We're just going to use our gate and cut through the Zoo," Reen advised him. "We decided while you were gone that it would be faster."

"Sounds good to me. Let's go."

CHAPTER TWENTY-ONE

The Zoo – Thor

The smell of sickness had begun to waft off the alpha the day before. Thor focused on it and stared at him. The stench had already become stronger, twisted with the hint of death and decay. If the other demiwolves noticed, they either didn't care or were simply waiting to see what would happen next.

The decay was something new. If Zoo creatures were wounded but lived, they usually healed quickly. He didn't understand why the alpha—like the beta—was now getting sicker instead of healing.

He didn't feel the need to challenge the pack leader. The older animal was still strong, despite the hints of his slow demise. His wound had not completely healed and he had ripped out all the fur around it. There was a puffy hole surrounded by a shock of pale, freckled skin. That, along with the smell and the pronounced limp, were the only signs he had given that the injury bothered him.

The alpha barked, the noise sharp and urgent, and he

immediately raced into the jungle. Thor followed and kept pace with him easily. The rest of the pack spread out behind them.

There was something appealing about the feeling of the vines whispering over his horns as he ran. The jungle seemed to create a tunnel around them and the greenery parted slightly to provide a path. Plants caressed the furred bodies as they passed like a mother's gentle touch.

Thor opened his senses and breathed in the intoxicating scent of the Zoo. He could smell the troop of monkey-like animals that followed above them and swung through the canopy.

The pack did not have a specific den they returned to, but they moved around more often than they had before. The alpha was restless. Thor had noticed this but he couldn't work out why. Running only weakened the animal, but he did it anyway.

He stretched his legs and began to run right beside the leader. The other demiwolf glanced at him and bared his teeth but didn't slow. If anything, he pushed harder and his claws dug into the soft jungle floor. He put on more speed. Thor remained alongside and after a short while, began to nose ahead.

The alpha snapped his teeth together and turned swiftly to the side to change the direction of the pack. The sudden move caused Thor to fall behind a step, but he soon recovered.

The larger demiwolf's breathing was more labored, but he didn't waver. Blood began to trickle from the wound, but he paid no attention to it.

Up ahead, Thor caught the familiar scent of the six-legged panthers that stalked through the jungle. The other pack members picked up on the scent as well. A shiver of excitement rippled through their ranks. They didn't seek them out as prey but they enjoyed fighting with the cat-like animals.

The alpha slowed his pace. They were a fair distance from the six-legged creatures but they wanted to maintain the element of surprise. A demiwolf's sense of smell was better than the panthers' but not by much.

The pack instinctively spread out and streamed silently through the jungle. Thor's mouth watered and anticipation made his eyes glow. He scented two of their quarry ahead. The creatures' irritation could be felt by their pursuers.

A scream sounded ahead of them. The demiwolves slunk forward, their bellies to the ground. They spread out and continued their approach to surround the unsuspecting creatures and narrow the possible avenues of escape.

The cat-like creatures were fighting one another. Claws slashed and milky saliva dripped from their black jaws. They howled and screamed as they clashed. The larger of the two was on top and pinned the other with its two middle legs while its rearmost limbs kicked and scored along the other's back to part the thick black fur and slice into flesh.

One of the demiwolves uttered a growl, and the two panthers froze in their battle. They raised their heads and searched the surrounding jungle with their glowing yellow gaze. The larger animal snapped back into the moment before the other. With a final thrust of its sharp claws, it leapt away and raced into the jungle. The remaining animal attempted to follow and make its own escape but didn't get far.

The alpha lunged forward, his head lowered. He rammed into the side of the feline. The sound of crunching bones filled the air. The creature screamed and catapulted to impact against the trunk of a large tree.

The demiwolves streamed forward. The leader, after the initial attack, let another pack member finish the kill. Already wounded by the other panther, it didn't have enough strength to fight off the predator that ripped its throat out.

Thor ran after the escaped beast. The excitement of the chase thrummed through his bloodstream. Several of his pack followed on his heels. He howled and the others took up the cry.

The panther crashed through the jungle ahead of them. Thor ran faster and barked and snapped his teeth. His prey screeched and scrambled up and over the massive trunk of a fallen tree. Its claws dug deep into the bark and it soon surmounted the obstacle.

He gathered his strength and hurdled after it. The other demiwolves ran around the fallen log. His claws weren't as sharp as the felines, but his leap had him almost at the top. He was soon over.

Their quarry wasn't far ahead of him now and his mouth watered. He stretched forward and snapped at the end of the animal's tail. His teeth closed around emptiness as, with a scream, the cat surged forward.

Thor could practically taste its desperation. It reeked of fear and adrenaline. The fight it had with the other panther before the demiwolves had found them had weakened it.

He could sense it lagging, digging into the last of its energy reserves to maintain its flight.

He howled in excitement. His fellows howled too and closed in on him and his target. The alpha appeared at his side and Thor sped up. This animal was his and he wouldn't let the leader take away the satisfaction of the kill. His bones vibrated with adrenaline, and he could practically feel the satisfaction of sinking his teeth into the panther's flesh.

The black animal stumbled when one of its legs gave out, but it had the other five and continued to run. The stumble brought it closer, however, and he took advantage and lunged forward. He used his body weight to knock the cat-like animal to the ground where they rolled together. The creature screamed and clawed while it tried to twist to disembowel him with its hind four legs, but he was ready. He snarled and evaded the razor-sharp talons, bit into its flesh, and ripped hunks from it. It howled and fought back, but he was filled with the bloodlust of the moment and didn't give the animal a chance to recover.

It was weak from its fight and flight and Thor had it overpowered in seconds. The yellow glow of its eyes died when he ripped its throat out. Its warm blood ran down his chin. He threw his head back and howled his triumph.

The alpha sat and watched with eyes that glowed deep-red. He returned the gaze unwaveringly.

The panther's blood was rapidly sucked into the earth and the Zoo greedily consumed its creation.

The pack raced through the jungle again. After the death of the panthers, they hadn't hunted anything for a few days and Thor was becoming bored.

The alpha's limp was more pronounced but still, the younger animal did nothing. He was waiting for something, although he wasn't sure what that was exactly.

They stopped at a watering hole. He stood back from the rest when something in the back of his consciousness pricked awake. His hackles rose and he raised his nose high and let his tongue loll out. He tasted the air. A familiar scent filled his senses. A confusion of emotions and feelings pounded into him. The distinct image of an old tire and a smiling man flashed into his mind.

Charles was in the Zoo.

Thor became overwhelmed with the desire to find the man. Part of him wanted to show off his long horns. He wanted to play with the tire again and to be scratched behind the ears—he'd always liked that. While he hadn't thought about those things in a long time, they now flooded him and overwhelmed the Zoo side that had been in control.

Without thought, he set off into the jungle in the direction Charles' scent was coming from. The other demi-wolves followed him and the alpha kept pace with him. He didn't seem bothered that he had taken the lead.

The man's scent wavered and the breeze that brought it to Thor weakened. He ran faster when a different feeling washed over him. He needed to find Charles as soon as possible.

CHAPTER TWENTY-TWO

The Zoo

"It's goddamn hot in here," Mick complained.

"Yeah, this armor sure doesn't have breathability going for it," Reen responded.

"No, it is breathable. It's just bleddy hot," Booker contradicted.

They traveled in a close column and made good headway through the jungle toward where the swamp was supposed to be.

"It does seem hotter than normal," Charles said. "Muggier."

"It's disgusting, is what it is," Roo muttered.

"How do you get stuck in a swamp?" Sophie asked Booker. She jogged along directly behind him.

He didn't like that she was so close to the front of the column where he was second in the line behind Charles, but he didn't want her farther away either. For whatever reason, he felt it was his responsibility to keep her safe,

235

although he knew the others were equally as protective of her. "You ever been to a swamp?"

"No. I have seen a marsh, though."

"Not the same thing. Swamps are denser, muddier, and a hell of a lot foggier too. Zoo swamps are their own particular kind of delightful. All mud and murky water and disgusting swimming monsters."

"Swimming monsters?"

"Yeah, but don't worry, I'll keep you safe." He didn't need to look over his shoulder to know she was rolling her eyes at him. "It's easy to get lost or trapped in a swamp. You can't see really well. Plus, true to Zoo form, everything in there is especially adept at killing. There are these lily pad things that drag you under and try to eat you. Sword-grass that thirsts for blood and is sharper than razor blades. Then there are the leeches."

"Leeches? Gross."

"Yeah. The bastards are pretty disgusting. Not to mention huge."

"Sounds delightful."

Charles stopped abruptly and held his hand up for the others to do the same. Sophie bumped into Booker and recovered quickly.

"Sorry," she muttered.

He ignored her and looked around as he adjusted his grip on his M5, raised the weapon, and tightened his finger on the trigger. Ahead, the fronds of a fern trembled. A sound like steel wool on metal sounded, followed by a hiss.

The others fanned out behind him. Charles moved alongside Mick and the two men kept an eye out behind them. Roo and Reen stepped forward to either side of the Brit. Sophie stayed where she was.

Another hiss issued from the fern before the fronds parted and a scaly, dark-green nose poked through. Its shiny, black tongue flicked out toward the BOHICAs. The spade-shaped head emerged from the fern. Four glowing yellow eyes, as big as dinner plates, stared at them and the black slits of its pupils cut the yellow perfectly in half. The snake-like creature hissed again.

The girl took a step back and tried not to hyperventilate. She was terrified of snakes, and the monster in front of them was something out of her worst nightmares. After a moment, she steeled herself and stepped forward again.

It reared and more of its thick, scaly body coiled forward. The sound of its scales rubbing together made the hair on their arms rise. It was almost as bad as nails on a chalkboard.

The creature raised its head into the air above them and hissed again. Foot-long fangs descended from its mouth and it flicked its black tongue again. Milky green saliva dripped from its maw.

Booker opened fire and severed the staring contest with the massive reptile. It lunged with a hiss and surged forward, its mouth open wide and ready to sink its fangs into its tormentor.

The rounds from Roo's VZ.58 struck the creature in the side of the head. Magenta blood spurted from the wounds. It hissed and changed direction toward him. Booker and Reen's rounds bit into its flesh. The Aussie stumbled back as the snake-like animal serpentined forward. Its mouth closed over nothing but empty air.

The monster zigged forward again. Its thick muscular body thrust Booker back a few steps and it darted amongst the BOHICA Warriors and targeted Sophie. She stood her ground and fired at the oncoming reptile. The scales on its face were too tough and the rounds glanced off. When she realized that it wouldn't stop, she flung herself out of the way.

The attacker hissed its frustration at missing another of the humans. It recoiled and prepared to strike again.

Charles stepped forward and delivered a slug into the base of the mutant's skull. Its pupils widened from the strike and consumed the yellow of its eyes. He fired again and the creature's whole body went into convulsions.

They leapt out of the way as it coiled and writhed in its death throes.

"You okay?" Booker asked and grasped Sophie's arms.

"I'm fine," she said. She stepped away and shook him off.

"Let's keep going," Mick said. "I'll take over on point."

"I have a confession," the girl whispered to Reen. "Snakes terrify me."

The woman smiled at her. "Well, it's a good thing that one isn't really a snake. And you held your own against it, so I don't think it really matters."

"What do you mean it wasn't really a snake? It sure as hell looked like one. A fucking overgrown one, but still a snake."

"It only sort of resembled one. Nothing is what you think it is here, remember that."

"I don't care if it's a normal snake or a freaking alien

one! It's all the same in the end. Gross tongues, large fangs, icky scales. Awful."

"Icky scales?" Roo asked.

She responded with an obscene gesture she could only have learned from him.

"It sure took its time attacking," Charles said.

"Good thing for us, too," Booker pointed out.

"Come on, people, we're getting close," Mick announced.

"How can you tell?" Reen asked.

"You smell that?" he asked.

They all paused to work out what he meant.

"It smells kind of like sulfur," she said finally.

He nodded.

"Smells like shit to me," Roo muttered.

"That'd be the swamp."

The team proceeded with more caution and the odor of their destination grew stronger. They jogged another klick and reached the edge of the morass.

"Looks like it's already starting to recede." Booker pointed at the stretch of mud before it turned into murky water. A few two-second frogs hopped around in the mire.

"But not enough to make tracking easy," Mick said. "It's gonna be a real bitch trying to find this prince."

"You can do it, though, right?" Sophie asked.

He gave a look that said she was crazy to question his skills.

"What is the best way to do this, do you think?" Charles asked.

"We'll have to stay close to one another. We can't risk getting ourselves lost or separated when we're in there.

We'll sweep, calling out for this I'nsan character and hopefully, he responds."

"Do you think he's still alive?" the girl asked.

No one answered her.

They stepped into the swamp and immediately sank into the mud with each boot-hugging step. The murky water swirled around their knees. They were surrounded by the sounds of the wetland. Things splashed and gurgled and unseen creatures hissed and screeched in the plants.

They spread out in a line, five meters apart from each other, and began to call for I'nsan. The sound of their voices seemed muted by the oppressive fog that clung to the water.

Booker sloshed to the top of a hillock and looked around. Mick joined him.

"Visibility is shit," the Aboriginal said.

His companion kicked away a fat leech that tried to crawl toward him. "Yeah. I can't see anything."

"Do you think he's out there?" he asked in a low voice.

The Brit watched Reen cutting through the swamp to their right. "I don't know. My gut's telling me he's probably dead."

"You're most likely right."

"Only one way to find out." He trudged forward.

The mud sucked at Roo as he sloshed through it. Surprisingly, the armor kept him dry. Something rippled in the almost knee-deep water beside him. He stopped and aimed his rifle at it. Bubbles popped on the surface a split-second before a slimy blob of a creature hurtled up from the water with its yellow teeth clacking. He fired and it exploded in a purple mist.

"That's fucking disgusting," he muttered. He looked around but couldn't see very far and almost by rote, yelled the prince's name again.

Off in the distance to his left, he thought he heard something. He stopped and squinted in the direction of the noise. "Hello? I'nsan?"

"Help...me," a voice called. Whoever it was sounded weak.

The Aussie couldn't tell exactly where the person had called from. "Shit. I'm coming! Where are you?" He turned fully in the direction of the voice. "Guys, you hear that?" he yelled over his shoulder.

He moved forward cautiously. The hairs on the back of his neck rose suddenly, and he stopped. "Where are you?" No one answered so he repeated the question but remained where he was. The only sounds he heard were the tell-tale signs of the others converging on him.

"I better not be fucking hearing things now," he muttered. "I'nsan?" He still made no effort to proceed.

"Did you find him?" Charles called.

"I'm not sure," he responded.

He stepped forward again toward where he'd heard the voice ask for help. Suddenly, a flash of light was followed by the unmistakable sound of an automatic weapon firing. Something struck him in the side and he spun helplessly. Pain ripped across his chest and he knew he'd probably broken a rib.

The others scrambled for cover. Charles lunged toward him and dragged him behind an outcropping of swamp grass.

"Where were you hit?" the big man asked.

Roo shook his head, winced, and shoved him away. He looked down at his side, but there was only a smudge where he'd been hit. The armor had successfully stopped the bullet, but it still hurt like hell.

"Doesn't the motherfucker know we're here to rescue him?"

Charles, satisfied that he wasn't bleeding, rose carefully from his crouched position. Once he could see above the grass, the unknown enemy opened fire. Reen fired in retaliation from where she had taken cover.

The American ducked again and kept his head low as rounds cut through the grass above them. "Fudge. What's going on?"

"I think we're under fucking attack."

"But why?"

"How the hell should I know?"

"Can you move?"

"My side hurts like a motherfucker but yeah, I can move."

Charles looked for the others. Reen was the closest. He signaled to her and she nodded.

"Okay, Reen's going to cover us and then we'll move to her," he said.

She nodded, stood quickly, and fired. Her teammates lunged toward her.

More weapons delivered a rapid volley at them through the mist. The two men had almost reached her hillock when a grenade landed in the water next to them and detonated, and both fell sideways. Charles grabbed the back of Roo's armor and dragged him forward. They collapsed beside Reen.

"What the fuck is going on?" she hissed. Another grenade exploded near them and showered them with mud and water. She wiped the muck off her face.

"We need to get out of here," the American stated.

"No shit, Sherlock. This is a fucking ambush." She lobbed a grenade of her own. It exploded and someone yelled. Other people answered the shout. The unknown attackers spoke in a language they didn't understand or recognize.

"How many of them are there?" Roo asked.

"How the hell should I know?" Reen asked. "More than one, that's for fucking sure."

Mick whistled to get their attention and they looked at him. Booker crouched beside him.

"Ready to move again?" Charles asked Roo.

"Are you?" he bit back.

Reen rolled her eyes. "Don't be such a pussy."

"I have a broken rib!"

"You'll live."

"I'm going to kill those fuckers," he promised belligerently.

More rounds whistled over their heads. Mick and Booker retaliated and drew the attention of the unseen gunmen. Their teammates used the brief cover and surged toward them.

Charles looked over his shoulder and saw human shapes moving forward out of the fog. He could make out four shadows, maybe, and fired his Remington. The shotgun thundered as the buckshot cut through the mist. Someone grunted and there was a loud splash like someone had gone down, but he couldn't tell for sure.

The three made it to Mick and Booker. They were all breathing hard.

"We've been fucking set up," Mick said.

"Really?" Roo snarked.

"Sarcasm doesn't look great on you, Aussie," Booker snapped.

His teammate ignored him

"Where's Sophie?" Charles asked.

"I'm here," she said from behind the Brit. She was covered in mud and had a scared but determined look on her face.

Men shouted to one another when the firing stopped. Booker tried to see what was going on but couldn't make anything out.

"So much for a goddamn rescue mission," he muttered.

Sophie pressed her lips together and scowled.

"What is it?" Reen asked.

"Those men aren't speaking a Baoulé language. They're speaking Fon."

"What does that mean?"

"It means that, whoever that is, they're not from the Ivory Coast. They're most likely from Benin."

"Are you fucking kidding me?" Roo hissed.

"This isn't her fault, Roo," Booker reminded him.

She closed her eyes. "No. It probably is. It's probably my father."

"You don't know that," he said.

A grenade exploded close by and another wave of debris washed over them. Reen flung a leech away.

Mick stood briefly and fired at the oncoming enemy. They were much closer than he'd like.

"We need to get out of this goddamn swamp," he said. "I don't know about you guys, but I'm not packing for a goddamn firefight."

"Has anyone been able to get a count?" Roo asked.

"I thought I saw four," Charles said. "But it's really hard to tell."

"I think Charles is right. There seem to be four weapons firing, at least. I can't pick the voices apart, but it does seem like there are four of the bastards," Mick agreed.

"How can you tell?" Sophie asked.

"Part of my special skill set," he replied. "When we're out of this, I'll teach you."

"This was supposed to be a rescue mission. I wasn't expecting to be attacked. By people, anyway," Booker said. He looked at Roo. "You were hit?"

"The armor took a lot of the blow and the round didn't make it to my skin. But I'm pretty sure I have at least one broken rib. Cracked if I'm lucky, splintered to all hell if I'm not. I'm not feeling very lucky, though, that's for damn sure."

The Brit nodded. "Okay. Let's get the hell out of here."

"I'll cover you and you guys make it to the next defensible spot," Reen said. "Ready? Go!"

She stood and sprayed a barrage at the attackers who sloshed steadily toward them. The others ran as best they could to another hillock. She dropped when they were safe and rounds ripped through the grass above her head while she hunkered lower.

"Reen!" Booker yelled, stood from his hiding place, and provided cover for her to join the team.

She sprinted toward them. A round grazed past her

arm. A grenade splashed into the water beside her and she dove forward to roll behind the hillock as it detonated. She came up sputtering and cursing but unharmed.

"They have terrible fucking aim," Mick commented. "And using grenades in the water? Fucking amateurs."

"It's a good thing, too," Charles responded.

"I don't think they're trying that hard," Reen said.

"You aren't making any fucking sense, Reen," Roo said. "They seem to be trying real fucking hard. If they weren't, they wouldn't be firing so much or tossing so many grenades."

"Quantity doesn't necessarily mean anything. Think about it. We're having a hell of a time hitting them and maneuvering through this goddamn swamp, and so are they. They're herding us out of here, or at least somewhere they can maneuver better to take us out."

"Shit, you might be right," Booker agreed. "They definitely came prepared for this. How much ammunition do you all have?"

"Not enough," Mick replied glumly. "I can engage maybe four more times—and that's if I'm being conservative with my rounds."

"Same here." Reen shrugged.

"It's not looking great," Charles added.

"Well, fuck." Booker grimaced. "Grenades?"

"I've used one already and only have the one left," she said.

"I have two," the American responded and Mick nodded.

"Same."

"I have six."

Everyone turned to stare at Roo. "Six?" Booker asked incredulously

"Yeah, I like to see things blow up."

"Jesus, all right. Well, that's great. And I have two."

"No one gave me any grenades," Sophie said. "I didn't realize that was an option."

"So, we've got enough grenades to take them out, probably," the Brit said and ignored her. "That's good news."

"Unless we can't hit them," Reen reminded him. "Their grenades don't seem to be doing much more than spraying nasty-ass fucking swamp matter everywhere."

Another grenade exploded near them, closer than before as if to demonstrate her point. The swamp water might be mitigating the grenades' ECR, but if even one landed beside any of them, it would mess up their day.

"Not that this isn't great, all this talk of grenades, but we need to get the fuck out of here. Those motherfuckers have gotten a hell of a lot closer," Roo reminded them. He fired at the oncoming attackers.

"Okay," Booker ordered. "I'll cover, you guys make a run for it. Roo, give Sophie one of your grenades."

He passed her one. "You just pull this here, throw it at the bad guys, and run like hell. Pretty simple."

She slipped it into a pocket at her hip. "Got it."

The Brit adjusted his grip on his M5 and nodded at them. "Ready? Go!"

He opened fire and they made for the next hillock. When they were half-way there, five men rose from behind their destination and opened fire. Sophie uttered a short scream and hit the fetid water with a splash. Reen lobbed a grenade, but her aim was thrown off when a round caught her shoulder and spun her with the force of the impact.

Roo and Mick returned fire while Charles snatched Sophie and Reen by the shoulders. He shoved them toward another small rise. The water wasn't as deep anymore. They were close to the edge of the swamp but now, another force of who knew how many people blocked their retreat to dry land.

The two Australians covered while the others managed to get to relative safety.

Booker had no cover and was now caught between the two groups of enemies. His teammates began to fire from their relatively protected positions. Mick and Reen worked on the group that had chased them from the swamp. Charles and Sophie fired at the new team. Roo pitched a grenade at the new enemy since they were closer to their location. The explosion, now on dry land, eliminated one of them. The others didn't even flinch at their comrade's demise and maintained their fire.

The Brit barreled to safety. One round hit him in the shoulder and he stumbled to his knees, but he scrambled up and pressed on. He didn't think he was bleeding, but it hurt like hell. Another round caught him in his right thigh, and he went down again. This time, he tasted blood. He'd bitten his tongue on the way down. It was harder to extricate himself from the mud that seemed more like sludge closer to the dry land.

A big hand caught hold of him and hauled him up. Charles half-dragged and half-helped him to safety. He took another strike in the side and when he tripped, he pulled his rescuer off-balance.

A round pounded into Charles' back. "Fuck!"

"Come on, big guy, we can't give up now."

"Who said anything about giving up?" he demanded through gritted teeth. He surged the last few feet and flung himself and his teammate behind the mound.

The firing stopped.

Sophie examined Booker but none of the rounds had penetrated the armor.

"Why'd they stop?" Reen asked.

"Whatever their reason, it can't be any good," Mick responded.

The Brit looked at the ground behind them. He couldn't see the edge of the swamp but the mist wasn't as thick, and the water was shallower than it had been before. They were close.

"This is our chance to get out," he said. "They're together now, which makes them outnumber us, but at least we aren't caught between the two forces anymore. We've got to make a break for it now."

"I can cover you," Charles volunteered.

"Okay. Let's get this show on the road," Booker said. "On my count, we're going to head toward that copse of grass over there. Ready? One...two..."

"Hello there!" A voice interrupted the count.

They all stilled. The man's accent was thick but he was still easy to understand.

"Have you given up?" he asked. His voice was deep and calm and he sounded almost bored with the whole affair.

"Go fuck yourself!" Roo yelled.

Reen punched him in the arm.

"What?" he asked.

"Shut the hell up."

"I'm going to ignore that and give you another chance. Give us Sophie Oladipupo, and the rest of you can live," the man said. "We only want her."

"Yeah, not fucking happening!" Mick said.

Sophie looked at them and shook her head. "I'll go."

"Like hell you will," Booker protested. "You're staying right where you fucking are."

"Booker, you guys have already done so much for me. I couldn't stand it if you got more hurt than you already are —or worse, killed. Just let me go."

"No fucking way," he stated bluntly.

"My patience is running out," the man called. "I'll give you ten more seconds to decide. Hand the girl over or die."

"I'll cover you guys, and you make it out of the swamp," Charles said.

"Charles, no. Let me do this. It's just me they want." She made a move to stand but he grabbed her and shoved her toward Reen.

"Not happening, Sophie. Don't go getting the idea of being a dumb superhero with all that sacrificial nonsense into your head. Everything's going to be fine, and we'll get out of here."

"Charles—" she started, but he shook his head.

"Nope. Not happening. Now, get ready to move."

"I've had enough of this," the man said.

Roo handed the American another grenade and nodded. The big man adjusted his grip on his Remington.

"Let's go," Booker said.

Charles launched himself upward and opened fire while the others moved away as fast as they could and stayed low. They added their firepower when they could, but he held his ground.

There were eight men in front of him. He could see them all now and they surged forward, preparing to close in for the kill.

"Not today, assholes," he said. One of his slugs caught a man in the center of his chest and he was eliminated.

He pushed forward, still firing, and emptied the shotgun. Calmly, he let his MCS drop to his side and exchanged it for the AK-47 he'd slung over his broad back. He aimed and held the trigger down. The barrage of rounds made the oncoming enemy pause and dive for cover.

Charles couldn't hear the others behind him anymore and he hoped they'd made it out of the swamp. He ducked behind an outcropping of grass, dropped the empty magazine, and shoved another home.

A man launched himself over his head and landed behind him. He fired the AK and double-tapped two rounds into the would-be assailant's chest. The man's body catapulted back and splashed into the muddy water of the swamp several feet away. The dark water around him writhed and black creatures swarmed the corpse, rushing for an easy meal.

From ahead of him, one of the attackers screamed. The shrieks were interrupted by splashes and hissing. It seemed the Zoo animals had taken an interest in what the humans were doing.

The American took advantage of the distraction to race to the next piece of cover.

A lanky man ran toward him as fast as the mud would let him. He fired two rounds, but his target saw him raise the barrel and flung himself aside, and the rounds whined harmlessly past him.

His enemy was out of sight, but he knew where he was. He pulled the pin on one of his last two grenades, tossed it to where he thought he was, and counted down the five seconds until the ordnance detonated. While he heard movement, he didn't know if that was the man in his death throes or simply getting farther away.

Charles knew he only had a few rounds left in the mag. He stood again, fired two shots, and broke into a run. The mud sucked at his feet and it took tremendous effort to keep his forward momentum. He paused to hurl his last grenade, hoping to slow down any pursuit.

Something careened out of the jungle and he instinctively jumped back. An enemy grenade landed in the mud next to him and stuck. He tried to scramble away but had only a managed a couple of meters when it detonated. Most of the shrapnel was thrown up over him, and his armor caught a couple of pieces, but three pinwheeled into his legs. He flung himself to the ground and the mad scramble knocked the breath out of him before pain lanced through his leg and made him grunt.

Several men ran past him in the heavy vegetation, but they either didn't see him or ignored him. He intended to make them pay. His expression grim, he raised his AK and fired through the bushes, but his magazine clicked empty after too few rounds

He reached toward his ankle and drew his Bowie knife. No matter what, he wouldn't go down without a fight, even if he couldn't seem to get himself to stand.

The lanky man who had been the target of his second-to-last grenade appeared in his line of sight, unscratched. He smiled at the American.

"You did well. I will enjoy killing you, which is something that hasn't happened in a while. It's too bad, really. Killing used to be so much fun," his adversary said.

Charles kicked at the man, but his muscles seemed uncooperative and his target easily avoided the kick.

"I'm Jam, by the way."

"I don't care," he said.

"No, I suppose you wouldn't. But I like my victims to know who I am before I kill them," he stated. He drew a 9mm Glock from a holster at his side and aimed at his forehead. "Any last words?"

"Fuck you."

Jam smiled an evil-looking smile. He made a show of tightening his trigger finger, then relaxing it, toying with him like a cat toying with a mouse. The man wanted him to break, he knew—maybe ask for mercy or even blanch. He refused to give him the pleasure and wouldn't look away.

The merc paused, and Charles thought there was the tiniest glimmer of respect in his eyes. He nodded, extended his arm, and brought the muzzle of the Glock a few meters from his head.

This is it. Killed by a human, not the Zoo.

Before he could pull the trigger, a massive black beast pounded into him from the side. The Glock went off and the round hurtled harmlessly into the mud of the swamp.

Charles tried to scramble to his feet and his whole body screamed in pain.

The air was filled with the sounds of howls and snarls

along with human screams. Giant wolf-like creatures attacked Jam and his men and savaged them with a determined kind of glee. The remaining men had to shift their focus and realign what they were doing, and that small fraction of time gave the advantage to the demiwolves. Several mutants were shot, but they swarmed the last few men and dragged the screaming humans down. One massive beast stood in the middle, a king surveying his legions.

Despite the pain and despite the danger, there was only one thought on the American's mind.

"Thor?"

The large demiwolf raised his head and his red eyes glowed. Jam's blood dripped from his jaws. Charles didn't recognize the long, spiraling black horns but he knew the tilt of the creature's head and the way it wagged its tail.

Booker splashed through the mud beside him and gripped him under the arms. "Time to go, mate. Did you think we were just going to leave you here?"

He pointed and the Brit froze. The vegetation hid much of the massacre, but there was no mistaking the dead bodies, human and beast. He started to raise his rifle when Charles forced it back down.

"Is that…Thor?" he asked.

"Yes."

The demiwolf tilted his head back and howled. The pack answered. Jam's men were dead, killed by Charles or ripped to pieces by the animals. Thor stood like a statue for a long moment and his eyes blazed red when he looked at the men.

He might be the same animal that Charles had rescued,

the same one with whom he'd played fetch with the tire, but this Thor was also different. He was *Zoo*, for lack of a better description.

And if he was Zoo, would he remember his friend?

The pack waited as if for a signal, and Booker fingered the trigger on his weapon.

With a soft yip that sounded sad to Charles, Thor picked up Jam's body in his jaws as if the man was a chew-toy and darted off into the jungle. The others followed suit and disappeared in an instant.

"Holy shit," the Brit said quietly.

Mick appeared at Charles' other side. "Let's get the fuck out of here."

With the two men's help, he was able to limp forward.

"This is a fucking nightmare," Booker stated.

"But we made it, didn't we? Did everyone get out of the swamp?" the American asked.

"Yeah, thanks to you covering us. Reen and Sophie are waiting," Mick added.

"What about the rest of those bastards? Are there any more of them?"

The Aboriginal pointed to the right where they could hear creatures squabbling like they did over a kill.

They slogged out of the swamp to join the others.

Finally, they reached where the rest had chosen to make their stand—a dense clump of brush on dry land—but it evidently had never come to that. Charles and Thor, and maybe some other Zoo creatures, had taken care of that.

Sophie punched the large man in the arm and hugged him. "You idiot. I thought you said no one was supposed to do anything stupid and sacrificial."

He smiled. "I wasn't doing anything like that."

"The wanker thinks he's some sort of hero," Roo said but he clapped his teammate on the shoulder. "Good to see you again, mate."

"Quit acting like I came back from the dead. Let's just get out of the Zoo."

"We sure showed them," the Aussie said.

"No, that was definitely the Zoo showing them," Booker contradicted. "So, let's get a move on before they decide to rip us apart too. We don't have enough ammunition for that."

Charles looked over his shoulder at the way they'd come. He could hear the sounds of creatures fighting over the remains. The animals snarled and howled their victory.

It had pained him to set Thor free and he'd worried about his friend's welfare, going out all alone like that. But he'd evidently done well for himself and now led a pack of his kind.

His kind, not humankind. He was where he'd be the happiest, even if it wasn't what would make Charles happy.

He took one last look at the killing fields the jungle had become. For a moment, he thought he saw a pair of glowing red eyes watching him leave, but when he focused on the place, they were gone.

CHAPTER TWENTY-THREE

The Zoo - Thor

Thor and the other demiwolves had reached Charles barely in time. He could smell that the man had been injured and knew the humans that had attacked him had death on their minds. They wreaked of malintent. Charles' scent was the strongest to him, the one that resonated the most. It clung with an intense familiarity, one that almost hurt. He recognized the scent of Booker and Roo. There were three other unknowns with Charles, but his smell on them lingered and protected them. It was a strange thought. These were friend-humans. The others were... not-friend-humans.

The other demiwolves didn't have the same drive as he did to protect Charles, but the feeling he had was so strong it prompted them to act. When Thor saw the human standing over Charles, his vision had gone red with rage. Everything in him told him to rip the man to shreds. It was the same feeling he got when a Pita plant was destroyed or taken.

He'd felt great satisfaction when he'd torn the man's throat out. The victory of the kill made his blood taste sweet.

The others decimated the other humans. Two of his pack were killed, but the end result was never in question. When Booker returned to help Charles, some of his pack-mates had moved in but Thor had growled a warning. The others were confused but the alpha didn't seem to care one way or another, so they moved on.

Thor carried the body out of the swamp. The pack watched but no one interfered. Demiwolves preferred not to eat humans, but he needed to eat this kill. The desire to make sure he'd conquered every part of the human who had tried to harm Charles overwhelmed him.

A vine snaked forward and wound around one of the man's ankles. It yanked the body away from him.

With a snarl, he lunged and dragged it back toward him. The vines resisted, and more tried to wrench the corpse from his jaws. Jam's arm ripped from the socket. Thor released it and grabbed hold of the body again, growling the whole time.

The pack watched him locked in his strange tug-of-war for the dead human.

The vines finally relented and claimed only an arm, and the rest of the body fell.

He howled his small victory and his pack howled with him. The alpha growled and the howling stopped, but Thor didn't mind.

Each piece seemed sweeter than the last. Charles was safe and this man couldn't inflict any more harm.

CHAPTER TWENTY-FOUR

The Wall, French Quarter

"What the fuck was all that?" Roo hissed when the door to the first wall shut and protected them from the Zoo.

They were covered in mud and blood and exhausted. Mick and Booker still had Charles propped between them. The wounds on his legs had stopped bleeding but he had difficulty standing on his own.

"It was my fault," Sophie said quietly. She stared blankly at the closed gate to the Zoo.

"How was any of that your fault?" Reen asked. She rolled her shoulder and winced. Even though they were almost out of the jungle, she checked Charles' bandages again while they waited for the door to open and let them into the Harvesters Camp.

It slid open and the guard stepped forward to help them through. "Do you need a medivac?"

"I can still walk," Charles said, although he didn't release his grip on Mick or Booker.

"You don't look too good," the man said. "You BOHICAs usually come out flying high. What happened?"

"Stop trying to get the latest fucking gossip," Roo said. "Mind your own goddamn business."

He held his hands up and simply watched them as they crossed to the next wall.

"My father sent those men after me. To kill you," Sophie said once they were far enough away from the guard to not be overheard.

"That still doesn't make it your fault," Reen said.

"But—"

"Enough, Sophie," Booker interrupted. "No one is blaming you. Now, let's all get to the infirmary and get patched up."

They returned to Fiddler's Green, tired but all in one piece. Charles still limped slightly, but the nurses had given him something for the pain and he said he was already feeling better.

"Those fuckers thought they could pull one over on us," Roo said. He sat with his arms folded behind his head and leaned back from the long table.

Reen rolled her eyes at him. "Now you're all bravado when they're all dead and we're out of the Zoo."

"Babe, when was I ever *not* bravado?" he asked and wiggled his eyebrows at her.

She shook her head and said, "That doesn't even make sense."

"How did the motherfuckers find us in the first place?" Mick asked.

"It was probably that asswipe who came and gave us the mission," she suggested.

"I guess we should vet these people more." Booker sounded disgruntled.

"I think the important thing is that we all made it out mostly unharmed," Charles reminded them. "The jerks got what they deserved for attacking us, and it's no big deal."

"What if they try again?" Sophie asked.

"Who?" Roo asked.

"They were definitely sent by my father. He won't stop. Especially now that another team has failed in killing me. My staying here will put you all in more danger."

"Hate to break it to you, Sophie, but we were already in danger before you got here. Your being here hasn't changed anything or made the stakes any higher. It's utter bullshit. You aren't going anywhere."

"Roo's right," Booker agreed. "You're one of us now, and we protect our own."

She shook her head. "I should go."

"Where would you go?" Reen asked.

Her eyes sad, she simply shrugged.

"You aren't going anywhere," the Brit stated firmly. "Whoever the fuck your father thinks he is, he has made the mistake of coming after all of us. It's personal now, and we aren't going to back down or run scared."

"You don't know my father."

"And the bastard doesn't know us," Mick said.

"Maybe we should take the fight to him," Roo suggested.

"You want to go back to Benin?" Reen asked.

"Don't be ridiculous, Roo," Sophie said. "You can't attack my father. He's...he's..." She frowned, unable to finish the sentence.

"He sure as fuck isn't untouchable," the Aussie retorted. "I've always liked the offensive."

"We aren't going to attack a wealthy businessman in another country, on his home turf, Roo," Reen protested. "Be reasonable."

"But he attacked us first!"

"And the asshole probably isn't worth all the trouble it would take to go down there and fish him out." Mick's tone was one of irritation. "I mean, I don't want to take what the wanker did laying down. But I'm no bogan. We'll just bide our time here."

"Mick's right," Charles conceded. "If this guy is really as crazy as he seems, he'll try again. We'll be better prepared next time." He stood from the table, winced, and stretched. "I don't know about you guys, but I'm beat. I'm going to turn in. I think this conversation can safely be put on pause until the morning."

One by one, they filtered out of the room until it was only Sophie and Booker left.

"You want a cuppa?" he asked. "I still have some tea I brought with me from Falmouth."

"Sure."

He began to prepare two cups and she watched him in silence.

"You really think it was your father?" he asked.

"Yes, I do. It has Arnaud written all over it."

"What makes you so sure?"

"Besides the fact that he's a coward and a Grade-A bastard? Do I need any more to go off of?"

"Probably."

"You don't believe me."

"I know we were purposefully attacked, but it doesn't mean that it was your father. We've pissed off a lot of people."

"Booker, they were specifically after me."

He passed her a cup and sat down beside her. "Well, that's true. Still wasn't your fault. I can see you want to argue with me on that still, but Teasy, you've got to believe me when I say you had nothing to do with this."

"But I was the one they were after!"

"Yes, but this is about your father, not you."

"I guess I don't understand what you're trying to say."

"I'm saying your father is the twat who decided killing his daughter was a good idea. You didn't put the idea into his head. You didn't tell him it would be a smart thing to hunt you. It's him and his hang-ups that are doing all of the damage."

Sophie traced circles on the tabletop with her finger. He watched her but didn't say anything more.

Finally, she looked at him. "I guess you're right."

"I am right."

"It still doesn't feel great."

"No, being the child of a fucked-up asshole never does."

"You the child of a fucked-up asshole, too?" Sophie asked, smiling at him over the rim of the cup.

He returned the smile, happy she seemed to be getting over her sullenness. "Yeah, my father is a certifiable douche."

"Did your father every try killing you?"

"Not on purpose or outright. On top of being a bastard, my father is also a coward who liked other people doing his dirty work for him."

She frowned, put her cup down, and placed her hand on his arm. He started at it.

"Did he hurt you?"

Booker shook his head, still staring at her hand.

"Booker."

"It's not important, Teasy. My family doesn't matter. They might be where I come from, but they sure as shit aren't where I'm going."

Sophie leaned back. "I wish you wouldn't call me that. It makes me feel like a little kid."

"You are a kid."

"No, Booker, I'm not. You might be older than me but you certainly aren't an old man. I'm not a child. I'm a woman."

"Sophie."

"What?"

"It's just…better, if I call you Teasy."

"Better for who?"

He didn't answer.

"That's what I thought," she said and smiled triumphantly at him.

Without thinking, he ran his finger across a small cut she had on her cheek. "Does this hurt?"

"No. It's only a scratch. You can kiss it better if you'd like," she said.

The light in her eyes told him she was teasing him, but he leaned forward and kissed her anyway.

CHAPTER TWENTY-FIVE

Fiddler's Green, Harvesters Camp

Charles found Booker on the first floor of the building, looking up furniture on the tablet. He sat behind the only desk in the large room with another chair pulled up in front of it. The American sat and shifted to get comfortable.

"What do you think of this one?" Booker asked and showed him a picture of a round conference table that could fit twelve chairs.

He shrugged. "It's fine."

"What about this?" He showed him a different table.

"Are you serious right now, Booker? You made me drag myself down the freaking stairs just to ask my opinion about furniture?"

"No, you're right. That's not why I called you down here." He put the tablet down and steepled his fingers.

"Am I in trouble?" Charles asked with a smile.

"What? No. Why would you say that?"

"It feels like I've been called to the principal's office or something. What's going on, Booker? I know you didn't ask me to help you pick out a table. And if you did, you better think of something else fast."

"Thor."

He nodded and leaned back in the chair, wincing a little. "That makes sense."

"How long have you known?"

"How long have I known what?"

"Come on, Charles. I know you're not dense."

"For a while, okay? Remember the mission Lester died on?"

"Hard to forget that."

"Right. Well, do you remember that giant trapdoor spider-thing that we crossed paths with but it was already dead?"

His companion frowned. "Not really."

"There was a giant bug, and we would've run right into its trap, but something killed it right before we got there. That something was Thor."

"You saw him kill it? I didn't see anything."

"No. I saw him after. I was Tail-end Charlie, and something made me pause. Thor stepped out and let me see him. He killed it. I'm pretty sure to keep us safe."

"You don't know that. Maybe he got caught and was fighting with it."

"That's possible, but my gut tells me it wasn't that."

"This isn't great, Charles."

He ran a hand through his short hair. "I know. I know it's not ideal."

"Not ideal? Charles, you were supposed to kill Thor because of what he did to the asshole he ate. Thor killed *and ate* a person, Charles. Another human being. If he was just a normal dog out in the world, he would've been put down for much less—just biting someone could have gotten him put down. I let it slide that you just released him into the Zoo. I know how hard that was for you, but I figured the Zoo would kill him. It didn't, obviously. And now we need to figure out what to do about it."

"Do we have to do something about it?"

"He's dangerous and obviously has a thing for killing people."

"Hey now, I don't think you can say that."

"Why not?"

"You're making it sound like Thor is just a maneater. He's not."

"He killed Bronson. Then he killed whoever attacked us. Who knows what else he's gotten up to? It seems he's joined a demiwolf pack. I shouldn't have to point out to you that all those things are bad, Charles. Very bad."

"He only killed Bronson because he was being attacked. It was self-defense. He killed that man, Jam, because he was going to kill me. He was just protecting me."

Booker pursed his lips and pinched the bridge of his nose. "Jesus, this is giving me a migraine."

"We aren't going to go hunt Thor. I'm sorry, Booker, but I won't do that."

"I know. We aren't going to hunt him down. But we should decide what to do if we see him again. We obviously can't tell anyone about this."

"What about the others? Roo should know Thor's still alive."

The Brit shook his head. "I think we should keep this

information between the two of us for now. It's sensitive. We'll just need to figure out what to do."

There was a long, pregnant pause before he continued. "You could have told me, you know."

"No, I couldn't. You'd have thought it was your duty to hunt him down."

"Maybe," he admitted. "Oh, I don't know."

"He's where he's supposed to be—in the wild, with his kind."

Charles didn't mention that he'd been trying to figure a way to reunite with Thor. He knew it wasn't right. Thor belonged with the other demiwolves but his heart ached for his friend.

"Okay. Is that all you wanted to talk about?" he asked in an effort to change the subject.

Booker cleared his throat but didn't look at him.

"Booker, what is it?"

"You know what, it's nothing. Never mind," the other man said and waved a hand in the air. "You can go on back to doing whatever it was you were doing."

He folded his arms and raised an eyebrow. "Spill it."

The man looked at him and exhaled a whoosh of air. "Fine. I kissed Sophie."

"You *what*?"

"Settle down! You're acting like it's the worst thing in the world. Fuck. It's not that bad. I just, sort of, you know. Made out with her."

"You…you made out with Sophie? Also, making out with someone and 'just a kiss' are two very different things, Booker. One kiss is okay, but if you're jumping down each other's throats it's time to pump the brakes."

"I don't like how shocked you are that I'm the one who kissed her. I have the same chance as Roo for that."

Charles laughed. "Roo definitely sees Sophie like a daughter." He grew serious again. "Booker, now I'm the one who needs to tell you the obvious—sex complicates things. Especially on a military team. We need to know that she isn't going to take priority with you. Or worse, if you two get into a fight, it can't compromise the rest of the team."

"I'm not having sex with her," Booker protested. "It was just a kiss."

"I thought you said you were making out?"

"Okay. It was a few heated kisses, but nothing further! It was a mistake. She was feeling down and needed reassurance and comfort. So, I just, you know."

"A hug or a pat on the back works, too."

"It's not that bad," he said defensively.

"Booker, it sounds like you're trying to convince yourself that it wasn't that bad. Do you have feelings for her?"

"I don't know."

"Well, you better figure it out. If we were any other place at any other time, I'd say, what the heck, go for it. But we're not. We're here, in the Zoo. I don't think it's a good idea."

"I know. I'll back off. I won't do that again."

Charles stood and nodded. "Good. I'm glad you told me, though. We'll figure it out."

The Brit watched him climb the stairs. He pinched the bridge of his nose and hoped he hadn't just lied to his friend.

CHAPTER TWENTY-SIX

**Cotonou, Benin**

The flash of cameras was almost blinding, which was why Arnaud Oladipupo wore sunglasses at night. He stepped out of the Rolls-Royce Phantom VI after his driver opened the door and put a hand up in a gesture he hoped would work to both say hello and deter the gathered journalists. They were like sharks in chummed waters.

Sophie's disappearance was the chum, of course. Which was what he wanted, although it didn't make being constantly photographed any better. It meant they were still interested, however, which helped his cause.

"Mr. Oladipupo! Mr. Oladipupo! Any news on Sophie?" one reporter yelled.

"Mr. Oladipupo, is it true you've put a bid in for the presidency?"

"Can you answer the rumors of you hiring mercenary teams to look for your daughter?"

He ignored all the questions and entered the cool silence of the lobby of his building. The door whispered shut behind him, effectively cutting off all questions. The heavily tinted, mirrored windows prevented anyone from seeing inside.

Arnaud strode across the lobby to his private elevator and took it to his office. Angelique stood waiting for him as the elevator doors opened.

"Not now," he said.

"But, sir, you're going to want to hear this," she replied and followed closely on his heels.

He poured himself a drink from his wet bar and held the amber liquid up to the light. As he stared out his window, he could feel her staring at him, waiting for him to turn and look at her. She was a good assistant but damn needy. That might have been his fault, he conceded. He probably shouldn't have slept with her.

Finally—when he felt sufficient time had passed to send a message—he turned and focused on her. She was a mediocre lay but a hell of an assistant. Her cat-eye reading glasses were in place and she held a pen poised over the small legal pad she carried.

"What is it?" he asked as he sat. He didn't motion for her to sit, so she remained standing and shifted slightly on her spiky heels. The ones she wore today were lime-green and prompted him to consider fucking her again.

"News has arrived back from the Zoo, sir."

"Excellent. I need good news. Tell me how Jam did."

"Well, sir, he failed."

Arnaud set his tumbler down carefully. "Come again?"

"He failed."

"Failed as in didn't kill those mercenaries?"

"Correct."

"Failed as in those assholes are still out there?"

"Yes."

"Where the fuck is he? I'm going to kill him."

"He's already dead, sir."

"They killed him?"

"Everything points to their death. They went into the Zoo for the mission and never returned. All communications were cut. His targets did emerge, though, bloodied but alive."

He considered throwing the tumbler but downed its contents instead and gripped the glass tightly. It was truly unfortunate that he'd used the last of his assets to send Jam after those bastards. He projected wealth and prosperity, but the truth was that he hadn't been in the black for a while now. But for now, he needed to maintain appearances. Once he became president, all his financial problems would be solved.

Angelique was still in the room.

"Is there more?"

"Yes, sir. See, it's believed that Sophie is still with the mercenaries. A young woman matching her exact description was relayed by Jam's team before they were all killed, and she came out of the Zoo with them."

"She's with the mercenaries? Did they kidnap her?"

"We don't know."

Arnaud did throw the tumbler that time. He aimed it at Sophie's face in the portrait. The crystal shattered and the glass over her face cracked and spidered out to hide her features.

"Get out of my office."

Angelique didn't need to be told twice.

"So, little bitch, you've decided to play mercenary?" he muttered to the distorted image. "I'll leave you to your games for now, but I will come for you. Don't worry about that."

He rose from his desk and looked out over the city. Despite his rage, he felt a bizarre swell of pride. His daughter was wily and she got that from him. If only she wasn't so hard to kill, it would make his life a whole lot easier.

CHAPTER TWENTY-SEVEN

Fiddler's Green, Harvesters Camp

"I'm not hurt that badly, Booker," Charles said. "None of us are."

"He's right. I feel fucking fantastic. I don't think we need R-n-R," Roo interjected.

Mick tossed the parachute cord with which he was trying to play cat's cradle onto the table. "Fuck it. I'm tired. It's pointless pretending we aren't. I'm with Booker. Let's take a bit of a rest. We can afford it. Right?"

"Yes, we can afford it," Booker confirmed.

"I feel like all we've been doing is resting!" the Aussie protested. "We've taken so many goddamn breaks, it's like we already are on some vacation. Come on, mate, let's stay with the action. We don't want everyone else saying the BOHICA Warriors have gone bloody soft."

"No one is saying that, Roo. Besides, we haven't been taking that many breaks. A lot has happened. We need time to recoup. I would rather not take a break, but we can afford it. What we can't afford is to take any more risks or big hits like that last one. I was reminded of my fucking mortality on that, and that's not something I like," Booker said.

"I'm also with Booker," Reen said. "We're tired. Tired people make mistakes. It's not smart to keep pushing. It's not like we're running against any sort of clock here."

"Do I get a say in this?" Sophie asked.

"It's already been decided," the Brit said.

"Has it?" Roo challenged.

Charles stood and didn't do a good job of hiding his wince. "Who am I kidding? What's a week off? It's not going to kill us. If anyone needs me, I'll be out working on the Mule."

Reen frowned at his retreating back. She caught Booker's arm and pulled him aside. "Do you know what's wrong with Charles?"

"How do you mean?"

"It's not like him to push so hard. He's usually good at reading himself and situations. Is he more hurt than we thought?"

"No."

"Then what is it?"

"It's nothing."

She didn't look convinced and dragged him down the hall to the armory so no one could hear.

"Are you two going to rut in another room? Is that why you're suggesting we take a fucking break?" Roo yelled after them.

Before they were fully out of the room, he caught sight of Sophie's glare and Mick's eye-roll.

"Fuck you, Roo!" Reen yelled over her shoulder. She

shut the door to the armory. "Spill it, Booker." She folded her arms over her chest.

He copied her pose. "There's nothing to spill, Reen."

"I don't believe you."

"I gathered that."

"It's just me, Booker. You can tell me."

"It's nothing. Honestly, Reen. He really is just tired, I think. We all are. It's nothing to worry about."

"You're saying there is something there, though."

The Brit didn't answer.

She took a step toward him and stared relentlessly at him. They were the same height and it was an easy thing for her to do, but he didn't relent. He kept his posture loose and non-threatening.

"Fine," she said. "Don't tell me. If you don't want to share, then it clearly isn't something that'll endanger the team. But if it turns out it *is* something that will endanger us, I'm going to fucking kill you. The both of you. Remember that." She stalked out of the room.

Booker knew Thor's presence in the Zoo was weighing on Charles, but he'd told him not to tell anyone else. The same rule applied to him but he considered her statement anyway and didn't think something like that was a danger to the team.

Not much, at least.

Sophie slipped into the armory. "Oh, you're alone." She feigned surprise.

"Teasy," he said.

She frowned at him. "I thought we were over that."

He grunted.

"What'd Reen want?"

"She's just worried about Charles."

"She came on pretty strong, hauling your ass out of the room like that. Is that all she wanted?"

"Yes, Sophie. That's all she wanted."

The girl stepped closer and brushed a piece of sand off his arm. "It's amazing how sand gets everywhere here. With the jungle and everything, you forget it's the middle of the desert." She didn't take her hand off his arm. "I thought you were the leader. Do you really just let everyone boss you around?"

"Hold up," he said and put space between them. "I'm not the leader. Sure, I take point a lot, but we don't really have a designated leader. Everyone else is former military. Reen was a US Marine NCO. She gives me quite a bit of defer-ence, but Marines take charge. It's part of their DNA, and she's led others as much as I have. It's not a competition. We're a team."

"I didn't mean to upset you."

"You didn't upset me." He pushed the door open and turned to her. "Look, Sophie, I think you're great. I'm clearly attracted to you, but we just can't."

"Why not?"

"It's better this way."

"For who?"

"The team. BOHICA Warriors. You."

"I think I can decide what's good for me and what's not, Booker," Sophie said. "Look, I get it. And you're right. Honestly? This is a fucked-up situation and we were just carried away in all the emotional high that came from the adrenaline dump we experienced. It's okay. It was fun. I wouldn't be opposed to doing that—or more—again. But you're probably right." She brushed past him on her way out the door.

He watched her go and frowned, unsure if the outcome was actually what he wanted.

"How's the leg today, Charles?" Sophie asked. She settled herself cross-legged on the Mule's bed.

He tinkered with the vehicle. Reen sat in the shade, cleaning under her fingernails with her knife.

"Fine," he said and stretched to his full height from leaning over the open hood. "It was only some minor wounds in the end, and that new stuff they have that's supposed to be all super-healing or whatever seemed to help. Either that or it wasn't as bad as anyone thought."

"Is there something wrong with it? With the Mule?"

"No."

"Then why are you spending all this time working on it?"

"Because."

"Come on, Charles. You know that's not an answer."

He grunted.

"You're really feeling better?"

"Yes."

"You feeling up to the gun range?"

Charles wiped his hands on a rag. "We were there yesterday."

"Is that supposed to make me not want to go today?"

The American shrugged.

"Well, it doesn't. I need all the practice I can get."

"You're doing fine."

"Fine isn't great."

Mick strolled up to them, whistling. He'd taken to disappearing for hours at a time during the past few days.

Roo came out and joined them. He raised an eyebrow at the Aboriginal. "So, you're back."

"Just went for a walk."

"Is that what you're calling it now?"

"I don't know what you're talking about."

"Oh, leave him alone, Roo," Reen said. "If the man doesn't want to share where his dick's been—I mean, where he takes his walks, he doesn't have to."

"Okay. I see how it is." Mick smirked. "You're all ganging up on me now, are you? Well, let me tell you fuckers, you won't get anything out of me."

She stood and stretched. "Let's not go to the gun range, Sophie, but I'll spar with you if you want."

"Great!"

The woman drew a large circle in the sand and stepped inside. "Remember the rules? If I can pin you for more than fifteen seconds, I win. If you step out of the circle, I win. If I can—"

"If you can get me into any position where I'd be dead, you win. Yes, I know," her opponent interrupted.

Reen smiled. "Let's begin."

The two women circled each other. Reen was calm and kept her stance loose, although her hands were up slightly. Sophie bounced with nervous energy, her lips pressed into a determined line and her brow furrowed in concentration.

The older woman lashed out first. She swept her adversary's legs out from under her with a well-placed kick. The girl landed hard but bounced up, her hands raised to guard her face. Reen smiled.

"That was pretty close to the edge of the circle. Roo, was she still in?" she asked.

"Yep, she's still in the game."

Sophie attempted a jab and her opponent easily dodged it.

"You're telegraphing," Mick said. "Everyone could see that move coming. You scrunch your nose up before you do anything, so keep that in mind too."

She nodded while keeping her eyes locked on the other contender.

Reen snapped out a front kick. Sophie stepped around closer to her and avoided taking the full force of the kick. She wound her arm around her adversary's leg and dropped to her back to catapult her over her head.

The woman landed lightly and rolled into a crouched position, still within the circle. She grinned. "Very good."

She'd no sooner spoken when she launched herself forward, her movements a blur. The younger woman did her best to block and dodge the punches but many of them struck home. She managed to land a few for herself but not nearly as many as she would have liked.

"Don't hold back," Reen said as she pinned her to the ground, her elbow putting pressure on Sophie's throat. "If you train holding your punches, chances are you'll accidentally hold your punches when it comes to the real thing. Follow through. I can take it."

"That's fifteen seconds," Roo announced.

Reen released her, stood up, and offered her hand. She let her help her up.

"Who's next?" the girl asked, panting a little. She was covered in sand and sweat.

"Why don't you try to take Charles down?" the other woman suggested.

"No way," the American said.

"Oh, why not?" Sophie asked. "You said your leg was basically better. We don't want you falling behind."

"I don't want to fight you, Sophie."

"It's only pretend fighting, Charles," she said.

"There's no such thing as 'pretend' fighting. There's full-power and half-power," he retorted.

She shrugged, and Reen said, "She needs to know how to take down someone bigger than her."

"Fine."

He stepped in front of her. She looked up at him and grinned.

"You ready?" he asked.

"Charles, you aren't supposed to ask me if I'm ready. You're just supposed to—" She stopped as his fist rocketed toward her face. Acting on instinct, she flung her forearm up and to the side and deflected the blow, but barely.

"Don't try to engage him directly just yet," Reen instructed. "He's a lot bigger than you are, and he has a whole lot more power. But you're potentially faster."

"Potentially?" Sophie asked and dodged another swing.

"Yes. I mean, right now he's still not at one hundred percent, which you should use to your advantage. As a general rule, big guys aren't usually lightning fast. Charles here is one of the exceptions, but like I said, he's still getting over his injuries."

The girl dodged again, breathing hard. Charles swung with his left hand. She ducked out of the way and to the side, landed a punch to his ribs, and immediately stepped away and out of his reach.

"Hitting him with your fist isn't going to be the best bet," Mick suggested. "The dude's built like a tank. You won't have much luck inflicting pain on anyone but yourself. Use your elbows. It'll still hurt, but probably not as much and it'll do more damage."

On her next offensive move, she did what he suggested and drove her elbow into Charles' side. He grunted.

"There you go!" Roo crowed. "Now kick his ass, Sophie."

The big man blocked her attempts to get closer to him. His blows landed but he held back the force of each one. She still felt it, however, and she was glad he hadn't actually tried to hurt her.

"Okay, Sophie. Let's try something new," Reen proposed. "You're going to take Charles to the ground."

"I am?"

"She is?" Charles asked and glanced at his fellow American.

"Yes, she is. Here's how it's going to work. Next time he punches, instead of deflecting his arm out, you're going to push his arm toward his body. Deliver a punch to his jaw. Swing around, step on the back of his ankle, then grab his face and break his nose."

"I don't know if I like the nose-breaking part," he protested.

Sophie frowned. "I'm not sure I get what you're asking."

"Watch," Reen said. "Mick, punch me. Just a straight jab to the face."

He looked reluctant but punched anyway and she demonstrated the move. She blocked his arm inwards with her right arm and wrapped her hand around his wrist to keep his arm out of position. Her left hand connected with the side of his face as she stepped forward, swung her leg around, and stepped on the back of his ankle. Both actions forced him to stagger back. She released his arm, wound hers around his neck, and drove her left elbow down, stopping short of the tip of his nose. It all happened in a matter of seconds.

"I don't know if I can do that," the girl said. "Hell, I'm not sure I know what you did."

Reen pulled Mick to the upright position. He glared at her and rubbed his neck. "We'll do it again, but slower this time."

After watching a few times at a slower speed, Sophie nodded. "Okay. Let me try."

Charles threw the punch more slowly than normal to give her time to attempt the maneuver. It worked and brought him to the sand with a grunt.

"Oh, shit, your legs! Sorry!" she said and hauled him up as best she could.

"Don't worry about it."

"Are you okay?"

"I'm fine."

"Do it again," Reen said.

She managed to fell him again. Each punch he threw

grew faster until he was almost at full speed and she could still take him down.

"Okay," he said as he pushed himself up from his knees and breathed hard. "I think I've had enough for today. Let's all take a break."

"What's going on out here?" Booker asked.

"Sparring," Sophie said. "Reen's teaching me how to take down someone of Charles' size."

"You won't be fighting anyone Charles' size. You won't be fighting at all. At least not people," he said.

"You don't know that," she challenged. "Besides, it's a good skill to have."

"Fair enough."

"Booker," Roo said, "we've been sitting on our hands here for almost a week. Charles is clearly better. When do we go back out?"

"Tomorrow. I got us a mission."

CHAPTER TWENTY-EIGHT

The Zoo

Mick hacked through the dense vines in front of him. He was glad he wore a visor as the orange goo from the vegetation splattered all over him.

"How much farther is this supposed to be?" he called over his shoulder.

"It can't be much farther. I mean, how thick can these vines be? We have to almost be to the center," Booker responded. He was behind and a little to the left of him and hacked at the plants with his own machete. They were clearing a path for the others—or trying to, at least. The vines seemed to grow back almost as fast as they were cut.

"What is it we're looking for, again?" his teammate asked and grunted as he sliced through a particularly thick creeper.

"Glowing mushrooms."

"Right."

"I don't like this one fucking bit, Booker. It's goddamn claustrophobic in here," Roo yelled and disentangled himself from a vine that had wound itself around his thigh. "Motherfucker." He sliced through it and it fell limply to the ground. Orange goo oozed from the fresh incision.

"Hey, Sophie, where are you?" Booker asked.

"I'm right—ouch—I'm right here," she answered from where she hacked her own path forward beside Roo.

"You okay?" he asked her.

"Yeah, I'm fine."

"I'm okay too, don't worry about me," the Aussie grumbled.

"Should I come back there and hold your hand, bunj? Would that make you feel less left out?"

"Fuck you."

"How's it going in there?" Reen's voice was muffled and sounded far away. She and Charles stood on the outside of the vine-laden tree the others attempted to cut their way through, standing guard in case the others' activity attracted the notice of other Zoo critters.

The American's gaze scanned the surrounding jungle while she tried to peer into the vines to see the rest of the team. A blur of movement caught his eye and he turned and caught a flash of black fur. He thought he saw red eyes deeper into the jungle, but they were gone too fast for him to be sure. To be safe, he kept his shotgun trained on the spot but didn't see any more movement.

"What is it?" she asked.

"I thought I saw something."

She squinted into the jungle but shook her head. "I've got nothing. You know what I've decided? This whole place gives me the fucking creeps. Everything here seems to be alive in the worst way. Even the goddamn plants want you dead. You just feel watched constantly because you are. It's the worst."

"You mad I recruited you?"

"Hell, no. Just making an observation."

They could barely hear the chops of the others' machetes anymore. The tree in front of them was massive, larger than the normal Zoo trees. Vines draped from it and coiled around it like a protective shell. It had been easy to locate, but reaching the objective had proven difficult. The small, glowing mushrooms they'd been tasked with retrieving grew on the bark of the tree at its base.

"Found it!" Mick called and slid his machete into its sheath at his thigh so he could maneuver better. He withdrew a small paring knife and jabbed it into the bark of the tree around the base of the round mushroom. It glowed an eerie blue that pulsed like a heartbeat. The trunk gave a shuddering groan when he stabbed it to slice the fungus free. Hundreds of them pulsed along its base. Booker stood shoulder-to-shoulder with him to harvest them. Sophie and Roo continued the assault on the vines to prevent them from closing in again.

"That smells like shit," the Aussie said. The deep blue sap that oozed from the holes in the bark gave off an unpleasant odor. "That better not be releasing some sort of poisonous gas."

Booker hesitated, then dropped another specimen into his sample container. He snapped the lid shut. "Shit. I don't know about that. Let's not stick around to find out, yeah?"

They fought their way out of the creepers and called out to Reen and Charles to get their bearings. The way they'd come had already been erased by the ever-coiling vines, despite their efforts.

"At least these fuckers don't have teeth," Roo said as he lopped through another twisted collection of fibrous tentacles.

They made it out and paused to catch their breaths.

"How was it?" Reen asked.

Mick and Booker gave their sample containers to Charles, who secured them in his pack.

"It was a regular fucking picnic," Roo said.

"Could've been worse." The Aboriginal shrugged. "The vines were a real bitch to cut through, but at least they didn't have teeth."

"Let's get going back to camp," Booker said. "I'd rather not be gone late. Franco is expecting these back. Not to mention, this weird sap stuff from the vines doesn't seem like a great thing to have on you for a long period of time."

Mick tried wiping some of the orange matter off on a nearby tree. He only succeeded in getting dirt and moss particles stuck to him. "Of course, that won't fucking work."

They started back to the gate. Mick had point and Booker took up the rear.

The Brit thought he saw movement to the right of their column from the corner of his eyes but when he turned to look, there was nothing.

The threat wasn't from the side. A roar split the silence and a large bear-like creature burst from the jungle behind them, bowled into Reen, and knocked her on her ass. She struggled to raise her rifle while avoiding sharp teeth and claws. It unhinged its jaws like a snake and uttered an eerily human-sounding scream as it leaned in to bite.

Sophie stepped forward and placed the muzzle of her M5 almost against the base of the bear-mutant's neck and fired twice. The rounds found their mark and bypassed the heavy skull as they plunged into its brain. The large animal collapsed onto the other woman.

It took both Roo and Charles to push the carcass off her. Reen scrambled to her feet and brushed herself angrily in an effort to get the creature's blood off. She cleaned her knife and picked tufts of fur free from where she'd stabbed it in the stomach. Her rifle had been a lost cause in the beast's embrace, so she'd switched to her blade and managed to land a single slash before Sophie made her efforts moot—luckily for her. It was doubtful that she could have gotten through the muscle and fat in time to do much damage.

"Quick thinking, Sophie," Booker said.

"Well done, Sophie!" Roo said and gave her a fist-bump.

"You okay?" she asked Reen.

"I'm fine. Thanks for the save, sister."

"Any time," she said, positively glowing as she relished the praise.

"Let's keep moving." Booker gave the huge creature one last baleful look.

Mick set the pace again, steady and fast. They didn't have any more close encounters on their way back to the gate. Sophie tripped over a snaking vine once but Booker caught her on her first bounce and hauled her back to her feet.

He hung back a moment with Charles as the others disappeared through the gate.

"I think we were followed," he said and nodded toward the edge of the jungle where a pair of glowing red eyes blinked at them before they vanished.

His companion nodded. "The whole time, I felt like something was watching."

"You think it was Thor?"

"I do."

"Hey! What's the hold-up? Come on!" Roo yelled from inside the wall. "They're going to get pissed if they have to hold the door open much longer."

"What do you think it means?" Charles asked as they strode across the sand to the gate.

"I don't know, but I don't think it's a bad thing. At least not yet. We'll just have to keep an eye on things."

CHAPTER TWENTY-NINE

The Zoo - Thor

Thor was still growing. He had outgrown all the other demiwolves and was formidable, his spiraling horns sharp and strong. With his increased size, he felt powerful—and he felt moved to action. But what kind of action?

The alpha watched him snap at a butterfly that flitted through the clearing they were resting in. His leg was the source of a dull throbbing pain that crept slowly into the rest of his body. He could smell the sickness there. As an alpha, he'd been hurt before but always, he healed quickly. This time was different, and he didn't understand why. With stoic acceptance, he didn't dwell on it but kept to his routine.

The other pack members had now begun to give deference to Thor. When he had decided to hunt and kill the humans, the leader hadn't protested, in a large part because he enjoyed a good chase the same as the next demiwolf. It had bothered him that the youngster had spared some of the humans. That was out of the ordinary, and it made him uncomfortable. There was some kind of connection between him and those particular humans, but he didn't understand what it was. He did understand that it was unnatural, however.

A she-demiwolf slunk up next to Thor and licked tentatively behind his ears. The alpha growled low reflexively. None of the others heard him. He knew his rival would continue to grow stronger. He wanted to eliminate him but knew that wouldn't be possible. There were pack forms that had to be followed.

Thor's interest in the humans was intriguing. The alpha recognized it for what it was—a weakness. He knew that he could exploit that weakness and only needed to learn how.

With this in mind, he left the pack and trotted into the jungle. While he knew leaving them under Thor's care might not be the best idea, it was necessary. He ran through the jungle and ignored the shooting pain in his hind leg.

His efforts were rewarded when he scented the humans. By now, he could sense the difference in humans, exactly as he did between the members of his pack, and these were the same ones his rival had spared. He crept forward to observe them. If they were Thor's weakness, he knew he needed to find out more about them.

He watched them and remained out of sight, although he was afraid he'd been seen by two of them. While he saw only those, he could smell others. They soon hacked their way out of the vine-covered tree and stood talking to one another. The alpha wondered what would happen if he leapt in and ripped their throats out now, simply to get it over with, but he chose not to. He knew that it wasn't the time for that yet.

Thor needed to be a witness to their deaths. He needed to see the humans' lifeblood draining from them. The alpha would make him see. He'd make the upstart watch and would re-establish himself as the be-all and end-all of the pack.

The animal kept pace easily with the humans as they crashed and thrust their way through the jungle. Humans were always so loud and careless.

The lone demiwolf scented the bear mutant before he saw it. Its odor was unmistakable, pungent and strong. They were stupid but deadly, nonetheless. He wondered how the humans hadn't detected its presence yet. Perhaps they were as dumb as the animal that was about to attack them.

He watched as the bear-like creature attacked the humans and knocked one to the ground, its jaws extended to kill, but that was not what happened. To his surprise, the demiwolf saw one of the other humans step forward and use their fire-stick. The animal collapsed and its bitter-smelling blood tickled his nostrils.

The humans rolled the creature off their companion and helped her up before they continued. The alpha hesitated. He'd contemplated attacking the two only moments before, but he'd forgotten that the humans could be deadly. Sometimes, they seemed so weak and helpless, easy to kill, but at other times, they did the killing.

At that point, he almost turned back, but he had to learn more and continued to follow them, but at a safer distance. The humans encountered no more attacks, which disappointed him a little. He'd hoped the rest of the Zoo would do the hard part of eliminating them, but it seemed it would have to be him.

Finally, he stopped when they reached the monstrosity of concrete and fire that was the wall. He'd tried to cross it with the gorgorexes but hadn't been so lucky. Now, he watched them from the cover of the jungle.

Two of the humans stopped before they entered the hole that had opened in the side of the wall. The alpha observed their interaction and used his eyes, ears, and nose to gather as much information as possible. He was sure that the taller and darker human was the one on which Thor focused. When that one had been threatened, he had gone into beserker-mode and destroyed the man who had attacked him.

This was the human who was most important to him. If he wanted to truly damage his rival, he would have to find a way to kill that human.

He lost interest when the humans disappeared inside the wall, turned away from the strip of sand, and ran back into the jungle, ignoring the ache in his bones. His mind settled on his choice. He would challenge Thor for putting worthless humans ahead of the pack and he'd make him watch him kill the human. Then, he'd rip the upstart's throat out.

CHAPTER THIRTY

__Fiddler's Green, Harvesters Camp – Three Months Later__

"How do you feel about adding more people to the team?" Mick asked and shoved his dinner plate aside. He'd wiped it clean of all remnants of food. Sophie had proven herself to be a more than capable chef, and the BOHICA team was grateful for it.

Booker didn't look up from his tablet. "I'm assuming you're only saying this because you have someone in mind."

"Whose turn is it to do the dishes?" Sophie asked.

"Charles'," Reen announced and nudged him with her elbow.

He grunted, but stood and started clearing the table.

"Who do you have in mind?" she asked Mick after Charles took his plate.

"I met this man, Tatsuki Chiyotanda. People call him Stone. He's a soldier of fortune and has been for a long time. I think he'd make a great addition."

Booker glanced up then. "Stone?"

"Yeah."

"And you like this guy?"

"He seems like he'd be a good fit. He's reliable."

"I don't think it'd be that big of a deal," Roo said. "I mean, after the fucking shitstorm that was Lester, maybe we should come up with a better recruiting method. We don't want a repeat."

"What about a trial basis?" Reen suggested. "For most other jobs, there's that period where you're trying to figure out if you like the employer and they're trying to figure out if they like you. We can have a three or four mission tryout period or something like that. We can see them in action and decide how they work with the team."

"That would be a good way to vet them," Sophie said. "Make sure they aren't from my father."

"We haven't had any attacks on us since that one swamp rescue mission. I don't think your father is actively seeking to kill us," Charles interjected.

"Don't assume that, Charles. You don't know him. But even if my father's out of the picture, it would be a good idea to evaluate peoples' loyalties."

"And capabilities," Reen added. "I don't want no lightweights with us."

"That is a good idea," Booker said. He didn't look up from his tablet and Sophie didn't acknowledge that he had spoken. The others exchanged a glance. It had become painfully obvious that the two of them avoided actually speaking or looking at each other when in the BOHICA Warriors' presence.

Roo kicked Mick's shin under the table and his friend nodded. Reen's eyebrow twitched.

"I don't see what harm it would do," the Brit said. "If you think the guy's legit, bring him in to meet the team, Mick."

Tatsuki "Stone" Chiyotanda was a somber man who appeared to be in his forties, although it was hard to tell. His head was shaved, and he had a tattoo of an onryō at the base of his skull. The creature's arms were spread wide, and its eyes seemed to blaze at anyone who attempted to approach the man's back. He wore all black and had a Howa Type 89 slung across his back and a Minebea 9mm machine pistol strapped to his front.

"Everyone, meet Stone," Mick said. "Stone, this is everyone."

The man studied the BOHICA team and inclined his head slightly. "Nice to meet you."

Reen stepped forward and shook his hand. "I'm Reen. This is Charles, Booker, Sophie, and Roo."

"So, what's your specialty?" Booker asked.

"Killing."

"Right." He scrutinized the wiry man. "Yes, but are you good at it?"

"I've lived this long. I'd say I do a decent enough job. I understand you're looking to expand your team?"

"We were thinking about it," Charles said. "You can stick around on a trial basis."

"Works for me," he responded curtly. "Do I bunk here or elsewhere?"

The Brit glanced at the others. "You could stay here,

although we don't really have that much space. We could put a cot downstairs for you."

He nodded. "I'll go get my things."

After he left, Mick raised his hands. "In my defense, I didn't expect him to come off so creepy and weird. He seemed perfectly normal in all our other conversations. Christ. Sorry."

"No big deal," Reen said. "That's why there's a trial period. Booker, are you really going to have him bunk downstairs? Isn't there extra space in the room you have now?"

"I'm not sleeping in the same room as that fucking weirdo," Roo said.

"I'm kind of with Roo on this one," Charles said. "He gives me the creeps a little. We'll have to see if he's not just overcompensating and trying to come off the way he thinks we want."

"Where'd you pick this guy up, Mick?" Sophie asked.

"The gun range."

"Sounds like a great place to meet people."

"He's a great shot. I'm sure he'll tone down the weird vibes once he's comfortable. Just give him a chance."

"We'll give him a chance because we said we would," Booker said. "I'm going to stop by Dan's and pick up an extra cot and some bedding for him. Anyone want to come?"

"Does it look like we're having a fucking slumber party? What, are you going to ask us to walk to the bathroom with you next?"

"All right, all right. Forget I asked. Jesus, you don't need to be such a bleddy wanker all the time, Roo."

"That's part of my charm."

Booker shook his head and walked out of the room. He hoped Stone didn't turn out to be as strange as the first impression of him had been. Still, he'd give him the benefit of the doubt for the moment. Maybe he had simply tried to project a persona, although it wasn't a great move with a team that had to work together as a machine. His answer to the simple question had been stupid. Any idiot could kill something. He wanted to know if a person had skills or anything else to bring to the group to make it better.

When he entered the shop, Dan was arguing with a young man in blue jeans and a t-shirt. He waited on the sidelines for him to notice him. The young man was dusty and had a mostly empty-looking duffle bag at his feet.

The supplier noticed him and waved him over. "Booker, maybe you can talk some sense into this fucking idiot."

"What's going on?" he asked.

"The kid just showed up without any money and is expecting to be put to work. He came here because he thought I'd be the best place to start." Dan scoffed. "What can I get you?"

"I'm going to need a couple of cots and some bedding to go with it," Booker said.

The other man nodded and disappeared to get what he'd asked for, grumbling about the kid as he went.

The Brit studied the stranger. He looked young, but he couldn't really tell his age exactly. While he could've been a teenager, he could've as easily been in his early twenties.

"I'm Booker," he said and extended his hand, "and you are?"

"Elijah Buchholz."

"Where are you from, Elijah?"

"Brooklyn."

"How old are you?"

"Twenty-five."

He raised an eyebrow.

"Twenty-two."

"What brings you to the Zoo?"

"You sure ask a lot of questions."

"Yeah, and you aren't in a position to have any snark about it, either. I can maybe help you out, but I have to figure out why you're here first."

"I heard you could make a shit-ton of money out here."

"You heard, huh?"

"Yeah. That, and I have nowhere else to go."

"Why didn't you join the US military?"

"Can't."

"And why's that?"

"Criminal record, man. They don't want that shit polluting their precious system. But fuck them. That's why I'm here. Besides, the military is a shitty place to earn money. I want to be rich."

"That's not exactly a great reason to do something like this, Elijah. I'll be honest, it makes you sound like a liability to me."

The young man grimaced but, with a contrite expression on his face, said, "Look, I'm a hard worker, okay? I was a dumb kid when I was arrested. I got mixed up in the wrong crowd. I'm just trying to earn a living, and it's fucking hard when people see *felon* on your resumé. I just assumed people here wouldn't judge, you know?"

Booker gave him a long look. The youngster didn't

sound like the pretentious asshole he'd projected a moment earlier. That was two people in a span of ten minutes who were trying to impress people—and made a bad impression.

"How's your aim?"

"Good. I mean, I'm no goddamn sniper, but I can hold my fucking own."

"How are you under pressure?"

"Cool as a cucumber," he said and a touch of his bravado crept back, all belied by the smile that had appeared.

Dan returned with the cots and bedding. The Brit paid quickly for everything without bothering to negotiate, which the supplier seemed bummed out about.

"How about picking those up?" Booker told Elijah.

"Why? I'm not your fucking ser—oh," he said when it dawned on him what was happening. "You're giving me a shot?"

"We'll have to put you to the test, kid. Think you can handle that?"

"Yes, sir!" he said and almost shouted it. "I'm just looking for someone to give me a fucking break, that's all."

"You might've gotten your chance. Don't get your hopes up too high, though. You have to be approved by the whole team."

"You have a whole team?"

"I'm part of a company."

"Which one?"

"BOHICA Warriors."

"No way! I've actually heard of you guys. I mean, around here, you're hot shit."

He grunted.

"That's pretty fucking awesome. And you're going to give me a chance?"

"We'll see. Like I said, everyone has to approve. We have another guy that we're trying out on a trial basis. You can be a part of that."

"Is this the day for strays?" Reen asked when he walked in with Elijah in tow.

The newcomer looked her up and down. She narrowed her eyes and bared her teeth at him.

"Don't even think about it," he said to the kid. "She'd eat you alive."

"Ah, fuck, who's this guy?" Roo asked.

"This is Elijah Buchholz. He's from Brooklyn. We might take him on a trial basis."

"Where'd you find him?" Charles asked.

"Dan's."

"Dan's pimping out people now?" Reen asked.

"No one's pimping Elijah Buchholz out," Elijah said. "I was looking for a job and figured the dude who supplied everyone's shit was the best place to start."

"Do yourself—and everyone else—a favor and *never* refer to yourself in the third person ever again," Sophie said and joined the others in their scrutiny of the fresh meat.

He looked at her in the same way he had Reen. Booker glared at him.

"What? Don't tell me all the chicks here will eat you alive," Elijah said.

"She might not, but she'd certainly try. And what she didn't get, Booker would finish off. And I don't think either of these two proven warriors appreciate being called 'chicks,'" Mick said. He held his hand out for the newcomer to shake. "You competent enough, bunj?"

"Bunj?"

"Mate."

"Oh. Oh, yeah. I grew up in the concrete jungle. I ran with a tough crowd. I know how to pull my weight."

"We'll see about that," Reen said. "But if Booker thinks you're good enough to have a shot, then I'll go along with it."

Stone returned and he and Elijah stared silently at one another as if sizing up the competition.

"Let's go to the gun range and see if you can put your money where your mouth is," Reen suggested.

The two hopefuls held their own. Elijah proved himself to be more willing to please and open to instruction than Stone was.

The Brit then had them run drills to work them into the team dynamic. He couldn't tell how it would go in a real Zoo situation, but the two both seemed capable enough, at first glance, to fit themselves into the team.

CHAPTER THIRTY-ONE

Franco's, Harvester Camp

Booker waited with the other team leaders for the dispatchers to come out of the warehouse. It was early, barely after sunrise, but there was already a large crowd. He knew they could've done jobs with larger companies, but with inhouse teams, jobs didn't get farmed out as steadily. Franco seemed to do his best to make sure he always left with a job. He wanted to keep the BOHICA Warriors around and not have them move to the greener pastures of the American sector.

The dispatcher immediately noticed him when he stepped out of the building. The other men started reading off their lists of flora and fauna jobs, but Franco waved him over.

"I'm glad you decided to show up today," he said. "I've got another mission with an old friend of yours."

"Friend?" Booker asked.

"Dr. Richard Leishman."

"The bug guy?"

"That's him."

"What's the mission?"

"You'll take it?"

"Let me hear what it is first."

"It's another harvesting situation. A new species has been discovered, and Dr. Leishman wants to study it. He and another colleague are going in, and they asked for you."

Asked for us? And you still get your cut, of course.

"Fauna?"

"Yes."

"What is it, exactly?"

The man looked around, then drew him farther from the group. The move surprised him somewhat, but he hid it.

"Dr. Leishman and his colleague, a Dr. Rosa Gonzalez, need to capture a creature they're calling a moss hog. It sort of looks like a tapir, just not as cute."

"A tapir?"

"Yeah, you know, those weird-looking little pig-like animals with the small trunks. From the Amazon, you know."

"Okay."

Booker was vaguely aware of the animal now. The Zoo rendition wouldn't be the same, of course, because, well...it came from the Zoo.

"The moss hog is, like I said, newly discovered but apparently, Dr. Leishman and Dr. Gonzalez think it has great scientific value. Something about the level of goop the creature has. It's a lot less fierce than, say, a gorgorex, or one of those giant lizards that spit acid. It's still deadly, though. It has long tusks and sharp claws, not to mention a nearly impenetrable hide."

"Sounds like a great fucking time."

"So, what do you say?"

"Dr. Leishman and this Dr. Gonzalez have to come along?"

"Yes."

"How much?"

"A hundred upfront. Fifty more on return, if it's dead. Alive, that ups the price."

"How much?"

"Can't say for sure, but it could be significant. Especially if the specimen is in good condition."

"Where are the good doctor and his accomplice?"

"They're around, gathering their gear together. They want to leave as soon as possible."

"They have the gear for this, or am I going to need to get more fauna capture equipment?"

"I believe they have the specialized tools you'll need. You'll take it?"

"Let me run it past my team first. We need to make the decision together, especially if we'll be taking in two civilians."

"I came to you first with this, Booker. I want to give the job to the BOHICA Warriors, but if I don't get an answer soon, I'll have to farm it out to someone else."

You came to me because they asked for us. You don't have the leverage you think, my friend.

"I'll let you know within half an hour. Just let me go discuss it briefly with my team."

"Half an hour," he agreed, returned to the building, and disappeared inside.

Booker jogged all the way back to Fiddler's Green, where the others were waiting around for the orders to leave.

"We get a job?" Charles asked when he walked in.

"Maybe. There's a catch," he said.

"That's never a good fucking sign. Spill it. What's the catch?" Roo asked.

"Remember Dr. Leishman?"

"The guy who wanted the locust legs?" the American asked.

"That's the one. He wants to go back, this time for another fauna capture."

"And he wants to come along again?" Roo sounded unamused.

Booker nodded. "And he has another friend."

"Shit. So, there'll be two of them?"

"Seems that way."

"What is this?" Stone asked. "Who is Dr. Leishman?"

"He's a scientist we took into the Zoo before. He had us harvest the legs off some of the locust-like creatures. He does research."

"What is it this time?" Reen asked.

"Something called a moss hog. It's new."

"What's the payout?" Mick asked.

He repeated what Franco had told him.

Elijah whistled. "Shit, that's a good chunk of change. Let's do it!"

The others ignored him.

"It's a big risk," Reen said. "He did decently enough last time, but it was still skin of our teeth shit."

"I know. But maybe he's learned his lesson and won't be dressed for a Hollywood safari."

"You think we should take it?" Charles asked.

"I don't see why we shouldn't." Booker nodded.

"Ah, to hell with it. The money's good. How hard can it be to catch a moss hog, whatever the hell that is? Let's just fucking do it," Roo stated.

The Brit looked at the rest of the team, who nodded their consent.

"Okay," he told them. "I'll go accept the job. I'll bring the doctors back here for a briefing before we head into the Zoo."

The other team leaders were gone by the time he returned to Franco's. One of the guards at the door stepped into the darkness of the building to call him.

The dispatcher exited with Dr. Richard Leishman—who wore dark-green fatigues—and a compact woman who Booker assumed was Dr. Rosa Gonzalez. She was dressed in almost the same outfit as Richard, but her steel-toed boots looked more worn than his.

The scientist smiled at him and shook his hand forcefully. "Booker! Didn't think we'd see each other again, did you?"

"I confess, I did not, Dr. Leishman."

"Richard, please."

"I see you've dropped the safari gear," he said with a grin.

"Yeah. God, I was an idiot. Oh, this is Dr. Rosa Gonzalez. She's a colleague of mine and an endocrinologist.

Gonzalez, this is Booker. He and his team helped me out last time I went into the Zoo."

Gonzalez shook Booker's hand, and he was surprised by the strength behind it. She was a shorter woman and wore her hair in a thick braid that reached to her mid-back.

"Endocrinologist? Wouldn't expect a doctor like that in the Zoo."

"You can expect the unexpected with me, Booker. Endocrinology is my expertise, yes, but I've studied a wide range of disciplines. I'm here because we expect the moss hog to have properties that will provide data to help us to synthesize medication that will balance out hormones in humans. The specimen needs to be fresh. So, if we are unable to take the animal out alive, I'll need to get samples on the spot and analyze them as best I can. It doesn't work well if the samples aren't fresh, we've discovered."

"We have a special cage I engineered for it," Richard said. "It's made out of the hinges of the locust-like insects, actually. It's a prototype."

"A prototype?"

"Yes. It's really fascinating, actually. You see—"

"Let me stop you right there, Richard. Before you get too carried away," Booker said. He noticed Gonzalez try to hide a smile. "The rest of my team will need to be briefed. I also need to know that the same rule applies to this mission as they did for the other one we ran with you."

"Rule?"

"My team gets paid whether you come back or not—and whether you're in one piece or not." Booker watched the two civilians to gauge their reaction. Gonzalez didn't flinch and Richard shrugged his shoulders in a jerky kind of way.

"Oh, yes, that rule. Of course, Booker."

"Great. The others are waiting back at our building. You can tell us what you know about the moss hog and then we'll head out. Sound like a plan?" he asked and looked from one to the other.

"We'll have our stuff sent to the gate," Richard said. "We'll go with you for the meeting and by the time we're done, everything will be squared away."

The BOHICA Warriors team was armed and waiting on the first floor of the building. Booker thought the uniforms he'd purchased really gave a cohesive impression. They looked skilled and formidable.

"Well, if it isn't good ol' Dick. How you been, buddy?" Roo asked.

"I've been great. I hear you've been great too. I'm sure it's also pointless for me to ask you to call me Richard, isn't it?"

"Sure is, Dick." The Aussie grinned.

"This is Dr. Rosa Gonzalez," Booker said.

"I'd like to be called Gonzalez," she said. She studied the team and her gaze lingered on Reen.

"I could think of other things to call you, but Gonzalez works," Reen said and winked.

Roo groaned and rolled his eyes dramatically. Sophie tried to hide her laugh in a fit of forced coughing. Reen made a show of patting the girl on the back.

"I can already tell this is going to be different than I thought," Gonzalez said. "It might even be fun."

"Okay," Booker said. "Let's get a few things straight

first. You two are civilians here and you follow our orders —no matter what we ask of you. Retrieving the specimen is priority, but your safety will also be in consideration. Just know it is not guaranteed. Now that that's out of the way, tell us what you know about the objective."

"Gonzalez, I'll let you take point on this one," Richard said.

She nodded and pulled out a small tablet-like device. She tapped a few buttons and projected the image of the specimen on the wall. "Okay. Some of this is conjecture as not much is known about them yet, but I think our conjecture is pretty accurate.

"The moss hog is dark-green with deep-purple spots, four clawed toes, and a set of nasty tusks it knows how to use. They average out to be roughly the size of a Great Dane and weigh about seventy kilos, give or take. They are omnivorous but eat mostly plants. The tusks and claws are used to fight off predators and each other. The moss hog is mostly solitary with a defined territory, as far as we can tell. They have a tough hide that acts like armor. They have soft spots where their legs connect to their bodies and at the base of their neck, where their sternum starts— although that's not especially important since the goal is to capture one alive. They have a large amount of goop in them, and we want to find out why. Also, the nature of the goop they possess suggests certain elements that could have a higher compatibility with human DNA. If we could study those and use them as a model to synthesize man-made medication, it could make it easier to help humans heal."

"How do we capture this thing alive?" Reen asked.

"I have a cage I designed especially for this," Richard said. "Actually, from the same materials you helped me harvest the last time I went into the Zoo. It's a prototype, but I've tested it plenty of times in the lab and have every confidence in it holding. It's easy to deploy and the moss hog's tusks shouldn't be able to penetrate it."

"Anything else we need to know?" Booker asked.

Gonzalez shook her head.

"Where's the territory?" Charles asked.

"A few have been tracked twenty kilometers in, near the Chinese Quarter," Richard said.

"With any luck," the Brit surmised, "we can get in and out in a day."

"That would be preferred," the doctor said.

"Let's hop to it, then." The American glanced at the team.

"You have gear?" Reen asked.

The other woman nodded and tossed her braid over her shoulder. "It's waiting at the gate."

"You know how to fire a weapon?"

"I was in the National Guard and then the Army Reserves when I was getting my doctorate. I didn't stay on with the military but joined the company Richard and I work for now. I never really stopped with PT to what extent I could, and I've kept my firearms license up to date."

"I thought you looked comfortable in your fatigues."

"I think you'll find I'm comfortable in them and out of them."

Roo's laugh was harsh and interrupted the women's

conversation. "I don't think we'll have enough time for that, mate."

"Ignore him," Reen said.

The doctors' gear was waiting at the gate. Charles noted that it was considerably less than what Richard had brought with him before.

"That first trip was a bit of a rude awakening. I've only brought the essentials this time," he said.

Booker distributed the gear amongst the BOHICA Warriors. Gonzales and Richard both had their own packs and carried their more specialized equipment.

He gave Elijah heavier items to carry. The young man was stocky, like Roo, and he'd proved himself to be quite the mule when it came to carrying heavy loads.

"Everyone ready?" he asked as they approached the gate. "Reen, you're with Gonzalez. Richard, you go ahead and stick with Charles."

They moved into position and started through the gate and into the jungle.

CHAPTER THIRTY-TWO

The Zoo - Thor

Ever since Thor had killed the human who had tried to hurt Charles, he'd led the pack in shadowing the group when they returned to the Zoo. The demiwolves' presence tended to ward off some of the other Zoo-denizens, so attacks on them were less frequent. This was becoming almost routine for the pack. Any time he sensed Charles in the Zoo, he shadowed the human and his mental imperative had begun to bleed out into the others.

The alpha was the only one who grated at chaperoning the humans through the Zoo, but he merely bided his time. He wanted to beat the humanity out of his rival and to strip all ties to humankind from the demiwolf. For now, he simply waited for the right moment. He knew the first step to doing that would be to kill the human Thor seemed most determined to protect—the largest of them who smelled like earth and machines.

Thor sensed the moment when Charles reentered the Zoo. He gave a yip of excitement and set off in the direction of the gate, knowing they'd intersect with the group that way. The demiwolves followed him, simply glad to be doing something.

He could smell four new humans with the team, but he took that in stride. They were with Charles, and that was all that mattered.

As always, he remained hidden in the brush and at a far enough distance to not alert the humans of his presence. He knew Charles was his friend, but he also knew it was better for everyone if the demiwolves were not close enough to engage. The rest of the pack seemed to accept his intentions but getting too close could trigger the Zoo-induced urge to kill.

Thor's tail wagged on its own at the sight of Charles. He almost whimpered from wanting to go to the man, but he restrained himself. The human had seen him multiple times in the past but had never called the demiwolf to him. If he had called, he would've gone willingly. As it was, he would wait.

The alpha watched his rival's excitement at seeing the humans. He growled low in his throat, and his eyes glowed a deeper red against his completely black fur. His leg wound had finally healed but it hadn't closed up properly and he was still in pain and weakened. For now, he was still larger than the younger animal, but not by much. In a few more weeks, Thor would most likely be larger than him.

His time to kill the human was soon. He knew it had to be. His window of opportunity to overpower the young upstart was swiftly closing. The alpha had seen the humans attack other Zoo creatures and realized that the head-on approach wouldn't work. He needed to lay in wait and let the humans come to him. His mouth watered in anticipation of ripping out Thor's favorite human's throat.

He would have the demiwolves' complete loyalty—he demanded it and felt it was his right. If killing the human didn't work, then he would have to kill the potential challenger too.

CHAPTER THIRTY-THREE

The Zoo

The deeper they traveled into the Zoo, the hotter it became. It was especially humid with the canopy closed in overhead, keeping the air trapped, and the low-growing plants transpired even more moisture into the air. Sweat dripped off Charles as he pushed through the jungle. He glanced constantly at Richard to make sure the scientist was okay. He didn't complain but was drenched in sweat and had begun to breathe hard. While he'd said he'd worked out and prepared for this trip to the Zoo, it was easy to see that whatever he had done, it wasn't nearly enough.

"You doing all right, Richard?" he asked.

The man gave him a thumbs-up.

Booker glanced over his shoulder and made eye contact with his teammate. He nodded and the Brit looked forward again.

The hair at the back of his neck prickled and he knew they were being watched. The feeling had intensified in recent outings into the Zoo. He knew it was Thor watching them. More than once, he'd caught glimpses of a demiwolf pacing them through the woods and he knew it was Thor. It couldn't have been any other.

Mick was on point, and he held his hand up in a closed fist to stop the column and pointed to the right. Booker and Sophie were behind him and Booker shifted slightly to put himself in front of her. She turned in the opposite direction and looked along the path to the left, confident that he had her back.

"I don't see anything back here," Stone said as Tail-end Charlie and peered back the way they'd come.

The boiling water sound was their only warning. Charles caught Richard by the arm and jerked him out of the way as a stream of acidic saliva streaked from the underbrush and began to melt the plants where the scientist had stood.

The giant green lizard stepped into the pathway and its spiked tail whipped at the humans. Reen dragged Gonzalez away from the animal's reach and opened fire. Stone and Elijah stepped forward to help form a wall of protection around the civilians.

Another lizard stepped out of the jungle and roared. It lashed its tail at Mick. He jumped out of the way at the last second and the spikes barely missed the side of his head.

Sophie held steady and waited for the acid sacs to expand. The first lizard whipped its tail at her. Booker opened fire to distract the creature for a moment. When its sac was fully expanded, she fired. Her round found its target and the acid exploded over the creature. It writhed as its own saliva dissolved its scaly skin and ate through flesh and bone.

The other lizard screamed in anger and lashed out at the humans. Its tail caught Stone in the side and hurled him away, but he scrambled to his feet and fired his Minebea to release a hail of the 9×19mm Parabellum rounds that only seemed to anger the giant lizard more.

Its claws raked the earth and its tail whipped from side to side in an attempt to spear the dodging humans.

Charles and Reen remained with Gonzalez and Richard and kept the scientists out of the enraged animal's reach. The others circled it.

The mutant turned and tried to see all the humans at once.

"Come on, you ugly bastard," Roo said. "Let's see you do your worst."

It hissed and its acid sacs expanded. Elijah sidestepped around it and maneuvered into an optimal position. Once its skin had thinned enough, he fired his AK-47, and the creature screamed when its acid sac exploded.

It whipped its tail one last time in his direction, but it was already dying. The momentum of the swing spun it before it collapsed in a bubbling heap.

"Everyone good?" Booker asked. He reached his hand out and brushed his fingers down Sophie's arm. She stepped away from him after a few seconds.

Howls came from a short distance away.

"Let's keep moving," Gonzalez said.

"You nervous?" Reen asked.

"I'd be stupid not to be."

"Good answer."

They started forward again. Stone and Mick took turns dropping monkey-like creatures from the canopy. Every time a body landed with a crunch and a thud, Richard winced.

"You holding up?" Charles asked him.

He nodded. "Hey, what's going on between those two?" he asked.

"Between what two?"

"Come on, Charles. I know you know who I'm talking about. Booker and your new member. Sophie, I think she said her name was."

Elijah moved in closer. "I'd like to hear the answer to this, too. I've been wondering. They're an item, right? They're just trying to keep it on the DL or whatever, right? But they have serious sexual tension vibes going on."

He looked to see if Sophie and Booker were far enough ahead of them in the column. "It's not my place to say anything about it."

"Confirmed," the young man said, a goofy-looking smile on his face.

The American frowned.

"I'd have to agree with Elijah," Richard interjected. "Your non-answer is as good as an affirmative."

"Honestly, if those two haven't bumped uglies by now I'd be surprised," Elijah continued. "I know they try to pretend not to look at each other or touch or anything, but it's pretty obvious they're fucking."

"We aren't talking about this," he said firmly. "Focus, Elijah. We aren't out for a stroll. This is a mission. Get your head in the game."

His new teammate fell back a few steps to his previous position.

"Well, good for Booker," Richard said quietly. "Robbing the cradle, but that's some baby."

Charles gave him a surprised look. He thought scientists were above that kind of locker-room talk. Evidently not.

They lapsed into silence again for a few more klicks.

The team froze when they felt the ground vibrate under their feet. It was either an earthquake or something heading their way—a rather big something.

A lone, sharp howl rose from the jungle to their right. It sounded like a warning, and Charles wondered if it was Thor giving them a heads-up that they were about to be attacked.

He didn't have much time to think about it. Three giant rhino-like creatures charged at them from the jungle. They were completely black but for the silver color of their horns. They bulldozed their way through the trees and splintered trunks in their path.

"Everyone, out of the way!" Mick yelled. The others didn't need to be told twice. They separated into two groups and the three giant beasts stormed through the center. As if they shared the same brain, they stopped, whirled, and attacked the humans again.

Elijah and Roo opened fire but the rounds bounced off the thick, black hides. The skin of the rhino-like animals was layered, almost like an armadillo's armor. Each had six yellow eyes that glowed brighter when they began their assault.

The mutants closed in on Mick, Booker, Stone, and

Sophie. They pawed at the ground and scored gouges deep into the earth. Two lowered their heads and barreled forward. The four humans scrambled out of the way and fired at the beasts. Mick narrowly missed being gouged by one of the silver horns. The animal rammed into the trunk of a tree instead and the trunk shuddered and moaned before it simply toppled. When its roots broke free of the soft, muddy earth, it sprayed them with dirt.

Momentarily blinded, Stone didn't see the third monster make its move. Charles and Reen attempted to stop it, but their rounds didn't affect it.

Sophie darted forward and hauled him out of the way. The horn snagged on his left forearm and pierced easily through the armor and fabric to his flesh. With a bloody rip and a crack when she pulled him one way and the animal jerked the other, his hand detached. It wasn't ripped completely off but dangled by a few loose tendons.

He screamed.

"Get out of the way!" Reen yelled. She hurled a grenade in front of one of the creatures. The animal stepped over it as it detonated and sprayed it with shrapnel. It roared in anger and antifreeze-blue blood pulsed beneath it. With another defiant bellow, it surged forward a few meters, stopped, and backed up before its hind legs collapsed.

"The belly is vulnerable," she shouted.

The other two attackers roared and snorted and launched another assault. The humans scattered to avoid the massive creatures that zigged and zagged amongst them. The animals were fast but not the most coordinated.

Sophie dragged Stone farther into the jungle. His face was ashen, and blood spurted from his mostly detached hand. Gonzalez appeared at her side, Reen right behind her.

"Do you want the hand attached or not?" the doctor asked him. He stared at her, his face blank with shock.

"Look, we probably aren't going to make it out in time to save your hand. It's only attached by a few strands of tissue. It'll be easier to address the wound if it's off completely. You're losing the hand either way. Do you want it gone now, or later?"

"Take it off." He gritted his teeth behind a grimace.

Sophie gagged. Reen pressed a grenade into her hand. "You go help the others. We don't need you here for this."

She drew her knife and Gonzalez held the man's arm down.

"You ready?" the doctor asked.

He nodded.

Reen severed the few remaining strands of tissue. There wasn't much left, only a shard of bone and some tendons. Stone screamed. She cut a clean strip of cloth and wound it around Stone's stump while Gonzalez held him still.

Charles kept himself between Richard and the snorting rhino-like creatures. The two remaining animals became more uncoordinated in their rage. He aimed his MCS at a mutant's head and waited for a clear shot at one of its eyes. The beast charged and skidded to a stop after its gouging attempt didn't work. He took advantage of its moment of stillness and fired. The slug drilled into the animal's orbital cavity, cracked the bone, and weakened its skull.

Roo followed up on the damage his teammate had inflicted with several rounds. The monster made a strangely hollow, groaning noise and tipped over.

The remaining attacker bellowed and reared in preparation to charge. Sophie lobbed the grenade Reen had given her under its legs. It detonated and shredded the tender belly of the creature. It fell in a daze and Roo threw another grenade to finish the job.

Silence fell over them again as the animal uttered a final death rattle.

"How's Stone?" Booker asked Sophie.

"Lost a hand."

Gonzales, Reen, and Stone emerged from the jungle. They'd rigged a makeshift sling for him and blood dripped from the binding around the stump of his left hand.

"I'm aborting," the Brit said when he saw his teammate.

"But we paid—" Richard started before he cut him off with an upraised hand.

"Safety first. We're heading back now. Stone, you coping?"

The man was pale and obviously in shock, but he nodded. "We keep going. We've come this far and going back now will only save us a bit of time."

"You just lost a hand," Charles said and moved forward to put Stone's good arm over his shoulder. "Don't try to be a hero."

The scientist started to argue, but the venomous look Roo shot him stopped him dead. The team turned and started back.

They'd gone only a couple of hundred meters when Stone grew noticeably weaker. He'd lost a lot of blood, but his skin had begun to look jaundiced. When he tried to move his legs, they could no longer support his weight.

"Hang in there, man," Charles said. "Just a little bit farther and we can have a rest."

He looked at Booker who mouthed the word "poison." That simply confirmed what he already knew. He could feel the life draining away from the man he supported.

Stone collapsed. The American stopped and threw his limp body over his shoulder. Mick stepped up and pressed his fingers to Stone's neck.

"His pulse is light and rapid. He's fading fast," he said.

"Do we have any kind of antidote?" Sophie asked.

Booker shook his head and continued to lead them through the jungle. Their only hope was to get him back in time for the doctors to do something.

Stone muttered and almost immediately convulsed on the big man's shoulders. Charles stopped and placed him on the dirt. They could see the web of his veins, black through the near translucence of his skin.

"Holy shit," Gonzalez said.

"Can't we...help him?" Richard asked.

Reen knelt and unwound the bandages. A rancid smell erupted and made them gag. The stump where his hand had been was completely black and looked like it was rotting. The poison had spread through his veins.

He convulsed again and his eyes rolled back in his head while foam bubbled from his cracked lips. Charles tried to hold him down but soon, the thrashing became too much for even his considerable strength.

"Make sure he doesn't contaminate you," Gonzalez warned. "Whatever pathogen he's been infected with could spread to you through that contact."

A gurgling scream wrenched from the wounded man's

throat and he went still. Charles checked for a pulse and shook his head. "He's gone."

Everyone stood and stared at the body, reminded that life was fragile, especially in the Zoo. Stone was their own mortality staring them in the face.

"Fucking animal that big, and it has to have poison, too? From its horn? What the fuck?" Roo muttered.

"Now what?" Richard asked, hope evident in his voice.

He refused to meet the big man's eyes when the American glared at him before he stooped to pick the body up. Slags of what had been flesh sloughed off.

"Put him down," Gonzalez said and stepped forward to push him out of the way and kneel beside the body.

"Amazing," she said as she peered closely but made sure not to come in contact with it. "I wouldn't believe that putrefaction could occur at such speed." She gave a sniff, then said, "No, not putrefaction. The poison itself is dissolving the flesh. Check yourself, Charles, and make sure that you have none of this on you."

The American jumped back and with Roo and Mick helping, searched his body for contamination. One of his magazine pouches had a splash of black ichor, and he took it off carefully and dropped it on what was left of Stone's rapidly dissolving body.

"I wouldn't touch his weapons, either," Gonzalez said, almost as an afterthought.

"Can we continue with the job?" Richard asked almost defiantly.

Booker took a step forward to get a better look. It was obvious that they were not going to be able to take the body back. There'd be nothing left of it by the time they returned.

"Any objections?" he asked the others.

Charles looked like he wanted to say something, but after one more look at Stone, he kept quiet.

"Okay, then. Let's move out. Just keep this as a reminder. The Zoo is always going to surprise us.

"Mick, how far now?"

"We're nearly there," he said. "I'd say another klick and we'll be in the moss hogs' territory. Any ideas on how to track the motherfuckers once we get there?"

"We have a special tool for that," Richard said. "If all goes according to plan, the Moss Hog will come to us."

"I thought you said these things were just discovered?" Sophie asked.

"They were, but we've done our research before this attempt to capture one alive. We've been able to study several dead ones and our teams have picked up other useful information. They are new, but we've become adept at gathering as much intel as possible in a short amount of time. It's our specialty," Gonzalez said.

"Then let's move out," Booker said. They all gave what was left of their companion one last look. Charles wasn't the only one to notice that none of the plants that usually tried to claim bodies were doing so now. It was as if the contagion that had almost consumed Stone's body was too much even for Zoo life.

They moved quietly through the jungle toward their destination, everyone shaken by their teammate's sudden death and what happened to the body. It was easier to simply focus on the mission.

The team crossed into the moss hogs' territory, and Richard stopped them at a large, bulbous tree that reminded Sophie of a baobab. There were deep scores in the tree's bark. It was clearly used as a scratching post for some animals.

"Here's as good as any place," the scientist said. He opened his pack and removed a folded black rectangle that looked like it was made of canvas mesh. He passed it to Reen before he retrieved a stainless-steel cylinder and unscrewed the cap. Mist poured out of it as if he had packed the cylinder with dry ice. A strange, unpleasant smell filled the air.

"What is that?" Roo demanded and covered his nose.

"It's the scent of a male moss hog—taken from an anal gland, to be precise. It was dead, so this isn't as strong, but it should be good enough," Gonzalez said.

"If that isn't as strong, I'd hate to get the real stuff," Reen said, holding her nose.

The doctor ignored her and continued. "It's a territory marker. This obviously isn't this male's territory, so whatever moss hog lives here will smell the intruder and come to chase it off. That's when we'll capture it," she explained. "Now, we just wait for it."

"How does this cage thing work, exactly?" Reen asked. She pulled on the corners of the rectangle and it expanded outwards.

"You pop it all the way open and drop it onto the creature. Pretty simple and straightforward. Once the animal is inside, the cage automatically shrinks to limit the moss hog's movements," Richard explained.

His voice trembled and he cleared his throat. Booker

and Charles exchanged a look over the man's head. For someone who'd pushed to get the mission back on track, he still seemed to be in a state of shock over Stone's death.

"Pretty simple?" Reen asked. "Seems unnecessarily unwieldy. We're playing ring toss with an angry hog."

"Oh," Gonzalez said and opened her own bag, "I almost forgot about these." She pulled out three black sticks. Each was a foot long and shaped like a Maglite flashlight. She passed one to Charles, Mick, and Roo.

"What are these?" the Aussie asked.

She took Charles' and gave the center of the device a quick twist and it expanded. Blue light crackled at one end. "Think of it like a boar spear, except it's designed to stun the animal, not impale it. It's electrified." She gave another twist and the device telescoped back to its original size. "That should make it easier to…uh, 'play ring toss' with the beast."

"That's pretty fucking cool," Roo said. He twisted his to full length and tested the weight of it.

They settled deeper into the underbrush in a semi-circle upwind of the cylinder.

Surprisingly, it only took about an hour for a moss hog to show up. It snorted and grunted, almost growling as it tried to find the intruder it scented. The creature looked like it weighed almost two hundred pounds with a stocky body on short, muscular legs. Its nose was long and hung down almost like a short trunk. A hump of muscle short-ened its neck. The thick, dark-green fur on its neck stood rigid and the rest of it bristled in anger. The tusks were about eight inches long and streaked with deep-purple and green, the same colors as the rest of its body.

It snuffled around and its beady gaze darted in all directions in an effort to locate its opponent. After a moment, it dug at the ground and began to spray to cover the scent of the other creature.

Mick, Charles, and Roo crept forward to pen the animal in. They extended their rods, which hummed with electricity.

The moss hog raised its head and froze. Its trunk trembled as it tried to identify the sound.

"Time to play rodeo," the Aborigine said and stepped out of concealment, followed by the other two.

The animal squealed and wheeled toward Roo. It charged, its head down, hackles raised, and tusks flecked with saliva.

He dropped to one knee and braced himself behind the rod, trusting that it wouldn't fail. The mutant collided with the electrified end head-first. The impact pushed the man back a few feet and into a furrow of mud. The target screamed as the current coursed through it, knocked it off its feet, and its body spasmed.

Charles and Mick lunged forward with their own electrified rods. The animal scrambled to its feet to buck and writhe away, twisting its body out of the reach of the devices. Like picadores at a bullfight, the three men closed the distance and lunged to block off any paths of escape.

The moss hog gave up the attempt to flee and went onto the offensive. It lowered its head and attacked Charles. He planted his feet in his best imitation of a young Maasai warrior-hopeful facing down a lion, and the animal bounced back with a frustrated squeal when his lance delivered its load.

Reen moved forward and eased into position with the expanded cage. Elijah and Sophie flanked her, their weapons at the ready.

Gonzalez had been told to stay back but she couldn't help herself. She crept closer to watch the capture. While she'd dissected a long-dead moss hog in her lab, she had never seen one like this in real life. She watched in fascination as the large animal tried its best to break through the human cordon. It feinted and charged and once, almost made it past Roo, but the electrified lances were doing their job. The more it was shocked, the angrier it became.

With the mutant dazed, Reen tried to drop the cage over the top of it, but the creature surged forward at the last moment and the edge bounced off its back.

"Try again," Charles shouted and grasped its hind legs to hold it in place, but the animal slipped free from his hold.

Mick shocked the animal, lunged forward to wrap his arms around its neck, and yanked back with all his strength. The animal squealed and reared. The momentum rolled it onto him, drove the air from his lungs, and forced him to release his hold. He tried to twine his legs around it to pin it, but the monster rolled free. It dashed away and screamed in anger before it hurtled toward the only exit it had. The path of least resistance was through Gonzalez, who stood wide-eyed in the gap created when the others tried to capture it.

Sophie and Elijah spun and fired, but it was too late. Without the body armor worn by the others, the doctor's green fatigues offered no protection. The moss hog bit down and tossed its head and the vicious action sliced

Gonzalez's belly open from chest to groin, even as the first rounds struck the creature. She was thrown down, her hands on her belly as she stared at herself in confusion.

The two fired again in unison, and the mutant managed four more steps into the jungle before it collapsed.

Reen rushed to the doctor's side and pressed on the woman's wound in an attempt to stem the bleeding. "Fuck! Shit. This wasn't supposed to fucking happen."

The woman blinked at her, then looked at Charles who was there an instant later. Both pressed against her belly to try to stop the bleeding, but there was nothing to press against. Her torn organs bulged at each attempt.

"I..." the mortally wounded woman whispered. She shook her head once and closed her eyes. A shudder ran through her body before she stilled.

Mick took her pulse and shook his head. "We lost her."

"Fucking hell," Roo muttered.

"Gonzalez?" Richard's voice sounded small and scared.

Booker steered the man away from the gruesome sight of his gutted colleague and friend. "Do you still want us to bring the moss hog back?" he asked. He gave the scientist a little shake when he didn't reply. "Richard. Do you still want the moss hog?"

"She's dead, isn't she?"

"I'm sorry. I know this is hard, Richard, but I need you to make the decision."

"We can't leave her," he said.

"We aren't going to leave her. We're going to get her out of the Zoo. You're going to get out. We'll do everything in our power to make sure that happens. Do you want the moss hog?" Booker asked again.

He simply shrugged.

"Fuck, he's shutting down," the Brit muttered.

"We'll take it with us," Reen said. "We've come this fucking far and lost two people. There's no way in hell I'm leaving that motherfucking animal behind." She slotted the cage over its body and it immediately contracted around the animal. She started to lift it, grunted, and set it down as she looked apologetically at Charles.

He nodded, swung it, and slipped his arms through the straps. She might have felt obligated to carry it back, but it was two hundred pounds of hog and the wall was many klicks away.

"Let's get the fuck out of here," Roo suggested.

Mick wrapped a pressure bandage around Gonzalez's torso and hoisted her body onto his shoulders. The bandage wasn't perfect, but it kept most of her organs with the rest of her.

The two men walked in the center of the formation with their burdens. The others surrounded them in a wedge formation, and they started back toward the gate with Sophie shepherding the unresponsive Richard.

The jungle around them buzzed with noise, more than there had been before. The Zoo was reacting to the killing that had taken place.

"Let us know when we need to rotate out who carries the weight," Booker said. He received only grunts in reply.

Sophie stayed beside the scientist and prodded him along. He was ashen and stared blankly ahead while he muttered inaudibly. She had to constantly pull him forward when he stopped moving, which was often.

"Come on, Richard. You've got to keep moving. Just put one foot in front of the other."

Booker made the decision to cut through a denser portion of the jungle that would be a more direct route to the gate. He started to hack his way forward and clear a path when necessary for the others. Roo pushed through. Sophie dragged Richard along. Elijah brought up the rear and watched their backs as they fought through the dense foliage.

Suddenly, a vine snaked out and twined around the Brit's ankle. It yanked and he fell heavily, his M5 knocked from his hands. He scrabbled at the earth but couldn't stop himself from being dragged away.

Sophie left Richard's side and lunged forward with a scream. She snatched up the machete her teammate had used and slashed wildly at the vines that attempted to drag him away.

"Don't you fucking dare! He's mine!" she shouted with the fury of an Amazon lumberjack as she hacked away. The creepers had no chance against her fury and they released him. She hauled him to his feet and examined him, turning him this way and that while her hands ran over him.

"I'm fine, Sophie," he said and brushed himself off. "Thanks."

She leaned up and kissed him.

Elijah whistled. "I fucking knew it."

He gave the newbie a funny look as he pulled away from her. "Let's get the fuck out of here."

Roo stared from one to the other.

"Close your mouth, Roo. You look like a fucking bogan," Mick said as he walked past.

"But—what the fuck?"

"Sorry, Roo. Everyone kind of knew but you," Reen said.

"I'm going to fucking kill him," he muttered.

"You can save killing me for later," Booker said. "Right now, we need to focus on getting out of this shithole."

The demiwolf pack shadowed the humans. Thor was satisfied that Charles was uninjured. He would have stepped in if the man had been in any serious danger but now contented himself with running along. He'd warned them of the danger, but that was all he felt he could do.

The alpha watched him trot happily through the jungle and follow the trail of the humans' scent. His hackles rose and his eyes glowed crimson. He surged forward and the pack followed him. This would be the moment he had waited for. He could scent the humans' weaknesses and he was ready to make his move.

CHAPTER THIRTY-FOUR

The Zoo

Charles' shoulders ached from carrying the moss hog. His arms began to tremble, but he clenched his jaw and pressed on. They had to be more than halfway to the gate by now. He was drenched in sweat and he could feel the heat and humidity getting to him.

Mick still had Gonzalez's body over his shoulders. He had to be struggling in the heat and humidity as well.

A couple of six-legged panther-like animals tried to attack, but a hyper-alert Sophie and Roo cut them down before they got close. Charles and Mick were still in the center of the group and relied on the others for protection as they plodded forward.

They converged on a path that either they or another team had made earlier. The foliage hadn't sprung up completely, and it made for an easier passage. They returned to a column formation.

He tried to blow some of the sweat out of his eyes. When that didn't work, he blinked it away. In that split-second, he caught sight of a flash of black fur before he was struck in the chest by a large animal that hurled him onto his back and thrust the breath out of him.

Charles kicked upward and punched at the animal's thick fur. Pain seared up his arm as the demiwolf's sharp claws raked him.

Howls and snarls filled the air as the pack moved in to attack, following their alpha's lead. Shots rang out and people shouted, but he couldn't tell what was going on. He fought to shove the animal off him so he could reach his weapons, but his attacker kept him pinned.

He'd lain in wait for this moment and now, he wanted to enjoy it. The alpha's jaws closed around the man's neck. The armor the human wore kept his teeth from ripping out his throat. With a low growl of frustration, he shifted his hold in search of the soft flesh. One fang penetrated and blood filled his mouth. This was the moment. The human prey was his. He opened his jaws and freed the one fang, ready to move up and break the man's neck.

Thor barreled out of the jungle. He pounded into the alpha's side and drove the demiwolf from his victim's chest.

He stood over Charles and growled at the attacker. The alpha bared his teeth and his hackles rose.

The other demiwolves stopped their attempts to attack the humans. Pack formalities took precedence.

Thor stepped away from Charles and circled the leader while he snarled and snapped his jaws together.

"Charles, get back," Roo shouted as he aimed at the two demiwolves.

"No! You'll hit Thor," he yelled in response, scrambled to his knees, and blocked Roo's line of sight. He held a hand up to stop Elijah from firing.

The Aussie hesitated. "Thor?" He looked at the two creatures locked in combat and his eyes widened when he recognized the black-and-brown animal.

The two lunged at each other and their horns clashed with a loud cracking noise. They bounced back, seemingly evenly matched. The pack growled but didn't interfere as the two combatants prepared to lock horns again.

Thor rose on his hind legs and thrust forcefully into the alpha. His adversary met him and surged upward to force him back a step.

Reen stepped forward to help Charles to his feet. She kept the muzzle of her weapon shifting to cover the pack. "Are you okay? Those goddamn demiwolves came out of fucking nowhere."

"Yeah," he said. "I'm pretty much okay. That big one was about to rip my throat out and Thor saved me."

The rivals collided again. Thor was forced back another step. The alpha lunged forward again, not giving him a reprieve. He slipped to the side of attack and threw the larger demiwolf off balance, then seized the moment and bit down on his shoulder to rip a chunk of flesh away.

The beast howled, twisted, and bit into his opponent's side. He'd been in too many fights, and he was well versed in all the tricks. Thor yelped but didn't release his jaws. He pushed forward and tried to force the leader to topple. The large demiwolf pressed back while he snarled and snapped at him. Blood oozed from Thor's side from the multiple bite wounds that had been inflicted.

Finally, he shoved the heavier the animal away and gained breathing space. His adversary's limp seemed more pronounced and Thor went on the offensive again, ignoring his pain. Anger coursed through his veins. The alpha had tried to kill Charles, and he intended to kill him for it.

He lunged, but his target was waiting for the attack and clamped his jaws down on his front leg, splintering bone. Thor yelped, jerked away, and reared on his hind legs. Instead of dropping to the ground, however, he twisted to slam his horns into the alpha's bad leg. His opponent yelped and his leg collapsed momentarily and threw him off balance. Thor repeated his assault and this time, pounded his horns into the demiwolf's side. He was rewarded with the crunching of ribs.

His adversary twisted and bit down on the tip of his right horn. Thor jerked his neck and drove the horn into the roof of the alpha's mouth, but the beast was too quick, snapped his powerful jaws, and broke off the tip of the horn. The younger animal screamed in anger, bit down on massive shoulder, and ripped the other demiwolf away.

Thor's front leg gave out and he dropped to the ground, the air heaving in and out of his lungs. The alpha limped toward him and stood above his defeated foe before he turned his attention to where the humans stood. He snarled and the other demiwolves shifted and began to close in.

The humans might have been willing to watch the fight,

but if the pack intended to attack, they would not meekly stand by.

As the others raised their weapons, the American only had eyes for Thor. Blood matted his fur from a hundred wounds, and he had at least one broken leg.

The alpha snarled at Charles and snapped his jaws open and shut.

Thor heaved himself upward and flung himself forward to take the other demiwolf by surprise. He clamped his jaws around the alpha's throat and locked in.

The animal snarled and struggled against him, raking his claws along his belly and sides, but he held on. He sank his teeth deeper into the alpha's neck. Blood filled his mouth and spilled between his teeth. His adversary's struggles weakened and Thor's canines worked their way in deeper. Blood and fur blocked his nose, making it hard to breathe, but he still didn't let go. Even after the alpha ceased the fight, he didn't release him.

The glowing light of his adversary's eyes dimmed. The pack knew their alpha was dead and gave one long howl in unison, which made the team aim in earnest. They merely looked at the humans and disappeared into the jungle.

Charles carefully approached Thor and the dead demiwolf and sat beside him.

"Hey, Thor. It's okay," he said, keeping his voice calm and even and his movements slow. "Everything's okay now."

Thor looked at him. His eyes stopped glowing crimson

and they looked the same as they had when he was a puppy —big and brown. The tip of his tail wagged once, twice, but that was all he could manage.

"Release, Thor," he said. "Come on. I know you remember. Release."

The others watched him talk to the demiwolf until he finally relaxed his hold.

"Holy shit," Roo said and squinted to see the color of the fur beneath the matted blood. "That really is Thor."

Charles scratched behind Thor's ear and the animal whimpered. He shuffled weakly and dropped his head into the big man's lap. He heaved a shuddering sigh.

"Good boy, Thor. Everything's okay now."

"Is everyone all right?" Booker asked, his weapon still held at the ready. "What the fuck happened?"

"Thor saved me," Charles said and stroked Thor's nose.

"I thought Thor was dead," Roo said.

He grimaced. "About that...I couldn't just kill him, okay? I released him into the Zoo because I thought that's where he belonged. I saw the videotape. It wasn't his fault with that asshole Bronson. He was just doing what he was born to do. He's been following us on almost all of our missions. I probably should've said something before, but I couldn't. I just couldn't kill him. He's my dog."

"Oh, Charles, he isn't a dog, though," Reen said and her eyes provided no indication as to her thoughts.

She had always been more "reg" than him, following the rules and regulations of the Corps. But he wouldn't let her do anything to Thor.

"I know."

"I'm glad he stopped those other demiwolves from

attacking us," Sophie said. "I mean, we could have fought them off, but you know," she added and nodded at Gonzalez' body where Mick and dropped her. "But why did you have to let him go in the first place?"

"We left the Zoo for a while and I had someone watching Thor, but he didn't do a good job. He abused Thor. He was beating him with a fire extinguisher and so he attacked. He killed the man. Then he ate him. When I got back and saw what had happened, I knew if any of the others in camp found out, they'd put Thor down. I wasn't going to let that happen, so I brought him back to the Zoo, where he belonged. He's a part of the Zoo, after all. But look at what that did. Thor couldn't just stay put. He had to protect us. Not just here. With the giant spider, in the swamp. He gave us a warning with the rhinos, but we didn't pay attention.

"I wasn't going to let anyone put him down," he said and his hand continued to stroke the animal's bloody head.

Sophie was doing well for someone who hadn't known that Thor existed until a few minutes before. She stepped forward and gave Charles a hug. "I couldn't've have let you do it either."

"What do we do now?" Mick asked. "I know this is terrible, but he's hurt pretty bad. I don't know if he's going to make it, and there's still the problem of Bronson. Are you just going to leave him out here again?"

"No way," Charles said.

Reen looked into the jungle. "Something tells me the rest of the pack isn't far off. Thor here seemed to have killed the alpha, which means he's the new one. But if he's wounded like this, maybe one of the others will see an opportunity for an easy challenge."

"Reen's probably right," Booker said.

"I don't like the idea of putting a dog out of its misery as much as the next dude," Elijah said, "but I especially don't like the idea of being attacked by a pissed off leaderless pack of alien dogs."

"I'm not suggesting we kill Thor," she snapped. "I'm saying if we leave him, he's wolf-fodder."

"Sorry," Elijah said. "I didn't mean anything by it."

Charles wrapped his arms around Thor and stood, cradling his large friend in his arms. His tail wagged weakly, and he stretched up to lick his face. "I'm taking Thor back with me. I am not leaving him. One of you can take that moss hog if you want. Up to you."

"Charles—" Booker started.

"Don't fucking say anything," he snapped. "He's my friend. He saved my life more than once. Yours, too and now, it's my turn. Thor's coming with me."

His teammate pressed his lips together but didn't say anything more.

Roo picked up the carcass and the group followed the American toward the gate.

CHAPTER THIRTY-FIVE

The Zoo

The guard looked at the half-dead animal in Charles' arms. "Why did you say you needed this thing again? There's already been so much research on the demiwolves, I didn't think they needed any more. They're not worth shit, I mean."

He clutched Thor closer. The guard had let the others and the bodies pass, but he was reluctant to let the two of them through.

"The animal is needed," Richard spoke suddenly. He seemed to shake himself from the fog he'd entered after the death of Gonzalez. "I am conducting research, for which I've been cleared, and Charles there is operating under my direct orders."

The man frowned. "I don't remember seeing that on the list."

"Research is fluid. If we don't make snap decisions, we won't learn anything. Now, I don't want to go through the trouble of getting your superiors involved, and I'm sure you don't want the trouble either."

"Ah, what the hell? I don't give a shit either way. Bring it in."

The American didn't stick around to see what else Booker and Richard discussed with the guard. He was focused on getting the wounded animal back to their building. His arms were going numb by the time he carried him into Fiddler's Green, but he didn't want to put the demiwolf down.

"I'm going to take care of you, Thor. Don't you worry."

His tail wagged once, and he closed his eyes with a sigh and pressed his wet nose into Charles' neck.

"How's the patient today?" Sophie asked from where she leaned against the door jamb. Charles had set up the armory to be a makeshift home for Thor while he nursed the demiwolf back to health.

He looked up from his whittling. "He's doing much better. Most of his wounds are completely healed. I don't know if the tip of his horn will ever grow back, and I think he'll probably have these scars, but otherwise, he's doing great."

Thor wagged his tail at her and uttered a whine. She laughed and stepped forward to scratch behind his ears. His tail wagged harder and thudded on the wooden floor.

"It's so weird. He really is just like a normal dog. I mean, apart from the horns and the whole glowing eyes thing.

Who would have thought that a Z…that he would be like this."

By unspoken agreement, no one referred to Thor as anything but "dog" or his name.

Charles laughed. "Yeah, that does kind of ruin the whole *normal dog* affect."

Booker appeared at her side. He ran the backs of his knuckles down her arm. "I was looking for you."

"Well, you found me."

He leaned toward Sophie and Charles cleared his throat.

The Brit looked away from her and blinked at his team-mate as if he'd just noticed him. "Oh. How's Thor today?"

"He's great."

"That's good."

"Did you want something?" she asked him.

"I'm sure I did. That's why I came to find you. I needed something from you."

"See you later, Charles," she said and hooked her arm through Booker's.

"Bye," he said, but the two had already walked off down the hall. He rolled his eyes to Thor who huffed out a breath in reply, which made him laugh.

"You're a fucking weirdo," Roo said as he walked into the room. "Were you just laughing with the dog like he's telling you jokes?"

"No," he said. "Sophie and Booker were just here."

"Gag me with a spoon."

"Oh, come on, Roo. It's not that bad, them being together."

"Not that bad? I fucking hate it. And they aren't

together. They're still pretending they aren't rutting, but we all know that's what they're doing."

"What bothers you more about the situation? That they're pretending they aren't together, or that they're having sex?"

"I'm putting an end to this conversation because I don't want to think about it at all, goddammit."

"You know she's an adult and can make her own decisions," Charles reminded him.

"Obviously I fucking know that, Charles. God, you'd think I was a fucking bogan. No. I just hope he's not stringing her along by not making it official."

He laughed. "I'm sorry, who are you and what did you do with the real Roo?"

"Shove off."

"It'll be fine," he assured him. "I don't think you have anything to worry about."

Roo shook his head, then looked from Thor to Charles. "You know you can't keep him as a pet, right?"

His teammate didn't reply.

"Charles. Thor can't stay here."

"I'm not going to talk about this with you. Thor isn't better yet. When he's better, we can have a discussion. Maybe."

The Aussie shook his head and left the armory. He wandered into the kitchen where Mick, Reen, and Elijah were drinking beer. She passed him one.

He sat with a sigh.

"Charles still doesn't want to talk about what to do with Thor, huh?" Mick asked.

"Nope. He won't hear it."

"Give him some time, guys," she said. "Charles is a smart man. He knows that Thor can't stay here."

"It's been almost two fucking weeks already! He loves that thing so goddamn much," Roo said. "It's like watching my daughter with her favorite stuffed animal."

"Yeah, except your daughter and her stuffed bunny rabbit are way fucking cuter than a grown-ass man and an alien dog monster," Mick pointed out.

"I don't know. That thing has really grown on me," Elijah interjected. "I don't even really notice the horns anymore."

"You should've seen him as a puppy. No horns. He just looked like a regular ball of fluff. Of course, he was a hell of a lot more coordinated than other puppies. Still cute. Charles always pretended to be tough on him, but he let that thing sleep on his bed every night."

"I wish there was a different course of action we could take besides, you know..." Reen left the last of that sentence unspoken.

"Don't even think of that. Charles loves you, but if he has to make a choice between you or Thor, I wouldn't want to be in your shoes," Mick said.

"Does he have to be put down?" Elijah asked. "That's what you're saying, right?"

"He killed a man. Then he *ate* the dude. In any normal circumstances, if a dog bites a person, they have to be put down. What Thor did was worse," Mick said. "I'm not sure what options we have. I mean, we can put him back in the Zoo when he's healed up, but I think Charles would stay there with him now."

"Whose turn is it to make dinner?" Roo asked and changed the subject when Charles walked into the room.

He looked at them with suspicion, so Mick passed him a beer.

"I feel like Sophie hasn't made anything in a while. She's the best cook out of all of us. Where is she?" Mick asked.

"Off with Booker," the American said.

"Of course," Reen quipped. "I'll go ahead and get things started, then."

Booker and Sophie entered the room holding hands. The others looked pointedly at the hand-holding.

"What? Hasn't anyone told you staring is rude?" he asked.

She laughed. "I think we've shocked them."

"So, you guys have decided to quit pretending, huh?" Mick asked.

"What are you talking about?" he asked and opened a beer for himself.

"You know, pretending you aren't an item, even though literally every fucking person who sees you knows."

Sophie stuck her tongue out at him.

"I don't think everyone knew," Booker said.

Reen laughed. "Everybody fucking knew, Booker. Don't kid yourself."

"Well, I'm all for it," Charles said. He tipped his beer bottle toward Sophie and she smiled.

"Thanks, Charles."

"Now that one elephant is out of the way, why don't we address the other?" Elijah asked.

"Look, new guy, I think you can keep your piece to your fucking self," Roo said.

"I thought you said we needed to talk about it!"

"Talk about what?" the Brit asked.

Mick raised an eyebrow.

"Thor. Right. We do need to talk about that."

"There's nothing to talk about," Charles said. "I'm not taking him back to the Zoo."

"That's where he belongs, Charles. He's a wild animal. Not even an animal. Not really. He's a fucking alien," Reen said.

"He can't stay here," Booker stated.

"I'm not giving up Thor," he said, folded his arms over his chest, and leaned back in his chair.

Sophie took a sip from Booker's bottle. She slammed her hand down on the table and almost choked.

He rubbed her back. "Shit, are you okay?"

"I have an idea!" she exclaimed.

Charles narrowed his eyes at her. "Am I going to like this idea?"

"Oh, yeah. It's a great idea that I think will make everyone happy."

EPILOGUE

Pendjari National Park, Benin

It was barely before dawn when the sound of a large vehicle woke Achille. He pulled on a pair of pants, grabbed his FAL, and stumbled onto the porch of the ranger shack. In the dim pre-dawn light, he could faintly make out the shape of an SUV bouncing up the dirt road.

"More poachers?" He growled belligerently. "They keep getting bolder and bolder."

He jogged forward and put himself in the SUV's way. The vehicle stopped and the metal ticked and popped as it settled. The ranger raised the FAL halfway, his warning that he was ready to shoot whoever stepped out of the vehicle if he had to do so to protect the park. He peered through the windshield to see who was there, then lowered the gun completely.

"Charles?"

The American slid out of the driver's side of the SUV with a big grin on his face. "Achille! How've you been? Still trying to shoot us, I see."

The two men embraced and laughed together. The back door of the vehicle opened and Booker exited. He turned and helped a young woman down, a nicety not always seen this far into the bush. The man slid a protective arm around her shoulders and tucked her close to his body. Achille recognized the body language of a man in love being over-protective of a woman carrying his child.

"Achille, old friend, how have you been?" the Brit asked. He released the woman momentarily to give him a hug and returned to her side. "This is Sophie."

She shook his hand, her grip strong and sure. "It's lovely to meet you."

"Sophie...this is the other girl that was kidnapped?"

"Yes. But they caught up to me," she said. "I think thanks to you."

He waved her off. "Where are the others?"

"On holiday," Booker said. "They went to Australia. Roo's showing his pool off to Reen or some such nonsense. Sophie and I are only passing through. Although I think Charles has a mind to stay a bit longer."

"Where's Mick?" Achille asked and looked toward the rear of the SUV to see if his friend would appear.

"With Roo and Reen. A quick visit home," Booker said.

"I have something to show you," Charles said. He opened the back hatch so Achille could see inside the SUV.

The ranger took a hasty step back when a giant dog-like animal stepped down from the vehicle. It had thick black-and-brown fur, although there were patches missing that revealed new scars. The size of the animal wasn't the most unusual thing about it. What stole his breath were the twin horns that sprouted from between the creature's ears.

They were in a tight spiral like those of a kudu, and they ran the length of its back. It sat and wagged its tail.

"What is it?" Achille whispered.

"This is Thor," Charles said.

Thor's tail wagged harder and thumped on the ground to create small puffs of dirt.

"He's friendly."

Achille held a hand out. Thor walked toward him and he saw he was limping. The demiwolf pressed his cold, wet nose into the palm of his hand. He carefully ran his fingers through the thick fur and scratched behind his ears. Thor's tail wagged harder and his dark purple—almost black— tongue lolled out, exactly like a regular dog.

"This thing," Achille said, "it comes from the Zoo. No?"

"Yes," Charles said. He told the ranger about how he'd found him abandoned in the Zoo and thought another person had left him there. He explained his history of violence and the rescue, all the way up to bringing him to Benin.

"But why here?" Achille asked. "Why the WAP?"

"President Okonkuo is doing us a favor," Sophie said as she and Booker joined the conversation.

"What favor?"

"The BOHICA Warriors have a new subsidiary," Booker said. "We're calling it BCA Conservation Research, Ltd."

"President Okonkuo has given BCA Conservation an exclusive contract over ten thousand acres of the park."

"What are you doing with the park?" he demanded, alarmed. "You can't turn it into another Zoo! I like you but I won't allow that."

Charles laughed and clapped him on the shoulder.

"Don't worry, friend. It's nothing bad. In fact, we're looking for someone to run it."

"A liaison, of sorts, between BCA Conservation and the park," Booker said.

"We want that person to be you," the American added.

"Me?"

"Yes. In exchange for your services, you'll get better equipment. Better housing. Higher pay, and more help," he explained.

"I'm a ranger," he said.

"And you will still be a ranger. This will just be your side-gig."

"Side-gig? I do not know what that is," the old man said, his eyes wary.

"A second job. A side-job."

Achille started speaking in rapid-fire French and Sophie answered him, her smile broad.

"There is one condition," Charles said after Achille had calmed.

"What is it?"

"Thor gets to make his new home here in the park."

Achille looked at the demiwolf, who returned his gaze while his tail thumped lazily on the ground. "I can do that."

Charles grinned.

"When does this all happen?" the ranger asked.

Booker glanced at his watch. "Basically, it started when we drove up here. And officially got going the second you accepted. Which means Teasy and I need to be making tracks."

"But you just got here," Achille said.

Charles pulled two duffle bags from the back of the

SUV and passed the keys to Booker. He shook his friend's hand and gave Sophie a hug.

"We're going to the UK. I have a connection there that was able to get Sophie a working passport," he said.

Sophie giggled. "It's going to be so much fun! My new name is Sonya Montag. I mean, how great is that? Sonya. I can't wait to see where Booker grew up and meet all his famous SAS friends."

The Brit gave a dramatic sigh but smiled and looped his arm around her shoulders again.

"What about you, Charles?" Achille asked.

He rolled his shoulders. "Well, I was hoping I'd be able to stay here for a bit. If that's all right with you. Make sure Thor settles in. Help you out with the transition and expansion. That sort of thing."

"Of course, you can stay!"

"Great."

Achille grabbed the bags despite his protests and took them to the ranger station.

"I'll see you soon," Charles said.

"We'll be seeing you, Charles. Don't you worry about that," Booker said. "I hope Thor likes it here."

"I definitely think he will. Thanks again for the brilliant idea, Sophie."

"That's why you guys keep me around. Good luck, Charles," she said and scrambled into the SUV.

The two men shook hands again.

"Ah, fudge. Come here, man," Charles said and pulled the other man into a hug.

Booker laughed. "Okay, Charles. This won't be the last time we see each other. No need to get all emotional."

"I'm not."

"Sure."

He slugged the Brit on the arm. "Now, get going. Your baby mama is waiting."

"Fuck you."

"Booker?"

"Yeah?"

"Be careful."

"Don't worry. The UK isn't quite as scary as the Zoo. I think we'll be all right."

Charles shook his head.

"I know what you're saying, Charles. I have every confidence in my friend's abilities to get Sophie into the country undetected. We'll be fine."

The American raised his hand. "See you."

Booker saluted and climbed into the SUV.

Charles looked at Thor. "You ready to see your new digs?"

Thor's tail wagged.

"Hey, Achille, I'm going to show Thor around. He needs to stretch his legs from being cooped up for so long."

"I'll be here when you get back," the ranger said.

Charles didn't know where to go, so any direction was as good as the other. He started down a path leading away from the station. Thor ambled beside him and absorbed the new place. The scents were tantalizing—different, but similar. He hopped around like a puppy, sniffing at everything, but he always ran back to him and was never away from the man's side for long.

They walked until Thor tired and then made their way back to the station.

He'd been grasping at straws when Sophie had told him her idea. While he hadn't been sold on the concept, he had nothing better. But out walking the bush with Thor, he knew this was right. There was enough wildness out there to keep him safe but let him live out his life in peace. This wasn't the Zoo with a danger behind every tree. This was… this was heaven.

Achille was waiting with dinner and a cold beer when they returned.

"You didn't have to do that," Charles said.

The man shrugged. "It's nice having someone else around. It's mostly just me."

They shared the meal before moving to the large porch and watched the sky turn almost violent shades of red as it dipped below the horizon. An elephant trumpeted and Charles watched as a herd of the large pachyderms walked through the tall grass.

"How long will you stay?" Achille asked.

"Not too long, at least this trip."

He planned to stay until Thor was settled in. Thereafter, he had things he had to do, not the least of which was to start extracting himself from the company. He'd keep his shares, but he was done with the missions.

After a trip home to put a down payment on a house for his sister and to get his mother the Tesla she'd dreamed about, well, he wouldn't have much to keep him in Des Moines. Or anywhere else. Watching the elephants slowly stroll past, he decided maybe the park wouldn't be a bad place to settle down. He'd be with Thor, at least, and at peace.

He scratched absently behind his furry friend's ear.

Thor's tail thumped on the wood of the porch and he heaved a contented sigh where he sprawled between the two men. While Charles scratched his ear, Achille leaned down to stroke the fur of his upper back. The sun dipped lower and the elephants wandered out of sight, but the two men and the demiwolf remained on the porch until the sky was filled with stars.

AUTHOR NOTES - C. J. FAWCETT

SEPTEMBER 18, 2019

This has been a special journey for me, just a fanboy who was given the chance to become a writer. It has been an amazing trip. I need to thank Michael and John for the opportunity, even if I might have caused John to pull out his hair with the rewrites, haha! Or as they say in Thailand, 555 (5 is pronounced "ha.").

I hope you'll all be seeing more of me.

C.J.

AUTHOR NOTES - JONATHAN BRAZEE

SEPTEMBER 19, 2019

When Michael and I discussed this series last year, I didn't know where it was going to go. Like most books, they tend to take a life of their own, telling the writers what is going to happen. This biggest divergence in this series from the initial inception was the rise of Thor.

Thor and Charles faced some pretty significant hurdles in Book 2, which we thought would be realistic given the events that transpired. Hopefully, they managed to overcome them in Book 3 in a satisfying storyline, yet in a manner which rang true.

As I read the ending, however, I knew there had to be more, so I wrote a novella that took Thor's story one more step beyond this book. I hope you'll give it a read, and more than that, I hope you'll receive the same sense of joy reading it as I did writing it.

CONNECT WITH THE AUTHORS

Jonathan Brazee Social
Website:
http://jonathanbrazee.com/

Email List:
http://eepurl.com/bnFSHH

Facebook Here:
https://www.facebook.com/jonathanbrazeeauthor/

Michael Anderle Social
Website:
http://lmbpn.com

Email List:
http://lmbpn.com/email/
Facebook Here:
www.facebook.com/TheKurtherianGambitBooks/
www.facebook.com/groups/320172985053521/ (Protected by the Damned Facebook Group)

OTHER ZOO BOOKS

THE BOHICA CHRONICLES